Praise for the Ghost Finders novels

GHOST OF A SMILE

"Packed with creepy thrills, *Ghost of a Smile* is a mighty strong follow-up in this brand-new series. Ghost hunting has never been quite this exciting. Recommended."
—*SFRevu*

"[With] plenty of action and chills, this book keeps pages turning even as a feeling of dread builds. The dialogue between the three characters is snappy and humorous, as is the chemistry between them." —*NewsandSentinel.com*

"*Ghost of a Smile* is a lovely blend of popcorn adventure and atmospheric thriller, and good for a few hours of distraction and entertainment. That's one of the reasons why Green's books always leap right to the top of my reading list."
—*The Green Man Review*

"[Green] gleefully tweaks the natural fear of experimentation (and the inscrutable motivations of the men behind it), bringing some real-world paranoia into his fantasy-laden playground. It's a gamble that pays off nicely . . . With his Nightside series ending soon, the Ghost Finders books are quickly proving to be worthy replacements."
—*Sacramento Book Review*

P9-EMQ-959

continued . . .

GHOST OF A CHANCE

"If future novels in Green's new Ghost Finders series are as engaging as this one, they will hold up admirably against his previous work . . . Readers will appreciate the camaraderie and snappy dialogue." —*Publishers Weekly*

"Terrific." —*SFRevu*

"Thoroughly entertaining."
—Jim Butcher, #1 *New York Times* bestselling author
of the Dresden Files

"It's fast-paced, filled with nifty concepts and memorable characters, and quite enjoyable." —*The Green Man Review*

"I'm a huge fan of Simon R. Green's Nightside novels, and he continues to impress with *Ghost of a Chance*. He continues to put out great stories and gives readers deeply flawed characters that you still want to root for. This book is a great start to a new series that I will keep reading."
—*Bitten by Books*

GHOST OF A DREAM

SIMON R. GREEN

ACE BOOKS, NEW YORK

THE BERKLEY PUBLISHING GROUP
Published by the Penguin Group
Penguin Group (USA) Inc.
375 Hudson Street, New York, New York 10014, USA

Penguin Group (Canada), 90 Eglinton Avenue East, Suite 700, Toronto, Ontario M4P 2Y3, Canada (a division of Pearson Penguin Canada Inc.) • Penguin Books Ltd., 80 Strand, London WC2R 0RL, England • Penguin Group Ireland, 25 St. Stephen's Green, Dublin 2, Ireland (a division of Penguin Books Ltd.) • Penguin Group (Australia), 250 Camberwell Road, Camberwell, Victoria 3124, Australia (a division of Pearson Australia Group Pty. Ltd.) • Penguin Books India Pvt. Ltd., 11 Community Centre, Panchsheel Park, New Delhi—110 017, India • Penguin Group (NZ), 67 Apollo Drive, Rosedale, Auckland 0632, New Zealand (a division of Pearson New Zealand Ltd.) • Penguin Books (South Africa) (Pty.) Ltd., 24 Sturdee Avenue, Rosebank, Johannesburg 2196, South Africa

Penguin Books Ltd., Registered Offices: 80 Strand, London WC2R 0RL, England

This is a work of fiction. Names, characters, places, and incidents either are the product of the author's imagination or are used fictitiously, and any resemblance to actual persons, living or dead, business establishments, events, or locales is entirely coincidental. The publisher does not have any control over and does not assume any responsibility for author or third-party websites or their content.

GHOST OF A DREAM

An Ace Book / published by arrangement with the author

PUBLISHING HISTORY
Ace mass-market edition / September 2012

Copyright © 2012 by Simon R. Green.
Cover art by Don Sipley.
Cover design by Judith Lagerman.
Interior text design by Laura K. Corless.

ISBN: 978-1-937007-73-7

ACE
Ace Books are published by The Berkley Publishing Group,
a division of Penguin Group (USA) Inc.,
375 Hudson Street, New York, New York 10014.
ACE and the "A" design are trademarks of Penguin Group (USA) Inc.

PRINTED IN THE UNITED STATES OF AMERICA

10 9 8 7 6 5 4 3 2 1

ALWAYS LEARNING   **PEARSON**

What ghosts really are . . .
is unfinished business.

The Carnacki Institute exists to Do Something about ghosts. Track them down, identify what's really going on, put lost souls to rest, and kick supernatural arse, where necessary. The Institute's been around for a long time and knows pretty much all there is to know about ghosts, monsters, other-dimensional incursions . . . and anything else that won't lie down and play dead like it's supposed to.

If the Carnacki Institute had a motto it would probably be: "We don't take any shit from the Hereafter."

PREVIOUSLY, IN THE GHOST FINDERS

One of the Institute's leading investigative teams consists of JC Chance (team leader and positive thinker), Melody Chambers (team scientist and girl geek), and Happy Jack Palmer (team telepath and general miserable pain in the arse). JC fell in love with a ghost girl called Kim. Love between the living and the dead is almost universally forbidden, for many good reasons. At the end of the team's last mission, Kim was stolen away from JC by unknown forces. He doesn't know why or if he'll ever find her again.

The team also discovered, on their previous mission, that the long-established and much-trusted Carnacki Institute had in fact been infiltrated and compromised by the Bad Guys. Secret people in secret positions who serve something called The Flesh Undying—a terrible creature that fell, or was pushed, from a higher reality into our world. The Flesh Undying sees this world as a prison, a trap, and is ready to destroy our whole reality in order that it might break free and go home again.

JC, Melody, and Happy are on their own. They don't know what to do or whom they can trust. Or where to look for their missing ghost girl. So for the time being, they're following their orders and doing their job, finding ghosts and Doing Something about them. And all the time looking . . . for a chance to get even.

ONE

....

ONE OF OUR TRAINS IS MISSING

The Past is only as dead and gone as we allow it to be. It has a tendency to cling, to hang on—like lovers who can't bring themselves to accept it's over. There will always be some who find the Past more comforting than the Present, people who look back on the way things used to be and make everything make sense with the benefit of hindsight. So it really shouldn't come as any surprise that there are always going to be people who prefer to give all their spare time, their personal time, to looking backwards instead of forward, investing all their happiness in re-creating some one special part of the Past.

Once upon a time, in the grand days of Old England, there were wonderful things called steam trains: huge steel beasts thundering across the great green countryside, connecting even the smallest of communities, one to the other. They roared like dragons, breathed fire and smoke, and the ground shook at their passing. But time passed, as it will, and steam reluctantly gave way to electricity. Less romantic, perhaps, but undeniably faster and more efficient. And then there came an infamous man called Beeching, in that far-off time called the sixties, and he shut down all the smaller stations, all the lesser-used branch lines, in the name of progress and efficiency. Sacrificing the needs of the smaller communities and the smaller people to better serve the needs of larger communities and more important people. And so the Age of Steam passed, and no-one realised what they'd lost until it was gone. The small railway stations were abandoned, left to rot and ruin in a slow, sullen silence. Ghosts . . . of an old way of life.

But wherever the Past is remembered, and sometimes even worshipped, it is never really gone.

          ,,,,,,,,,,,,,,,,,,,,,,,,,,,,

The Ghost Finders came to Bradleigh Halt, in Yorkshire, on a cool autumn evening. Once a small but thriving railway station, in the very north of England, Bradleigh Halt was left behind when the map changed, and its trains were sent somewhere else. Now it was a few abandoned buildings, full of dust and shadows and rusting rails covered in weeds. Set in the bottom of a deep, dark valley between two tall, grassy walls, with wide mountainous slopes stretching away on the one side and great stony inclines on the other; a cold wind blew fitfully through the station gap and sighed mournfully in the single tunnel-mouth.

You could drive right past and never know Bradleigh Halt was still there; and for many years, most people did.

An old-fashioned black taxi-cab delivered the Ghost Finders to the top of one grassy slope, after a lengthy journey down many winding roads, from the main-line railway station at Leeds. The taxi-cabby slammed his vehicle to a halt a more-than-comfortable distance away from the top of the valley and sat grimly in his seat, refusing to emerge, even to help his passengers with their luggage. He stared straight ahead, as though concerned with what he might see, dourly still and determinedly silent, as JC Chance, Melody Chambers, and Happy Jack Palmer clambered out the back of his cab, stretching slowly and massaging aching back muscles. Melody dragged her scientific equipment out of the boot while JC paid the driver, and Happy took in the new surroundings with his usual miserable and put-upon expression. The taxi-cabby snatched his fare the moment it was offered and departed at speed, not even bothering to check if JC had added a tip. The three Ghost Finders watched the taxi depart, then looked at each other. JC smiled vaguely, Happy sniffed loudly, and Melody turned away and gave all her attention to her precious scientific instruments. It was a late evening in early September, under slate grey skies. The light was beginning to drop out of the day, and there was already a definite chill in the air.

Not far-away stood the original station sign: old lettering on old wood, much reduced by long exposure to wind and weather and many years of neglect. The sign should have read *Welcome to Bradleigh Halt*, but someone had recently put a painted slash through the word *Halt*, and replaced it with *Hell*.

The three Ghost Finders stood together at the top of the steep, grassy slope, looking down into the valley below, taking in the sights, such as they were. Battered stone-and-wood buildings stood slumped together on either side of the sunken railway lines, the long platforms hidden under accumulated junk and rubbish and lengthening shadows. To the east, the railway tracks disappeared into the gloom of the tunnel-mouth, and into the long-disused tunnel that passed through and under the great, sprawling slopes known locally as the Grey Fells. The lines reappeared on the other side, many miles away, in another abandoned station halt, that no-one cared about any more. To the west, the weed-choked rails stretched away far and far, disappearing into the distance, between two sets of stony grey slopes. Going nowhere and taking their own sweet time about it. The whole scene had a quiet, wistful air, though adding the word *peaceful* would probably have been stretching it. Even without knowing what the Ghost Finders already knew, Bradleigh Halt didn't even try to look inviting.

Birds sang on the evening air, insects buzzed industriously, and the gusting wind murmured querulously to itself. The sun was sinking slowly in the sky, in a warning sort of way. There was a pervading sense of the world's having moved on, leaving Bradleigh Halt behind.

JC Chance stood at the very edge of the high slope, smiling thoughtfully, hands thrust deep into his jacket pockets. It had to be said, he lacked a lot of his usual cocky bravado. Recent events in the secret hidden world

had conspired to knock a lot of his usual over-confidence
out of him. And the stealing away of the love of his life,
the ghost girl Kim, had punched the heart right out of
him. But he persevered. Because he was a Ghost Finder,
because it was his job and his calling. And because he
had nothing else to do.

JC was tall and lean and perhaps a little too handsome
for his own good, or anyone else's, for that matter. He
was well into his late twenties, with pale, striking features under a rock star's great mane of long, wavy, black
hair. He had a proud nose, a grim smile, and he wore
very dark sunglasses all the time, for very dark reasons.
He also wore a rich cream white suit, of quite extraordinary style and elegance, along with an Old School tie
that he might or might not have been entitled to. JC never
let little things like authenticity get in the way of looking
good. He also had a tendency to strike a pose, whether
anyone was watching or not. Though, to his credit, he
would knock it off at once if it was pointed out to him.

On any case, on any mission, under any circumstances,
JC could always be relied on to be the first to charge into
danger, looking around eagerly for some new trouble to
get into. Losing his one true love had slowed him down,
some. He wanted to be out looking for her; but since he
didn't have a single clue where to start, he insisted on
taking any case the Carnacki Institute could provide . . .
On the grounds that it was better to be doing something
than to be doing nothing.

Melody Chambers stood a little way behind him,
studying JC carefully but saying nothing. Melody was
the big-brain scientist of the team and proud of it. Fast

approaching thirty with the brakes off and loudly not giving a damn, Melody was conventionally good-looking in a threatening sort of way. Short and gamine thin, she burned constantly with enough raw nervous energy to run a small city for several weeks. Melody was a great one for getting things done and walking right over anyone and anything that threatened to get in her way or slow her down. She wore her auburn hair scraped back in a severe bun, glared at the world through serious glasses with dull functional frames, and wore clothes so anonymous they actually by-passed style and fashion without noticing them.

She gave up worrying over JC as a bad job, returned her full attention to the assorted technical apparatus she'd hauled out the boot of the taxi, and piled it all onto a small self-assembly trolley of her own design. Without anyone else's help. Admittedly, mostly because Melody had a tendency to strike people viciously about the head and shoulders if they touched her things. She preferred machines to people, on the unanswerable grounds that when machines decided not to do what they were supposed to do, you could fix them or hit them until they did. People were more complicated. Melody had a first-class mind, more balls than a tennis court, and a sex drive that would have frightened Casanova into early retirement. It's always the quiet ones you have to keep an eye on . . .

Happy Jack Palmer stood alone, glowering at the world in general. Happy was the team telepath, observer of the hidden realms, and full-time grumpy bugger. He'd only recently hit thirty, and thirty was hitting back. He was short, stocky, and prematurely balding, all of which he took as proof positive that God hated him personally. He might have been attractive enough if he'd ever stopped scowling, slouching, and saying inappropriate things in a loud and carrying voice. He wore grubby jeans, a staggeringly offensive T-shirt, and a battered leather jacket that had probably looked better when it was still on the cow. Happy's marvellous mutant mind allowed him to see and hear things no-one else could detect, and even have long conversations with them, and, as he was fond of saying, *If you could see the world as clearly as I do, you'd be clinically depressed, too.* Neither of his fellow team members knew who had originally named him Happy. They could only assume his school days must have been an absolute hot-bed of irony.

Happy used to take an awful lot of pills, potions, and special medications, mixing and matching as necessary to keep the world outside his head. Because both the real and the hidden worlds were full of things he didn't want to think about. He was trying to do without his little chemical helpers these days because they got in the way of having lots of sex with Melody. Happy and Melody were something of an item; and it would be difficult to decide which of them was more surprised. The things we do for love. Love, or something like it.

"I really don't like that sign," said JC after a while. He indicated the *Bradleigh Hell* sign with a jerk of his head. "That sign speaks of well-established phenomena, ghosts and hauntings and general weird shit, seen by far too many civilians. As in, ordinary everyday people completely untrained or unused to dealing with bad things on the move. I say we withdraw and nuke the whole place from orbit. It's the only way to be sure."

"If I hadn't seen your lips move, I would have sworn I said that," said Happy.

"We all know you don't want to be here, JC," Melody said carefully. "We're worried about Kim, too."

"I'm not," said Happy. "I mean, come on; it's not as if she's in any danger, wherever she is. She's a ghost! She's dead! What else can happen to her?"

"For you, tact is something other people do, isn't it?" said Melody.

"What?" said Happy.

"Mouth is open, should be shut."

"Oh. Okay."

"Somebody has her," said JC. "Somebody took her from me. And if they have the power to hold a ghost against her will, who knows what else they can do? I swear . . . I will move Heaven and Earth with a really big stick to get her back. I'm only staying with the Carnacki Institute so I can make use of their resources."

"I don't trust the Institute any more," said Happy.

"You never did," said Melody. "In fact, you are famous for never trusting anyone or anything, including yourself."

"And I was right!" Happy said loudly. "I was dangerously paranoid even before we found out the Institute had been infiltrated by Big Bads from Beyond! Imagine my shock when all my worst dreams were proved true. I was so much happier when I only thought I was crazy . . ."

"Let us all concentrate on the mission at hand," said JC, not unkindly. "Since we all have so many things we'd rather not be thinking about . . . it's best to keep occupied. And hopefully come across something here so sufficiently nasty we can justify kicking the shit out of it in the cause of justice and therapy. I feel like hitting something."

"Never knew you when you didn't," muttered Happy.

JC led the way down the steep, grassy slope, leaping and bounding along with cheerful abandon. Happy followed after, far more cautiously. And Melody brought up the rear, lowering her trolley of piled-up special scientific equipment foot by foot while filling the air with foul language every time something inevitably fell off, and she had to stop and put it back on again. She glared after the others, but knowing better than to ask for help. JC and Happy could break delicate equipment merely by looking at it the wrong way. Bradleigh Halt loomed up before them, still and silent, holding shadows and secrets within. It didn't look any better as it got closer.

"Talk to me, my children," said JC as he descended. "Tell me things I need to know."

"Starting with, what the hell are we here for?" said Happy.

"Just once, I wish you two wouldn't leave it to me to read the briefing files," said Melody. "We all spent hours on the train getting here . . ."

"I had some important dozing to be getting on with," said JC.

"And you know I don't like to read anything scary," said Happy. "It gives me nightmares. And wind."

Melody sighed, loudly and pointedly. "All right. One more time, for the hard of thinking at the back. This one seems straightforward enough. Until very recently, Bradleigh Halt was another run-down, long-time-closed, small-time railway station. One of the many shut down by Dr. Beeching, back in the sixties. But, the halt was due to be renovated and reopened, by the Bradleigh Preservation Trust—a bunch of old-time steam-train enthusiasts. The volunteers had only started work here, rebuilding and repairing and generally putting the place in order for a Grand Reopening . . . when they started seeing things. And hearing things. All the usual disturbing supernatural phenomena . . . More than enough for the volunteers to down tools and run for the hills. Somebody in the Preservation Trust knew enough to get the bad news to the Institute, and somebody at Carnacki apparently loves steam trains, too . . . So here we are."

"Yes," JC said patiently. "Got that. But what about the details, Melody? All the helpful little details, so we can figure out exactly what we're dealing with here? What exactly did the volunteers see and hear? Revenants? Poltergeists? The Blair Witch on a Broomstick?"

"I don't know," said Melody. "Nothing in the briefing. Only a note to say that we are to be met here by one of the volunteers from the Preservation Trust. Who will hopefully tell us what we need to know."

"Wouldn't put money on it," growled Happy. "Civilians . . . Always more trouble than they're worth."

"Oh hush," said Melody. "You know you love the chance to feel superior to someone."

"Almost as much as you love a chance to lecture us," Happy said sweetly.

They looked at each other and exchanged a smile.

Shared emotions were unfamiliar territory for both of them; but perhaps it takes one broken soul to mend another.

"I can hear you two smiling at each other, and I do wish you wouldn't," said JC, not looking back. "You know your entire relationship creeps me out big-time. Young Ghostbusters in love. The horror, the horror . . ."

"And this from a man in love with a ghost," said Melody. "At least Happy and I can touch each other."

"And we do," said Happy. "Often into the early hours . . ."

"And you call my relationship unnatural," said JC.

"The living and the dead aren't supposed to get that close," said Melody. "For all kinds of worrying and unsettling reasons."

"It'll all end in tears," said Happy.

            ııııııııııııııııııııııı

They reached the bottom of the grassy slope pretty much at the same time and stepped carefully down onto the end of the waiting platform. JC peered easily about him, pretending to look the place over, giving Happy a chance to cough up half a lung getting his breath back, while Melody counted all her precious bits of equipment, twice, to make sure she hadn't left anything important behind. It had to be said: the Station Halt didn't appear particularly welcoming. Some attempt had been made to clean up the place, but with only limited success. Soap and water and industrial-strength detergent can only do so much in the face of decades of dust and grime and disinterest. Various rubbish and debris had been brushed roughly to one side of the platform; but the standing structures, the original station buildings . . . looked distinctly uninviting.

The old stone walls, sourced from local quarries, were stained and discoloured the exact shade of old piss, and the wooden facings, shutters, and doors were all pitted and rotten, looking almost diseased in the limited light. Newly replaced glass windows gleamed brightly enough in the gloomy surroundings, and a few new doors stood proudly open, showing only darkness within. Freshly painted signs hung here and there, saying *Ticket Office*, *Waiting Room*, and the like, in clear but still traditionally old-fashioned lettering. No-one had done anything for the buildings on the opposite platform. The slumping, single-storey structures across the tracks looked dim and distant, as though they were miles away.

It was all very still and silent, without even the birdsong and insect buzz from above to add a sense of life to the place. At the bottom of the valley, between the two steep slopes, it all seemed so much darker; as though the light had to struggle to reach so far down. The wind seemed stronger, though, gusting along the open platform with sudden loud murmurings, like a hound on the trail of a scent. The pit between the two platforms was choked with weeds run wild though efforts had been made to clear a short length of track. It seemed to JC that efforts to clean up the halt had stopped and started several times before something drove everyone away . . .

"First impressions, Happy?" JC said brightly, on the grounds that someone had to be bright and cheerful before they all burst into tears.

"Nothing obvious," said Happy, glowering about him. "I'm not picking up any manifestations, no stone-tape imagery . . . But it does seem a lot darker and gloomier down here than it should, as though we've left the evening behind, up above, and come down into the night. Look up. Does that look like an early-evening sky to you? Wait a minute, hold everything, drop the anchors. Did anyone else hear that?"

They all moved closer together and stared down the long platform. A light had appeared in the window of the furthest building, the Waiting Room. It was a warm, golden glow, calm and cheerful and quite out of place in the generally forbidding atmosphere. The light moved out of the Waiting Room and quickly revealed itself to be an old storm lantern, held high in the hand of a dim figure. JC looked sharply at Happy, who shook his head and mouthed the word *civilian*. The figure came walking slowly down the platform towards them, taking its time, holding the lantern out ahead. The advancing golden glow quickly revealed an old man, in comfortable clothes and sturdy working-man's shoes. He finally swayed to a halt in front of the Ghost Finders and looked at them. He didn't give any impression of being particularly impressed. He squared his old shoulders, lowered the storm lantern some, and nodded brusquely.

"About time you got here," he said, in a rough, worn-out voice. "Ronald Laurie, representing the Bradleigh Preservation Trust."

"Here to help us of his own free will," murmured Melody. "Try not to frighten him."

Ronald Laurie was a tall but stoop-shouldered old

fellow, well into his seventies, in a battered tweed suit of a kind that men of a certain age like to wear when gardening, or doing odd jobs, until their wives decide they can't stand the sight of it any more and drop it off at a charity shop when their husband's out and can't object. Laurie wore a battered cloth cap on a bald head, troubled here and there with a few wispy grey strands. He had a deeply lined face, a pursed mouth, and piercing steel grey eyes. He managed a small smile, for each Ghost Finder in turn, but didn't offer to shake hands. He still held the lantern high as though to be sure he was spreading the light as far as he could. And he took his time looking the Ghost Finders over, as though he wanted to be sure they were what they appeared to be.

He's seen something, thought JC. *What have you seen, old man?*

"So," Laurie said finally. "You're the experts, are you?"

From the way he said the word, it was clear he didn't take much assurance from it. In his world, experts were people who came down on orders from the bosses to meddle in things they didn't understand.

"That's us," said JC as positively as he could. JC was usually the one who got to talk to civilians and put them at their ease, as much as was possible. Happy and Melody didn't have the knack. Or the inclination. JC offered Laurie his hand, but the old man nodded brusquely again.

"You took your time getting here," he said. "It's late. Getting dark. But then, we're a long way from anywhere. These days."

"We got here as soon as we could," JC said smoothly.

"Hope you haven't been waiting too long. It was good of you to agree to meet us and help out."

"Aye. Well," said Laurie. "Didn't seem right to let you just walk into this ungodly mess without at least a warning."

"I want to go home," said Happy. "Right now."

"So this is a bad place?" Melody said to the old man. "Nice to have that confirmed. What have you seen here?"

"This is Melody Chambers, girl scientist and plain speaker," murmured JC. "That cheerful soul is Happy Jack Palmer, professional worrier. Don't get too close or try to feed him. And I am JC. I lead this team, for my many sins. Let us all play nicely together, people. We've a lot to discuss and not much time before night falls. It would help us a great deal, Mr. Laurie, if you could fill us in on exactly what's been happening here. We do have official reports, but we prefer to get our information from first-hand sources, wherever possible. From people who've actually experienced the events in question. Whatever they may be."

"Details," said Melody. "We want details."

"And you can leave the rumours and gossip at home," said Happy.

"Hush, children," said JC. "Daddy's working."

"Who are you people?" said Laurie, looking back and forth between them. "All I was told was to expect some experts. Are you with British Rail?"

"Not in any way, shape, or form," said JC. "We are all experts in the field of unnatural situations. We investigate bad places, determine what's going on, then do something about it. We are here to help, Mr. Laurie."

"Aye. Maybe." Laurie still didn't look convinced, but he made a clear effort to be reasonable and get along. He tried his brief smile again, then looked up and down the long, gloomy platform. A low murmuring sound issued from the tunnel-mouth at the opposite end, and they all turned to look. There was nothing there. Only the tall, brick-lined arch, the deep, dark shadows, and a few leaves blown back and forth by the breeze. Laurie looked back at JC. He seemed suddenly older, even fragile.

"You can't trust anything around here. Can't turn your back on anything. You know why no-one else from the Trust is here to meet you? Because I'm the only one who'll come here any more. None of the rest of them'll set foot here, for love nor money. Not after what happened." He looked sadly at JC. "Must be nice, to be an expert. To be a scientist and understand everything, so there's nothing left to scare you."

"Don't you believe it," said Happy, immediately.

"It's only sensible, to be afraid of things that are dangerous," JC said carefully. "But you can't let it stop you from doing what needs to be done. We are all of us trained to deal with . . . extraordinary situations. Please tell us what it is that's happened here, Mr. Laurie."

"I never used to believe in the supernatural," said Laurie. "Or ghosts."

"That's all right," said JC. "They believe in you. In fact, that's pretty much the definition of supernatural— things that insist on happening, whether you believe in them or not. Have you seen ghosts here, Mr. Laurie?"

"I want this taken care of," said Laurie. "I want this

unholy mess dealt with, forced out of here, so I can take it easy again . . . and the Trust can get on with opening up the station. Used to be a fine old place, this, back in the day. Always liked it here. Nowhere else I'd rather be." He glared quickly about him, as though defying the shadows to do anything. "I'm the only one who'll come here now, and I can't stay. Not once it starts getting really dark. No-one will stay here once it starts getting really dark. I'll tell you what's what, show you where everything is; but then I'm gone. You're lucky I stayed to meet you, this late in the day."

"But what is it?" said JC. "What is it that scares you, Mr. Laurie?"

"We thought it was kids, at first," said Laurie. "Teen-agers, with nothing to do, nothing to occupy them . . . messing about, making trouble. You saw the sign, up top—Bradleigh Hell? Aye. That was them. The last thing they did, before they ran away. They used to come here after dark, you see, to do all the things their parents didn't need to know about . . . but you couldn't drag any of them back now. Not after what they saw."

"What did they see?" JC said patiently. "What happens here once it gets dark?"

"I think maybe . . . everyone sees different things," Laurie said slowly. "I think maybe this place shows you whatever it is that scares you most. Because that's the best way to get rid of you. The volunteers woke something up; and it wants us gone. You'll see. All of you. Whether you want to or not. Come with me. I'll show you where everything is, then I'm out of here."

"Please don't rush off, Mr. Laurie," said JC. "Stick with us for a while. You'll be perfectly safe, with us. After all, no-one knows this place better than you."

Laurie managed his small smile again. "Aye. Maybe I have been here longer than most. I can still remember when Bradleigh Halt was a going concern, and the old trains came through here regular. Marvellous it was, the sight and sound of a steam train coming into the halt. My old dad used to work here, in the Bookings Office. I used to bring him his lunch every day, when I was a kid, along with a bottle of beer now and again."

"Do you ever see your father among the ghosts?" said Melody.

"No, lass," said Laurie. "I would have liked to . . . but it's not spirits, as such, you see. I'm not sure whatever walks here now has anything human left in it. Whatever's not finished with this place, it's nothing to do with human needs or human business. No . . . Something bad is coming. And it's getting closer all the time." He broke off abruptly to glare at JC. "Why in God's name are you wearing sunglasses at this time of night, boy?"

"Sensitive eyes," said JC. "Work-related injury. You know how it is."

"Hello!" Happy said suddenly. "That's new. That's . . . really quite nasty, actually."

He'd moved away on his own, staring into the dark tunnel-mouth. He was frowning hard as though trying to focus on something he couldn't quite identify or pin down.

"Excuse me a moment, Mr. Laurie," said JC.

He moved quickly over to join Happy and laid a heavy hand on the telepath's shoulder.

"What is the matter with you, Happy? I was starting to get some useful information out of the old man! Have you been indulging yourself with mother's little helpers again?"

"It's not the pills," said Happy. "Wish it was. No; when the old man said something bad was coming, I got a flash . . . There is definitely something Out There, outside the world we know . . . dragging itself closer, struggling to break in. Something connected to this station, but not in any way human . . ."

JC waited, but Happy had nothing more to say. "From now on, keep it to yourself," JC said quietly. "We do not want to freak out the natives till we have to. Mr. Laurie is our only source of first-hand information, and I don't want him spooked."

He moved back to join Laurie, smiling easily and re-assuringly. "No problems. Everything's fine. Oh yes. Happy's a little . . . highly strung. Now, you were about to tell me what's really going on here."

"No I wasn't," Laurie said stubbornly. "You're not ready yet. It's not like I've seen anything definite . . ."

"None so blind as those who will not see," said Happy. "Ow! That hurt!"

"It was meant to," said Melody. "Carry on, JC."

"Most people never encounter the hidden world," JC said carefully to Laurie. "Never see a ghost, never hear voices in the night. It takes the right kind of person, in a really bad place, at a very bad time . . . to actually see anything from out of this world. Ghosts are rare. Mostly, the dead go where they're supposed to. Please don't ask me where. I don't know, that's not my department. It's my job to deal with the problems of this world, not the next. No, only very rare people, under very rare circumstances, become ghosts; otherwise, we'd be hip deep in the things by now. Like you said: it's mostly people with unfinished business. Hanging on to places like this, that mean a lot to them."

"Aye," said Laurie, unexpectedly. "Like I'm fond of this place because me dad worked here, and my son is so keen on reopening it."

"And most ghosts can only be seen by the properly trained," said JC. "People with the proper skills . . ."

Laurie looked at him steadily. "Who are you people? Really?"

"You don't need to know," said JC, just as steadily. "In fact, you don't want to know. You'll sleep more easily that way. Think of us . . . as the clean-up crew. And that's all that really matters. Isn't it?"

"Aye. I suppose so," said Laurie. He nodded briskly, as though he'd made a decision. "Suppose I'll stick around for a while. Come with me. I'll get you settled, get you started. Fill you in. But I'll tell you now, for nothing—this isn't a good place to be, even before the sun goes down. Ghosts or whatever, there's something in this place that wants us out. Doesn't want anything human here. No-one's actually died of fright here, not yet; but if I was a betting man, that's where the smart money would be going. Because whatever's here will stop at nothing to have this place to itself."

"I want to go home," said Happy.

....

Ronald Laurie led the Ghost Finders through a propped-open door and into the main station building. There was no sign hanging over the door, old or new. Laurie held his storm lantern high to spread the light and indicated the single lighting switch to JC. Who turned it on, with a dramatic flourish, and was pleasantly pleased when stark, modern light filled the room. Everything inside had been cleared away and cleaned up, leaving a bare, open room with more doors leading off, and a lingering smell of disinfectant. The doors to the Ticket Office and Waiting Room were clearly labelled, and there was no dust, no cobwebs, no unnaturally dark shadows. There was still . . . an uneasy feel to the room. As though none of them was really welcome.

"Pleasant enough setting," said Happy, determinedly. "I'm not getting any bad vibrations, not much of anything, really. I don't like the place, but how much of that is me and how much the room . . ."

"This is as far as the volunteers got," said Laurie, and the others all jumped to find he'd moved silently forward to join them. He'd left his storm lantern behind and was looking around the refurbished setting with a pleased, almost proprietorial air. "Don't go in the Ticket Office, though. It's a dump. This is as much work as got done, before everything went to hell in a hurry. The Trust were going to make everything spick and span again . . . working from old photos, taken back in the day. They had the exact right shade of paint, specially remade furnishings, the lot. And then . . ."

They all waited, but he had nothing more to say.

"I saw an old signal box further down the track, when

I was up top," said JC. "Anything there we should be concerned about?"

"No," said Laurie. "This is it. This is the bad place. I think . . . something really bad happened here, long ago, and part of it is still happening."

"What do you think is behind all this, Mr. Laurie?" said JC, still being very patient because it was either that or scream out loud and stamp his foot. "You must have a theory. You know the history of this station. Has there ever been a bad crash here or some natural disaster? A murder, or a mystery . . . ?"

"There is an old story," said Laurie, reluctantly. "Not something most of us around here care to talk about. Dates back to Victorian times. Summer of 1878. A train was seen to enter the tunnel, on the other side of the Grey Fells, heading for Bradleigh Halt. Twenty, maybe thirty people saw that train enter the tunnel, going strong and steady, leading six, maybe seven carriages, packed full of passengers. A routine journey. But no-one ever saw the train come out of the tunnel, at the other end. It never arrived here, at Bradleigh Halt.

"It got later and later, and people started to worry. The signal box sent warnings up and down the line, stopped all the other trains. At first people thought there might have been some kind of accident. Maybe a crash though there shouldn't have been anything else on the line for the train to hit. The way was clear. The other station put out the alarm, and volunteers came running from towns on both sides of the Fells. Everyone would turn out, in those days. There were no real emergency services then like there are now. The men entered the tunnel from both ends, slowly and cautiously, taking their own lights in with them. A train crash in a tunnel could be a terrible thing back then. A crash meant fire, you see; and there was nowhere for the heat to go. The enclosed space of the tunnel would turn it into an oven. A furnace.

"So the men walked down the tracks, holding their lights out before them, calling out . . . and hearing only the echoes of their own voices. In the dark. In the tunnel. Until, finally, they saw lights and heard voices. But it was only the other volunteers, coming the other way. They met in the middle of the tunnel, deep under the great wide weight of the Fells; and for a long time they stood there, looking at each other. Because there was no sign of the train anywhere. Or the carriages, or the passengers. There were no side tunnels, nowhere the train could have gone.

"All those people saw the train go in; but no-one ever saw it again. Local legends have it that the train isn't really gone, just lost. Delayed, somewhere. And that one day it will return, thundering out of the tunnel-mouth and into Bradleigh Halt. A ghost train, carrying dead men and women as its cargo, all of them driven mad by all that time away . . . The train will come back, they say, come home, to announce the end of the world, perhaps.

"There are those who say you can still hear the train travelling at night, sounding its awful whistle as it enters the tunnel on the other side of the Fells; but no-one's ever heard it here. You can always find someone in a pub, ready to tell you the story for the price of a pint, how they've heard steel wheels pounding along tracks that aren't there any more. That old steam-whistle, like the scream of a soul newly damned to Hell . . . Cutting off abruptly as it enters the tunnel, going nowhere . . ."

"But no-one here's actually seen it?" said Melody, looking up from assembling her equipment.

Laurie shrugged briefly. "Who would want to? Local feeling is, if you can see it, then it can see you. And it's never good to attract the attention of something from the dark side."

"So that's why we're here," said Happy. "A late-running train. How very unusual."

Laurie gave him a hard look. "Was a time I would have said it was only another tale, for telling on a windy night by a roaring fire. Like Black Shuck, the huge black dog that wanders the back lanes late at night, confronting people and telling them their fortunes—always bad. Or like the local mine-shaft they had to close down because miners working on a new seam heard sounds of someone else digging on the other side. Or maybe the graveyard up the road, so old they're buried three deep in places; where it's said the dead rise out of their graves on Midsummer's Eve, to dance till dawn. There are always stories . . . and after what's been seen and heard here, I don't know what I believe any more."

He sighed heavily, turning his back on the Ghost Finders to look about him. "The Trust had such plans for this place. A fully refurbished Bradleigh Halt, after all these years. They'd made contact with other steam enthusiasts, made arrangements to have a proper steam train run through. There are still some out there, you know, running private services. My son Howard had it all set up; we were going to have regular excursions coming through . . . And now, no-one will come here. No-one dares."

"Don't give up yet, Mr. Laurie," said JC. "We'll sort things out and put them right. That's what we do."

"Mostly," said Happy.

"Don't think I can't reach you from here," said Melody. She consulted her various pieces of equipment, arranged before her in a semi-circle, on a collapsible stand of her own design, and seemed pleased enough. Sensors and scanners, computers and monitors, and more than a few things that only made sense to her. Laurie looked it all over with a sceptical eye. Melody stared him down. "This isn't as much as I'm used to, Mr. Laurie, but this was all I could fit into the boot of the taxi. More will follow, if necessary."

"All very shiny and impressive, I'm sure, miss," said Laurie. "But I can't guarantee you how much of it'll work here."

"I don't need to rely on your local power supply," Melody said easily. "My babies have their own generator."

"There's a sentence you won't hear very often," said Happy. He strode across to the Waiting Room door, pushed it wide open, and looked inside. Shadows looked back at him, quiet and unmoving. Happy sneered at them, shut the door carefully, and looked back at Laurie.

"So what are we waiting for? What's going to happen? Is it going to involve ectoplasm? Because if it does, I'll put my heavy coat on. Messy stuff . . ."

"It's the small things you notice, at first," said Laurie. "You'll see. The doors here don't like to stay closed. Or open. Any of them."

They all looked back at the main door they'd come in through, giving out onto the platform. It stood wide open, spilling bright electric light out into the evening. They all studied the door carefully for a long moment. Nothing happened. And then Happy frowned suddenly.

"Wait a minute . . . I shut that door behind me when we came in. Didn't I?"

None of the others had an answer for him, one way or the other. Happy scowled, strode quickly over to the open door, and slammed it shut. Then he backed quickly away from it to rejoin the others, not taking his eyes off the door all the way. It didn't move.

"Look at the Waiting Room door," said Laurie.

They all turned, and looked. The door was standing all the way open. Happy swore softly.

"Okay; I know I shut that one a moment ago. Doesn't necessarily mean anything, though. Could be the door isn't hung right, or the floor's off at an angle . . ."

"No," said Laurie. "That's not it."

JC strode unhurriedly over to the Waiting Room door, studied it for a moment, and produced a small wooden wedge from an inside pocket. He forced it into place under the bottom of the door, stepped back to look over his work, then went to the open main door and did the same thing with a second wooden wedge. He smiled cheerfully across at the others.

"That should hold it," he said. "The simple answers are always the best."

"Might work," said Laurie. "Might not. The Trust volunteers tried that as well, at first. Because it was small things, to begin with. Small, disturbing things. But if it were as easy as that to deal with, we wouldn't have needed you . . . There. See?"

They all looked around sharply, as the single naked light bulb overhead began to go out, the harsh electric light dimming, bit by bit, as though it had to come from further and further away. The light went out of the room, and the shadows pressed forward. The bulb went out, then the only light in the long room was the late-evening light, spilling through the new glass windows and the wedged-open door.

"You can replace the bulb, if you like," said Laurie. "It won't make any difference. It'll keep going out. Any bulb, in any room, anywhere in the station . . . My son Howard helped install the new lights, and the new wiring; nothing wrong with any of it. It seems that there's something here that doesn't like the light."

Melody snorted loudly, hit some switches on her display, and half a dozen small floods kicked in, blazing light from her instrument stand. Not enough to fill the whole room but more than enough to force the shadows back where they belonged. Melody smiled triumphantly at Laurie, then, one by one, the floodlights began to fade out, too. Melody swore harshly, her fingers stabbing at the keyboards set out before her, bringing all the power in her generator to bear. The floods stopped fading, but they didn't regain their former brilliance, either. Melody's eyes darted back and forth before she finally nodded, reluctantly.

"Nothing on the sensors, nothing on the scanners—short- or long-range. All of my tech is specially protected from Outside influence; but something's got to them. I've never had my lights go out on me. It shouldn't have happened."

"Will the lights stay on?" said Happy.

"They will if they know what's good for them," said Melody.

"What readings are you getting?" said JC. "Anything useful, or even interesting?"

"I'm getting electromagnetic fluctuations, other-dimensional energy spikes, and really strange barometric pressures," said Melody, her eyes darting from one monitor screen to another.

"If you don't know, say so," said Happy.

Melody stuck out her tongue at him. "The readings are clear. However, I don't know enough about local conditions to make sense of them. Yet."

Laurie managed another of his small smiles, for JC. "Been together long, have they, those two?"

"You can tell?" said JC.

"Oh aye," said Laurie. "I was married, once. But I got over it." He looked about him. "Your machines are impressive, but you'll do better with candles. The Trust laid a stock in—over there."

He nodded to a small cupboard, set to one side. JC moved across, opened it, and brought out a dozen large candles, each in its own separate holder. JC set them about the room at regular intervals, lighting them one at a time with his Zippo. He didn't smoke any more, but he liked to have something in his life he could depend on. He came back to join the others, looked about him, and nodded, pleased at the gentle, golden warmth the candlelight added to the room. Soft as butter, golden as buttercups.

"Keep an eye on the candles," said Laurie. "They have a tendency to go out. When it's most inconvenient."

And then he broke off and looked hard at JC. Around the edges of JC's heavy, dark sunglasses, a bright light was shining, sharp and distinct.

"Dear God, man," said Laurie. "What happened to your eyes?"

"Laser surgery," said JC. "I'm suing. Don't worry about it."

"JC," said Happy. "Look at the main door."

They all looked. The door JC had so carefully wedged open was now closed. The wedge lay alone on the floor, some distance away. JC studied the situation for a moment, then strode across the room, yanked the door with one hand, and pushed it all the way open. He then retrieved the wedge and forced it back into place, using all his strength. He studied the wedge, breathing hard, and knelt to check that the wedge was as securely positioned as he thought it was, testing it with his bare hand. He nodded, satisfied that he'd have a job getting it out again without the assistance of a hammer and chisel. He stood up, brushed himself down a bit fussily, and smiled easily at the others as he came back to rejoin them.

"Didn't bang it in properly, the first time," he said. "So, Mr. Laurie, doors that don't like to stay open or closed, lights that don't like to stay on. What else can we expect?"

"It gets cold," said Laurie. "Cold, for no reason. Cold as the grave."

"No central heating here?" said Happy.

"Remember where you are, lad," said Laurie. "They

didn't have such things, back in the day. Didn't believe in them. My old dad always said central heating made you soft. And who's to say he was wrong? There's a decent-sized fire-place if you need one in the Waiting Room. And an authentic paraffin stove, in the Ticket Office. Not much fuel in it. So don't waste it. Never know when you might need it."

"Hold everything." Melody looked quickly from one set of readings to another. "Something here, or very near here, is interfering with my equipment. My short-range sensors keep locking onto something, then losing it for no good reason. There's something here with us, JC. Can't tell you what it is yet, but it's weird and powerful and very slippery . . ."

And then Happy cried out—a sudden, shocked sound. They all turned to look at him. He was pointing with a trembling hand at a small mirror hanging on the far wall. It was an ordinary, everyday mirror; in a straightforward ornamental frame. Afterwards, no-one could be sure exactly what they saw there, only that there was a face in the mirror, watching them. And it wasn't the face of anyone in the room. The image disappeared the moment they all rushed forward to look at it, and by the time they all got there, the reflection showed only their own faces, looking back at them with wide eyes and shocked, startled expressions. At what they'd seen, or thought they'd seen. It took the Ghost Finders a moment to realise Laurie wasn't there with them. They looked back; and he was standing right where he had been. He nodded slightly and shrugged one shoulder, as if to say, *What did you expect?*

JC very firmly turned the mirror over, to face the wall, then looked thoughtfully at Laurie.

"This isn't the first time that's happened, is it? You've seen this before?"

"Aye. Everyone has, who's spent any time here. Someone is always watching us. But don't ask me who."

"What did you see in the mirror?" said Melody. "Who did you see?"

"Once," Laurie said slowly, "I thought I saw myself; as I might look after I'd been dead and in the ground for a good few years."

"It's mind-games," JC said briskly. "Everything we've encountered so far has been nothing but supernatural parlour tricks, designed to scare us off. Whatever's here can't be that powerful, or it wouldn't need tricks. It'd simply kill us, or throw us out of here. But it hasn't because it can't. That's why it's hiding from us."

"It?" said Laurie, pointedly.

"Oh, there's always an It," said Happy.

"Details," said JC, advancing purposefully on Laurie. "I need details, on everything that's happened here. Tell me about the experiences of the other volunteers, Mr. Laurie. The time has come to tell the tale, supernatural warts and all."

"Sounds," said Laurie. "Voices. Saying . . . disturbing things. The sound of footsteps, walking up and down the platform; but when you go out and look, there's never anyone there. Station announcements, over speakers that aren't there any more, for trains and services that haven't run in decades. Voices in the room next door, blurred and indistinct, like the words we hear in dreams . . . They sound like old friends, or dead relatives, desperately trying to reach us, to warn us about something terrible that's coming. And there's always this feeling of someone here that shouldn't be, watching from the shadows, or from just behind you. And you never turn round to look because you know, you just know, there's nobody there . . . or at least nobody you'd want to see. I've spent years in this place, and never once felt threatened or in any danger, until now . . . The last volunteer to leave said he was convinced there was always someone sneaking up behind him, looking over his shoulder . . ."

By now Happy was trying to look in so many different directions at once that he was turning round and round in circles. He was breathing heavily, his eyes painfully wide. He realised that the others were looking at him and stopped abruptly. He took out a handkerchief, wiped the sweat from his face, and smiled weakly. Then he put the handkerchief away, marched over to the nearest wall, and put his back to it, arms folded defiantly across his chest.

"I'm fine!" he said loudly. "Fine and dandy, oh yes! And no, I'm not picking up anything. Which is odd, because I should be getting something by now. So I can only assume that whatever particular It is haunting this place, it's pretty damned powerful. And I'd really like to get the hell out of here before It turns up and shouts Boo! in my face. Please pretty please."

Laurie looked at Happy, then at JC. "I thought you people were supposed to be experts."

"Oh, we are," said Melody, not looking up from her instruments. "But then, there's experts, then there's experts."

"You have to make allowances for Happy," said JC. "Because if you don't, he sulks. Or gives you ulcers from the sheer frustration of trying to keep up with his many and various mood swings. Happy is a sensitive soul, and not nearly as heavily medicated as he used to be. Feel free to hit him. We do."

"At least I've got enough sense not to hang about in places where I'm clearly not welcome," said Happy.

"Then you are very definitely in the wrong business," JC said cheerfully. "Now quiet down and be a brave little ghost finder, and there shall be Jaffa Cakes for tea. Go on, Mr. Laurie, I'm still listening. What else has happened?"

"Isn't what I've told you enough?" said Laurie.

"Information is ammunition," JC said solemnly. "Which we can use to kick the arse of our paranormal enemy. Ghosts deal in uncertainty. Things we see out of the corners of our eyes, come and gone in a moment, are always going to be more frightening than some blurry shape in a doorway, not even solid enough to rattle its chains."

"Most of what I'm telling you is only stories," said Laurie. "Things the volunteers talked about, among themselves. Some did say they'd seen, or at least glimpsed, a figure. Never up close, and none of them saw it clearly, but they were all very sure they'd seen something. And some of them said it wasn't human. As such."

"Now we're getting somewhere," said JC. "You ever see this figure yourself?"

"I might have glimpsed it, from time to time," Laurie said reluctantly. "An old-fashioned type, tall and thin, dressed like a gentleman from my grandfather's time."

"And you never thought to mention this before?" said Melody, sharply.

"You stick around this place long enough, and your senses will start playing tricks on you, too," said Laurie. "But if I did see what I thought I saw . . . there was something wrong with its head. Like maybe . . . part of the head was missing."

JC considered this. "Does this . . . disfigured figure fit in with any of the local legends?"

"No," Laurie said firmly. "This is something new. Something else. Even if it does have its roots in the past."

They all suddenly stopped where they were and shivered violently. The temperature in the room had plummeted in a moment. Their breaths steamed heavily on the still air, and they all hugged themselves against the sudden, bitter cold. Great whorls of hoarfrost spread slowly across the walls, like massive fingerprints. Frost and even solid ice formed on Melody's instrument panels and monitor screens. She frantically wiped it away with her sleeves, but it came back again. The room was so cold now, it burned exposed faces and hands and seared the lungs that breathed it in. Of them all, Laurie seemed the least affected. Probably because he was northern, one of those hardened souls who claim not to feel the cold and only put a vest on when there's an actual blizzard outside. Melody fired up the heating elements in her support system, scraping the frost off her sensor screens with her fingers, so she could make out the new readings.

"I am seeing serious cold, JC!" she said, forcing the words out between chattering teeth. "And I'm talking deep cold here, unnatural cold! But according to my sensors, only in this room!"

"Now this is what I call a cold spot!" said JC, beating his hands together, then rubbing them briskly. "This is more like it! Traditional ghost sign; something is draining energy out of the immediate surroundings to fuel an imminent manifestation. Take up your positions, people; we have a ghost heading this way."

"Yes," said Laurie. "It's here . . ."

JC beckoned Happy forward, and the two of them stood back-to-back, looking quickly about them. Melody ignored the room completely, giving all her attention to what her sensor readouts were telling her. Laurie stood alone, looking out the open main door at the platform beyond. All around, shadows were moving slowly, subtly, creeping forward, pushing back the light. The room was full of a sense of movement, of things that came and went, gone the moment you looked at them directly. And there was a growing sense of *presence*, an overwhelming feeling that they were no longer the only ones in the room. That something new was approaching from an unknown direction, to join them.

"Told you," said Laurie. He was the only one not looking around him, apparently entirely unconcerned. "It's not safe to be here, not now it's got dark."

"Please stand your ground, Mr. Laurie," JC said firmly. "Don't go, not when things are starting to get interesting. You really mustn't let these things bother you. It's all smoke and mirrors, when you get right down to it— meant to soften us up for the main event. To put us in the proper mood for when our ghost finally deigns to make his entrance. Never met a ghost that wasn't a drama queen. Melody, tell me something!"

"Power readings are off the scale, JC," said Melody, her eyes darting from one monitor screen to another. "Room temperature's stabilised, even starting to rise again. A little. Which would suggest our mysterious prime mover now has all the power it needs to materialise. Something is coming. Heading our way from a direction I can't even describe. From Outside, from far beyond the fields we know. Hold it . . . hold it . . . I'm getting something. Something drawing near. I can't say what it is or how it's related to what's been happening here . . . but I'm quite definitely detecting a weak spot in reality, in our Space/Time continuum . . . Outside, at the far end of the platform, down by the tunnel-mouth. I think . . . it's a doorway, or at the very least a potential door, an opening between here and Somewhere Else."

"Great!" said Happy, miserably. "Fantastic! Just what we needed—more complications. I may cry. Why isn't anything ever simple and straightforward?"

"Because the world isn't like that," said JC. "Ours, or anyone else's. Okay! Everyone come together, in the middle of the room. And, yes, that very definitely includes you, Melody. Your precious toys can look after themselves for a moment. Come along, come along, hoppity hop! In a circle, please, shoulder to shoulder, looking out at the room."

"We're not going to have to hug each other, or hold hands, are we?" said Happy suspiciously. "You know I've never been keen on that hippy touchy-feely crap."

They all stood close together, shoulder pressed against

shoulder. JC could feel the tension in Happy's shoulder on the one side and the cold, hard presence of Laurie on the other. Happy glared about him, a bit more focused now he had something definite to disapprove of. Melody's hands had closed into bony fists, more than ready for a close encounter with the mortally challenged. JC couldn't keep from smiling. He lived for moments like this, a chance to grab the supernatural by the shoulders and give it a good hard shake till it agreed to start making sense and give up its secrets.

"Ignore the advancing shadows, and the strange shapes jumping at the corners of your eyes," he said loudly. "It's all misdirection. We're meant to look at them, so we won't see what's really important. Keep your eyes open and listen to my voice. Consider. What made Bradleigh Halt such a bad place, so recently? A *genius loci* and a centre for bad happenings? What's powering the unnatural events in this out-of-the-way place? It has to be connected to the train that disappeared into a tunnel. Snatched out of this world and taken away to Somewhere Else. Because that's the only story, the only event, that contains a general-weird-shit event and general loss of life. The usual prime causes of a haunting.

"I think the train is still Out There, somewhere, locked in place, preserved, like an insect trapped in amber. Held there, in equilibrium, unable to go forward or back. And then the Preservation Trust volunteers started work here, ripping out the old to install the new. Changing things . . . changing the situation. Enough to upset the delicate balance and blast the trapped train right out of its holding pattern. You should never move things, Mr. Laurie; it leaves gaps. And, sometimes, it attracts the attention of things from Outside."

"What are you saying?" said Laurie. "What's happening here? What's going to happen?"

"I think your little lost train is finally coming home," said JC. "All the time it was trapped and held Somewhere Else, it's been trying to get home. Straining against the bonds that hold it. Think of it as pressure building, like steam in a kettle. Building up a head of steam powerful enough to break free at last. And, as Melody said, there's now a weak spot in reality, right by the tunnel-mouth. Where the train will come through . . . When the accumulated pressure finally blows it wide open. So that the train and its carriages and passengers can finally come home. Which might be a good thing, or a bad thing, depending on what state the train and its passengers are in. Whether they were trapped in a time-less moment, or whether they had to endure every bit of the long years they've been missing, in that Other Place.

"And, of course, there's always the problem of what the train might bring back with it, from that Other Place. There are always terrible things lurking on the threshold of reality, waiting for a chance to break in. To feed or destroy. Or, much worse, make us over into things like them."

"If the train was trapped in a moment out of Time, then the passengers could return without knowing any-thing at all has happened to them," said Happy. "They could come home safe and well. They'll need debriefing, of course, but . . ."

"Dear Happy," said JC. "Always hoping for the best."

"And nearly always being disappointed," growled Happy. "Why can't we have a happy ending, for once?"

"Because it wasn't temporal energy I was picking up," said Melody. "Or I would have said. My instruments were registering powerful other-dimensional energy spikes. And besides, trains don't simply disappear. Something reached into this world and took it away. And, given the way things have been acting up around here, I don't think that train was taken with good intentions. Do you?"

"Why can't we all get along?" said Happy, plaintively.

"So," JC said firmly. "A train with carriages packed full of people, taken Outside of Time and Space, and held Somewhere Else, for over a century. And no way of telling for what purpose. After being held for so long, under unknown alien conditions, there's no way this can turn out well. I think the best we can hope for is that everyone on the train is dead."

"What?" said Laurie, looking around sharply.

"You can't live under alien conditions without being changed in alien ways," JC said patiently, and as kindly as he could. "You can't live in an alien place and stay human. The only way to survive is to change and adapt. After all those years away, completely cut off from Earth-normal conditions; who knows what shape the train's passengers will be in? Physical or psychological? The shock of the return might be enough to kill them."

"So . . . you're saying we should try and stop them coming back?" said Laurie, frowning.

"I'm not sure that's an option any more," said JC.

"Not with so much pressure building behind it for so long."

"Then what do all the manifestations and things here mean?" said Laurie.

"Simple," said JC. "Someone, or Something, was disturbed when the volunteers started changing things in the station, and it has been working ever since to drive everyone else away. It doesn't want things to change enough for the train to be able to return; or, failing that, it doesn't want anyone here when it does."

He broke off; and they all looked around at the wedged-open main door and the platform beyond. Slow, steady footsteps were advancing down the platform from the far end, heading straight for them. Heavy, regular footsteps, not hurrying, taking their time. As though whoever was responsible wanted them to be heard, for the people hearing them to have a chance to get away. There was something off, something not quite right, about the footsteps. Too loud and too heavy for any single man to make; and each and every echoing tread seemed to linger that little bit too long, as though every step had something of eternity in it. A sound that was always there, even when you couldn't hear it.

A dark figure walked past the window. It looked like a man, but its movements were wrong. It took too long to make its movements, as though the body wasn't affected by things like gravity or inertia any more, as though it accepted no authority but its own. A human shape, broken free of the ties of this world. And though everyone in the room only saw the dark shape at the window for a moment, they all thought the same thing. *There's something wrong with its head* . . . It passed by the window, then, after a heart-stoppingly tense moment, it came in through the door, and stopped there, facing them. The ghost of Bradleigh Halt.

It looked like a man, standing tall and slender and proud, dressed like a proper gentleman of Victorian times. A smart, even elegant, outfit, but . . . hard worn, as though it had been put to use for much longer than it should have. A middle-aged man, with a grey, sad face and fixed, staring eyes. His arms hung unmoving at his sides, the pale, long-fingered hands twitching slightly. For all his stillness and silence, there was a dreadful urgency to the man. You couldn't not look at him; by being there, he weighed so heavily on the world that he drew all the attention in the room. Because simply by being there, he was the most important thing in it.

"See?" Laurie said quietly. "The head. Look at his head."

They looked, and they saw. The top part of the ghost's head was gone. Missing. As though someone had sawn the top of his head right off, directly above the bushy eyebrows. A very neat cut, with not a single jagged edge; a very professional job indeed.

JC moved slowly forward, and the ghost didn't react. It stood there, glaring at them all. Step by cautious step, JC walked right up to the ghost, until he was face-to-face with it. JC's breath steamed thickly on the bitter cold air, but no breath moved from the ghost's lips. JC lifted himself up onto his tiptoes, and looked down into the ghost's cut-open head. And then he stood down again and carefully backed away from the ghost, never taking his eyes off it.

"Well?" said Happy.

"Well," said JC. "That's . . . really quite interesting, actually. There's nothing inside his head. His brain has been removed."

TWO

LAST CALL FOR THE DEAD

"Removed?" said Melody. "You mean surgically?"

"Could be," said JC. "Or it's the most extreme case of trepanation I've ever seen."

"What?" said Laurie.

"Where you drill a hole in your head to make yourself smarter," said Happy. "Trust me, it doesn't work."

"Hold everything, shout halleluiah," said Melody. "I think I know who that is. I've seen that face before . . . in an old photograph. Nothing to do with this case . . . another case altogether . . . Yes! Got it! People, we are looking at someone who used to be very famous indeed. This is all that remains of that great Victorian medium and spiritualist, Dr. Emil Todd!"

"You never forget anything, do you?" said Happy, admiringly.

"The name rings a vague bell," said JC, which was his

way of saying he'd never heard of the man but was willing to admit that Melody had. "Still, a dead Victorian medium, and a missing Victorian train. Has to be a connection. But why is he here now?"

"Ask him," said Happy.

"You ask him," said JC. "You're the team telepath. Look inside his mind and see what this is all about."

"I can't," said Happy, frowning. "And not because there's a whole bunch of fresh air where his grey matter used to be. This is a really powerful manifestation, and it's very powerfully shielded. I wouldn't even know this ghost was here if I couldn't see it standing there scowling at me, and I do wish it would stop doing that."

"You really think you can get answers out of that thing?" said Laurie.

"Why not?" said Melody. "It's a ghost. Most of them only stick around because there's something they need to say to someone. Even if it's simply *Look what you made me do, aren't you sorry now?*"

"You can leave now, if you wish, Mr. Laurie," said JC. "You shouldn't have to deal with things like this. Coping with ghosts is our business. We're trained to deal with things that go Boo! in the night."

"No," said Laurie, after a moment, staring steadily at the ghost before him. "Now I've seen what it is, up close, it doesn't seem that scary, after all. It's a man, isn't it?"

"Or what's left of one," said Happy. "That's all ghosts ever are, really—people with unfinished business. If you weren't scared of a man while he was alive, why be scared of him once he's dead? Even when they walk through walls, or rip their own heads off, they're only indulging a thwarted theatrical streak."

"So why is this man running around with his head empty?" said Laurie.

"Because that was the last important thing that ever happened to him," said Melody. "A ghost's shape and aspect is determined by its most significant memories."

"And *that* certainly made one hell of an impression on him," said Happy.

"Is this figure what the other volunteers saw, Mr. Laurie?" asked JC.

"I don't know," said Laurie. "Maybe. I never saw anything like it before, and I've been around here longer than most."

"Why isn't he saying anything?" said Melody.

"He's a Victorian gentleman," said Happy. "Probably waiting to be properly introduced."

The ghost of Dr. Todd stood very still, glaring at them all impartially. JC stepped forward again.

"What are you doing here, Dr. Todd?" he said carefully. "What holds your spirit here? Is there anything we can do to help?"

The ghost didn't speak, didn't move. His eyes didn't blink; his mouth remained a flat grey line. He might have been alone in the room.

"This is like when we have an argument," Happy said to Melody. "And you go stomping around the room, being mad at me but refusing to say what's wrong because I'm supposed to know. And I never do."

"There's no blood on the doctor's face," JC said thoughtfully. "Which suggests that the . . . rather dramatic cranial damage occurred sometime after his death. Ghosts usually like to show off their death-wounds, especially if they're a bit gory."

"They do?" said Laurie.

"Oh sure," said Happy. "Ghosts are all about the show. Bunch of drama queens. *Look what happened to me! Aren't you impressed?*"

"It could be surgical," said JC. "Given the neatness of the job. How did Dr. Todd die, Melody? Do we know?"

"According to the records I am accessing right now," said Melody, from behind her bank of instruments again, "the files say . . . nobody knows. He disappeared. Body never found. Big mystery, back in the day."

"Ah," said Happy, wisely. "One of those . . ."

JC nodded to Happy, and they both moved in close, looking the ghost over carefully at point-blank range. He didn't blink, or flinch, in the slightest. And then they both started shivering violently and quickly backed away. A thin layer of new frost covered both their faces. They wiped it away with their sleeves, looked respectfully at the ghost, and backed off some more.

"Damn, that was cold!" said Happy, beating his hands together to try to force some feeling back into them.

"I could feel the heat being sucked right out of me," said JC, stamping his feet hard on the wooden floor. "Melody?"

"My short-range sensors are registering a major heat-sink," said Melody, frowning. "Dr. Todd is still draining energy out of the room to maintain his presence in the material world. Get too close, and he could shut you right down."

"But it's not like he's doing anything!" said JC. "What does he need all that energy for?"

"I think he's used to scaring people off, simply by turning up," said Happy. "He isn't used to people who don't go all to pieces the moment they see a ghost. I have to wonder: is this all he's got, or does he have a second act?"

He didn't have long to wait for an answer. The main-entrance door began to force itself closed. It pushed itself forward, pressing against the wooden wedge set in place to stop it, straining forward in sudden jumps and surges, determined to close. The wooden wedge squealed loudly as it scraped across the wooden floor, and smoke curled up from the contact point. JC moved forward, another wedge already in his hand, only to stop himself abruptly as the wedge under the door exploded, blown apart by the sheer pressure behind it. JC turned his face away as wooden splinters flew through the air like shrapnel. The door surged forward triumphantly. JC ran forward, grabbed the edge of the door with both hands, and threw his weight against it. He struggled for a moment, setting his merely human strength against the implacable unnatural force behind the door. Then JC ripped the door right off its hinges and threw it to one side.

The door hit the floor with an echoing crash, loud enough to wake the dead; and then it rocked briefly back and forth before lying still. But no-one was looking at the door. Everyone was looking at JC. He was looking at his hands, turning them back and forth as though he'd never seen them before.

"When did you turn into the Incredible Hulk, JC?" said Happy.

"Beats the hell out of me," said JC. "I'm as mystified as you. It was as though the door suddenly didn't weigh anything at all." He looked at the shattered brass hinges, hanging loosely from the solid door-frame. "It would appear that the change started in me, by my contact with the Outside, is an ongoing process. That isn't finished with me yet."

He knelt beside the door, tried to lift it with one hand, and found he barely had the strength to raise it off the floor. Whatever more-than-human strength had moved in him moments before, it was clearly gone. JC stood up, turned his back on the fallen door, and smiled briefly at the others.

"As long as I'm not actually turning green and exhibiting a more-than-usually-surly disposition . . . I wouldn't worry about it."

The ghost of Dr. Todd advanced suddenly on Happy, striding forward with uncanny speed. The cold, grim expression on the ghost's face didn't change at all. Happy quickly backed away, but the ghost went after him, rapidly closing the gap.

"Don't let him get too close!" said Melody. "He's still sucking the heat out of everything!"

"I had worked that out for myself, thank you!" said Happy, back-pedalling fast. "I'm trying to hold him off telepathically, but I can't find anything to lock onto. I'm not even convinced there's anything there to reach, with his brain gone. All I'm picking up is his presence, a shape impressed on reality through sheer force of will. He shines so bright, JC! Looking at him is like being blinded by a spotlight!"

"Then stop looking at him!" said JC. "Put up your shields! Keep him out!"

"I'm trying! I'm trying! Damn, he's strong!"

Happy's back slammed up against the far wall. There was nowhere left for him to go; and the ghost was still advancing. Melody came rushing out from behind her instruments and put herself between Happy and the ghost of Dr. Todd. His expression didn't change; but he stopped dead, right in front of Melody. His hands came up from his sides and clutched her shoulders. She cried out, in shock as much as pain, as the terrible cold hit her. She shook and shuddered under his touch, the fierce cold stabbing through her like knives. A layer of frost formed on her face, covering her eyeballs like cataracts.

JC ran forward, grabbed Melody by one arm, and hauled her out of the way. The ghost had no physical strength to hang on to her. He didn't even look aside as Melody disappeared from in front of him. His cold gaze remained fixed on Happy. Melody fell to one knee, shaking and shuddering. Happy moved quickly out from in front of the ghost to kneel beside her, throwing his arms around her, using the warmth of his own body to drive the cold out of hers. The ghost turned to glare at him. JC moved to put himself between the ghost and his partners, whipped off his very dark sunglasses, and showed what he had for eyes to the ghost of Dr. Todd. They glared brightly, fiercely, in the gloom, like the sun come down to touch the Earth; and Dr. Todd could not face the light. He backed away, slowly, seeming to glide as much as walk, until he came to a halt on the far side of the room.

Melody scrubbed roughly at her face with both hands,

brushing the frost away. Her skin was blue-white, almost bruised, but already fierce spots of angry colour were returning. She moved restlessly inside Happy's arms, and he immediately let her go and stood up, letting Melody get to her feet under her own strength. She could be funny about things like that. JC replaced his sunglasses.

"Dear God, man," said Laurie. "What the hell happened to your eyes?"

"Work-related injury," said JC. "I let some demons get too close to me during a haunting down in London's Underground. They very nearly killed me; but something from Outside reached down and touched me, giving me the strength I needed to save myself. I'm more than I was; and you can see it in my eyes."

"Something from where?" said Laurie. "From Heaven?"

"Undecided, as yet," said JC.

"Don't you think you should try to find out?" said Laurie. "You've been marked. But is it a sign of grace or a sign of ownership? I think you owe it to yourself to find out the true nature of your benefactor—if only for your own peace of mind."

"Trust me," said JC. "It is right there on my list of Things to Do." He looked across at Melody and Happy, and they both nodded quickly to show that they were themselves again. "Happy, keep trying to read that ghost. Get something out of him. But don't let him get inside your head. Melody, it's research time. I need to know everything you can find about Dr. Emil Todd. What's his story, and what connection does he have to Bradleigh Halt?"

"I'm on it," said Melody, already back behind her rank of instruments, fingers stabbing stiffly at her keyboards as she accessed the relevant files on her computer. "The Institute still has an open file on Dr. Todd, as an unsolved case . . . But it is really heavily restricted, JC, for several pay grades above ours. This is the kind of information the likes of you and I aren't supposed to even know exists."

"You've been hacking the restricted files on your own time again, haven't you?" said JC.

"Yes," said Melody.

"Good girl," said JC. "Now tell me things I need to know."

"Dr. Todd disappeared, late in the year 1878," said Melody. "Same year as the missing train . . . And according to this file, it's all connected to something called the Ghost Caller. This is pretty obscure stuff, JC. Old-time information, much of it second hand; I'm not sure anyone at the Institute knew about this stuff before we were sent in."

"Except we can't be sure of anything where the Carnacki Institute's concerned, these days," Happy said darkly.

"The Ghost Caller," said Melody, talking over Happy with the ease of long practice. "Also known as The Call For The Dead. No definite information here about what it was or how it worked. Presumably some kind of Victorian steampunk break-through, to produce a machine we have yet to duplicate."

"Mostly because any sane person would have more sense than to build anything that calls ghosts," said

Happy. "Anyone with two working brain-cells to bang together knows it's in everyone's best interests to keep the dead at arm's length."

"Ah, but it wasn't always like that," said Melody. "The Ghost Caller, this incredible machine, was the brain-child of Dr. Emil Todd, (almost certainly not his real name,) one of the greatest and most popular mediums of Victorian times. When they were all going mad for Spiritualism, and raising the ghosts of the departed, so they could make contact with loved ones on the Other Side. Dr. Todd toured the country with his act, appearing in all the biggest theatres, putting on spectacular shows. He produced spirit voices, visions, ectoplasm, and extended conversations with the dearly departed of people in his audience. Charged a pretty price for admission but always gave the people their money's worth. He was, briefly, a national sensation. But he'd barely been in the big time a year before he was exposed as a fake and a fraud. He really did do most of it with mirrors. And ventriloquism, conjuring tricks, and plants in the audience. All very obvious, in retrospect. A jumped-up showman, with delusions of grandeur. He was ruined, abandoned by the audiences who'd adored and believed in him. He was hounded from the stage and forced into early retirement. Had to go into hiding, for his own safety.

"And then he disappeared. As suddenly and completely as one of his own stage effects.

"With anyone else, the story might have ended there, but Dr. Todd was made of sterner stuff. He was determined to restore his reputation by presenting the public with something undeniably real. So he took the extensive fortune he'd amassed and spent pretty much all of it in having the Ghost Caller created for him. An apparently very impressive device, for which no contemporary description survives, but powerful enough to call ghosts to it, like moths to a bright light.

"However, before Dr. Todd could demonstrate the Call For The Dead on stage, he was shut down by the Queen's champion of that time, the legendary Victorian Adventurer, Julien Advent. He confiscated the Ghost Caller because of the threat it posed. Not to the Nation, but all Humanity. Apparently, the machine was so powerful that once its Call began, anything, and by that I mean anything at all, could be summoned into our reality from any of the Outer Reaches. Ghosts, demons, abhuman monstrosities—you name it. An irresistible Call, a summons with no limit to its reach . . . Who knows what that might have let in. There are always things Out There, lurking on the threshold of our world, waiting for an invitation . . ."

"We're talking about the Great Beasts, aren't we?" said Happy. "The Abominations, the Entities from the Outer Reaches."

"You might be," said Laurie. "I haven't a clue what you're talking about."

"Be grateful," said Happy.

He moved away, to be on his own for a moment. One hand deep in his trouser pocket closed around a pill bottle. Melody had worked hard to keep Happy from depending on chemical supports, mostly by having lots of sex with him whenever he looked like weakening. But really, all she'd done was distract him. And she couldn't be there all the time. The problem remained the same: that Happy saw, heard, and sensed far more of reality than was good for him. He needed his special medications to shut his telepathy down to bearable levels, to keep the hidden world and all its horrors outside his head. He'd hoped that sex, and maybe even love, might be enough; but they couldn't give him the peace of mind the pills could. Or the strength. Happy was not a strong man. He never had been. And he knew it. He had done his best to keep off the pills because it meant so much to Melody; but at times like this, faced with imminent dangers from Awful Things from Beyond . . . Happy reached for the only real strength he'd ever known.

His hand closed tightly around the pill bottle; but he didn't take it out. Not yet.

Happy didn't know, but JC had already talked with Melody about providing Happy with some kind of experimental tech support. Some kind of machine, to keep the bad stuff outside Happy's head. But Melody had been forced to admit she'd already tried everything she could think of, and she could think of some pretty extreme things. Not one of them had worked. She'd failed Happy and failed herself. She wasn't used to that. JC and Melody hadn't told Happy any of this. They didn't want him to give up hope. Because Happy needed hope more than anything.

And Happy wasn't the only one.

"This . . . Ghost Caller," JC said to Melody. "Is it something I could use, to call Kim back to me?"

"Not a good idea, JC," Melody said quietly. "The Ghost Caller was, by all accounts, anything but subtle. You can't choose whom you want to call. There's an On/

Off switch, to open and close a Door. And God alone knows what might be waiting on the Other Side."

"Hold everything," said Happy, turning back to face them. "Didn't I hear something recently about an Apocalypse Door? A Door to give you direct access to the Hereafter? Am I remembering that right? Could that be something like our Ghost Caller?"

"Not really," JC said patiently. "The Apocalypse Door allowed you to open the Gates of Hell. It was destroyed by the Droods."

"Why would anyone . . . ?" said Laurie.

"Don't go there," said JC.

"The Ghost Caller doesn't give you access to the Hereafter," said Melody. "It sends out an open call to the restless dead. Of which there has never been any shortage . . ." She thought for a moment, then sniffed loudly. "What we could really use is a Ghost Repellent. Something to send ghosts away."

"Some kind of spray, perhaps," Happy said brightly. "Something in a can—Ghost Away! I'd pay good money for a can of that."

. JC gave Melody a look, and she resumed telling Dr. Todd's story.

"It seems that Julien Advent took the Ghost Caller away from Dr. Todd, despite his strong and even violent objections. And put the device on a train, under guard, to be taken to a place of safety. Where it could be studied, and, if necessary, dismantled. The files don't say where this would have taken place . . . Probably the original Dark Heir Headquarters, down in Cornwall. That was the main repository, back then, our very own Area 51, for all the really dangerous weird shit that the world wasn't ready for. Is it Area 51, the Americans use, these days? I get mixed up, there are so many stories . . ."

"It's Area 52," said Happy, unexpectedly. "Situated in the Antarctic Circle, up past the McMurdo Sound. So if anything should go suddenly and unpleasantly and explosively wrong, there's no-one around to be killed, maimed, or nastily transformed. Except a few penguins."

"There aren't any penguins in the Antarctic," said Melody.

Happy glared at her. "They had some moved in, for camouflage."

"You've been working your way through the forbidden files I downloaded, haven't you?" said Melody. "Good boy. There will be treats later."

"Young rebels in love," said JC. "The horror, the horror . . . Get on with the story, Melody. It's getting late."

"Later than you think," said Laurie. The others looked at him, but he had nothing more to say.

"Anyway," said Melody. "Pressing on. Enter Dr. Todd, again. It seems he was now so scared of the Ghost Caller, and what it could do, that he wanted it gone. Destroyed, or at the very least, made safe. Apparently he didn't trust what Her Majesty's Government of that time might do with it. So he made a deal with Someone, or Something, presumably the same Power that made the Ghost Caller for him in the first place, and had them send the Ghost Caller . . . Away. You have to understand, though, all of this is conjecture, put together after the fact. No-one knows anything for sure."

"Oh, I think we can make some pretty good guesses,"

said JC. "The Ghost Caller was placed on a train, which entered a tunnel, and was never seen again! Because it was sent Away, out of our reality, to some Other Place. So no-one else could have it. And Dr. Todd's ghost is here to guard the station, to frighten people away . . . so no-one could do anything that might bring the train back again. He's stood guard all these years, to protect us all from the terrible machine he made.

"But the volunteers came and made changes in the station, changing the conditions that helped keep the train Away . . . And now there's a dimensional weak spot where the accumulated pressure has burst through. A doorway, or at least a potential doorway, between here and Away."

"You think the missing train is coming home, at last?" said Laurie.

"And bringing the Ghost Caller with it," said JC.

"All right, I'm sort of with you," said Happy. "But none of that explains why the top of Dr. Todd's head is missing."

"One thing at a time," JC said cheerfully. "Let's go out onto the platform again. See what there is to see."

"It'll all end in tears," said Happy. "Probably mine."

::::::::::::::::::::::::::::::

They went back out onto the station platform, JC leading the way and looking cheerfully about him. He'd recovered a lot of his usual cocky bravado. Happy wasn't sure whether he approved or not. Yes, it was good to see JC back to his old self again; but the old JC did have a distressing tendency to rush in where angels wouldn't show up on a bet. Usually while shouting *Follow me!* to Happy and Melody. Happy looked nervously up and down the platform, sticking close to Melody. It was very late evening now, not much light left in the sky. Hardly any of the station room's candlelight followed them out through the doorway, and the lights built into Melody's instrument rack had dimmed right down. Even the sound of their footsteps seemed muffled, far-away. There was a terrible stillness to everything, as though everything in the station was waiting for something. An almost unbearable sense of anticipation, of something important and significant, about to begin.

Laurie stayed in the doorway, looking at the three Ghost Finders as much as the station.

JC strode right up to the edge of the platform and stopped, the tips of his shoes protruding over the drop, and the tracks. He bounced up and down happily, peering into every dark and concealing shadow as though he expected something to emerge and present him with a box of chocolates. He studied the weed-choked tracks, and the heavily rusted rails, before finally giving his full attention to the gaping tunnel-mouth. He studied it thoughtfully for some time. Darkness looked back at him, complete and implacable.

"This where you detected the dimensional weak point, Melody?" he said, without looking back.

"Not so much a door as where a door could appear," said Melody. "And the more the pressure builds, the bigger that door's going to be. And the greater the impact it will have upon our reality. You can't force an opening between worlds without some inevitable spiritual fall-out."

"Such as?" said Laurie from his doorway.

"Rains of frogs, spontaneously combusting cows, and the dead coming home to roost," said Happy. "The universe doesn't like being messed about with and has a tendency to act up cranky, in protest. Is there any way we can stop the train's coming back, JC?"

"We don't want to," JC said briskly. "The train wants to come home, where it belongs. And we want that pressure relieved because it's been building for over a century; so when the doorway finally opens, it's all going to happen at once, in a big way. Best we can do is hope to control the situation and keep the nasty side effects contained, here within the station. That train is on its way back, finishing its long journey at last, and nothing in or out of Heaven or Hell will stop it now."

"The train isn't the real problem," said Melody. "Don't get side-tracked, JC. The real problem is the Ghost Caller. It was dangerous enough when it was first placed aboard the train; by now it could have accumulated enough power to blow a hole clean through the Space/Time continuum. If the stress of the return activates the machine, we could be talking about a mass psychic summoning. One last call for all the dead that ever were."

"I am leaving now," said Happy. "Try and keep up."

"Stand still! Show a brave face, Happy," said JC, sternly. "There are civilians present."

"Oh, don't mind me," said Laurie. "I told you, no-one with any sense stays here once it gets dark."

"See!" said Happy. "See!"

"We should get danger money," said Melody.

Happy stopped and looked at her. "It would help," he said finally.

"Hold it," said JC. "We have company."

They all looked around, to find the ghost of Dr. Todd had joined them out on the platform. He stood on his own, some distance away, staring unblinkingly into the dark tunnel-mouth. JC calmly strode forward to join him, looked into the tunnel opening, then right into the ghost's face.

"Why are you here, Dr. Todd? You've failed to prevent the train's return, so why are you still here?"

The ghost looked straight through him, as though he weren't there, and said nothing at all. JC glanced back at Happy.

"Are you sure you aren't picking up something from him? Anything at all?"

"No thoughts, no personality . . . it's as though he's so far-away, I can barely see him. Something really bad happened to Dr. T; and I don't think it was only the head injury. I think part of it is still happening. There's a definite connection between the ghost, the missing train, and the Ghost Caller. I can sense it, feel it; this whole setting is soaked in information. And JC . . . I can't feel Dr. Todd, but I can feel something that I'm pretty sure is the Ghost Caller. It's not simply a machine. It's close now, closer than it has ever been, ready to break through . . . And I think it needs Dr. Todd to be here when it arrives. He's not here through his own free will; the Ghost Caller holds him here."

"Why?" said JC. "What's the connection?"

"I don't know!" said Happy. "I'm getting a headache trying to process all this. It's something to do with the price Dr. Todd paid for the creation of the Ghost Caller."

"No-one move," Melody said quietly. "But look around you. The fog is rolling in."

They all looked carefully up and down the platform. A shimmering grey fog had descended on both ends and was creeping slowly and remorselessly along the platform towards them. It rose out of everywhere at once, curling and coiling thickly on the still evening air, pulsing with its own eerie light. The tunnel-mouth was already lost to sight. In a few moments, the fog was already so thick that none of them could make out the opposite platform. The pulsing mists spilled along the railway tracks, covering them up in a thick grey tide, and soon the Ghost Finders and Laurie and the ghost of Dr. Todd were surrounded by a grey sea of impenetrable fog, filling the station with its own sour and bitter light.

Laurie stepped back, into the main station building, as though he felt safer inside, in the candlelight. Dr. Todd drifted back before the fog, to stand with the Ghost Finders. He still stared unblinkingly through the thick grey mists, at where he believed the tunnel-mouth to be. The fog was cold and wet and intimidating. It felt like being trapped underwater, cut off from the rest of the world, every sound eerily muffled. The foggy air smelled of smoke and coal dust and times past. It grew slowly, steadily thicker.

Happy suddenly put both hands to his head and pressed hard against his ears to keep out some terrible sound only he could hear. His face screwed up, and he stumbled away from the others. JC yelled for him to come back, but Happy couldn't hear him. He disappeared into the curling folds of the fog, becoming a dark and indistinct shape.

And then he disappeared from sight completely, as his feet took him over the edge of the platform, and he fell.

But Melody was right there behind him.

She'd followed him into the fog, and when he fell, she threw herself forward and grabbed his out-flung hand at the last moment. She slammed facedown onto the platform, driving all the breath out of her lungs with the impact; but still she held on to Happy's hand with desperate strength.

"Don't let go!" yelled Happy, his voice rising from the deep gap between the platforms. "I'm not sure there's anything here, any more! The fog's eaten it all up! There's nothing underneath me!"

"Oh hush up, you big baby," said Melody, between gritted teeth. "I've got you. I've always got you. Haven't you learned that yet?"

While they were busy with each other, the fog took advantage of the moment to surge forward, from both ends of the platform at once. A great grey wave swallowed up everything. JC lost sight of Melody, grimly hanging on to Happy's hand. And when he looked back, he couldn't see Laurie or Dr. Todd. He was cut off from everyone, standing alone in a great grey sea that was becoming steadily thicker all around as though it was walling him up.

And then Kim Sterling came walking out of the fog, heading straight for him. His lost love, his ghost girl, striding towards him, smiling. The fog fell back from her, as though intimidated by her presence, as though it couldn't touch her. Kim came walking through the fog, and her feet on the platform didn't make the slightest sound. She slowed to a halt before JC, and his unbelieving smile slowly widened to match hers. He took off his sunglasses, so he could meet her eyes with his, and the blazing light from his altered eyes blasted the last of the fog away, illuminating Kim like summer sunshine in a church. She stood tall and easy before him, a magnificent pre-Raphaelite beauty with long red hair, in a shimmering, long, white dress. She had a high-boned, sharply featured face, and her wide mouth was a red dream with a smile always tucked away in one corner. She looked so fine, so wonderful, so full of life . . . JC reached out to take her hand, and she reached out a pale hand to him . . . but his hand passed right through hers. Because only he was really there. The living and the dead were never meant to touch.

"Where have you been?" said JC; but Kim smiled sadly at him.

She gestured at the sunglasses in his hand, then looked right into his eyes in a meaningful way. JC nodded slowly, looked around him at the fog, and said, very distinctly, *I can still see the platform.* The fog rolled back before him, giving up its hold on the station, unable to withstand the otherworldly glare of his eyes. It slowly faded away and disappeared, as though it had lost its grip on the world. JC looked around for Kim; but she was already walking away, back down the platform. By the time the fog was completely gone, so was she. As though she had never been there.

"I'll find you," said JC. "I'll never stop looking."

JC didn't waste time with regrets. He hurried over to where Melody was still lying facedown on the platform, one hand over the edge, grimly hanging on to Happy. JC knelt and grabbed Happy's other hand, and, between them, he and Melody hauled Happy back up to the platform. Happy scrambled up onto his feet, breathing hard, then retreated quickly away from the edge. Melody went with him, while JC took his time getting back onto his feet, brushing fussily at his marvellous ice-cream white suit.

"What the hell did you hear," Melody said to Happy, "to make you go rushing off like that?"

"A steam-whistle," said Happy. "Like a howl out of Hell, getting closer by the moment."

Melody nodded, then turned away to look back at JC. "Before you ask. Yes, I saw her, too."

"Saw who?" Happy said immediately. "What did I miss?"

"Kim," said Melody. "She was back. She helped save us from the fog, then disappeared again."

"She looked exactly the way she did when I first saw her," said JC. "Down in the Underground."

"Everyone else has a guardian angel," growled Happy. "Trust you to be different and have a guardian ghost. Did she say anything to you, like where she's been all this time? Who was holding her; how she broke free?"

"No," said JC. "She didn't say a word. But at least now I know . . . she's not lost. Not gone. She's . . . out there, somewhere."

"Then where's she been all this time?" said Happy; but JC wasn't listening. He looked across at Laurie, standing stiffly in the candle-lit doorway. JC considered him thoughtfully for a long moment, then looked across at the ghost of Dr. Todd, back where he used to be, staring into the darkness of the tunnel-mouth. JC moved away from both of them and gestured for Happy and Melody to join him.

The three Ghost Finders stood close together, speaking in quiet voices.

"The train is coming back," said JC. "We can't hope to stop it, so I say we do all we can to encourage it and keep all the weird shit limited to this one location."

"Good idea, oh great boss and leader," said Happy. "You get on with that while I sprint for the nearest horizon. Be sure and send me a nice postcard when it's all over and let me know how it turned out."

"Unfortunately, I can't do this without you," said JC. "So stay where you are, or I'll nail your feet to the platform. Or maybe I'll only nail the one and watch you walk round and round in circles."

Happy scowled at him. "You would, too, wouldn't you? Bully. All right. What do you want me to do, and I know I'm going to hate it."

"I will use my amazing eyes to find the weak spot in reality," said JC. "And then you will use your amazing mutant mind to force it all the way open. Lance the boil before it bursts."

"You have such a way with words," said Happy. "And all of them bad."

"You really think that's going to work?" said Melody.

"Oh yes," said JC. "The train wants to come home. The Ghost Caller wants to come home. They've been Away too long. All we have to do is open the door a crack, and they'll force it open the rest of the way, from the other side."

"I'm more worried about what might come through with them," said Melody.

"I should have been a plumber, like Mother wanted," Happy said miserably. "Always good money, in plumbing."

,,,,,,,,,,,,,,,,,,,,,,,,,,,,,

In the end, it really was that simple. JC and Happy stood together on the platform, concentrating on the dark tunnel-mouth, while Melody hurried back into the Station building, gathered up her precious instruments, and hauled them out onto the platform. Laurie watched interestedly, but he had apparently observed enough of Melody in action not to make the mistake of offering to help. The ghost of Dr. Todd ignored them all, still orientated unwaveringly on the tunnel-mouth. JC and Happy gave him plenty of room. It was cold on the platform, but the natural cold of an evening shading into night, not the unnatural chill Dr. Todd had brought to the Station room. Presumably he didn't feel the need for any more energy; and JC and Happy were quite content for him to go on feeling that way.

JC took off his sunglasses and stared meaningfully into the tunnel-mouth. The deep dark shadows seemed to stir uneasily under the touch of his augmented gaze. Happy stood half-crouching behind JC, concentrating, reaching out with his mind. Feeling for something that strictly speaking wasn't actually there yet.

"You're right, JC. There's definitely something . . . almost there. A dimensional door with something very powerful pushing up against the other side. There is a light at the end of the tunnel but not necessarily in a good way."

"Something's coming," JC agreed, smiling confidently. "So close now, even I can feel it. Melody! Can you tell me what direction it's coming from?"

"According to my instruments," said Melody, breathlessly, as she slammed the last bit of high tech into place, "whatever it is, it's coming from every direction at once! Forget spatial coordinates; this is coming from Outside our reality. Still, if I were the betting kind, which I'm not, but if I were . . . the odds do favour its coming through that tunnel-mouth. Completing the journey the train began all those years ago. The Universe has a fondness for circles and neatness. But JC, I have to tell you . . . it's not only the train that's coming. Something really powerful is hitching a ride with it, something so big, so intense it's overloading all my sensors!"

"Yes," said Happy, almost absently, all his concentration focused on the tunnel opening. "I can See it, I can Hear it . . . Like a bright Light, like a great Voice . . ."

"The Ghost Caller," said JC.

"The Light is shining very brightly now," said Happy, in a far-away voice. "I don't like it. That's not a proper Light. And it's not a good Voice. It wants to tell me things. Things I don't want to know . . ."

"Is it calling you?" said JC, quickly.

"No," said Happy, almost reluctantly. "It doesn't care about me. I'm just in the way. Its attractions are not for the living. I think both the Light and the Voice are lies, lures . . . It calls to the dead, to trick them away from the true Light and the true Voice . . ."

"Okay," said JC, surprisingly gently. "That's enough of that. Come home, Happy. Come back to me, or I'll have Melody come and bring you back."

"I'm back!" said Happy, scowling at JC. "I can look after myself, you know."

"Really," said JC. "You do amaze me. Have we done enough to open the door?"

"Oh yeah," said Happy, scowling at the dark tunnel opening. "All I had to do was pry at the edges, and the train did the rest. The train and what's coming with it. Still not too late to gather up our skirts and run, you know."

"We don't run," said JC. "We are the Ghost Finders, and we don't take any shit from the Hereafter."

"What's this *we* stuff, white man?" said Happy.

"It's close!" said Melody, staring raptly at her sensor readings. "And I mean, really close. My instruments are going crazy! In fact, one of them melted . . . I'm getting really weird energy spikes, other-dimensional radiations . . . Time and gravity and . . . and temperature readings that don't make any sense in our world . . . Holy crap!"

She backed rapidly away from her bank of instruments as, one by one, they burst into blue-white flames, then exploded, unable to cope with what they were experiencing. Melody tried to get back, to shut everything down, but the sheer heat drove her away again. She reluctantly abandoned her precious toys and hurried down the platform to join the others. The railway lines down in the valley between the platforms were jumping and juddering, ripping free of the thick weeds that had grown around and over them. The platform vibrated fiercely under the

Ghost Finders' feet. Signs hanging on steel chains swung heavily back and forth. And all the doors in all the buildings slammed open and shut, again and again. Laurie was forced out onto the platform, looking at the tunnel-mouth with wide eyes.

Until, finally, a great light appeared in the tunnel, blasting out of the tunnel-mouth, red as all the fires of Hell; and out of that unnatural light the steam train appeared at last, thundering out of the old tunnel-mouth. It was huge and dark, with gleaming steel and brass, smoke pumping out of its chimney and its whistle screaming like a soul newly damned to the Pit. Strange-coloured sparks rose where its steel wheels met the rusting rails; and then all the wheels screamed and squealed as the brakes slammed on, and the train and its carriages bucked to a shuddering halt, all along the platform of Bradleigh Halt.

Come home, at last.

JC and Happy and Melody stood close together, looking over the steam engine and its seven carriages as they settled to a halt. There was a loud ticking of cooling metal, and great gusts of steam rose on the still, evening air. A thick viscous liquid dripped steadily from every outer surface, bubbling and boiling in reaction to Earth air and Earth conditions. Some alien substance, covering all the train, brought back from the Away place, as though the train had been born again in some strange, alien amniotic fluid. The stuff fell slowly and reluctantly away from the train, dissipating, giving up the ghost, unable to hold itself together in this new kind of world. The whole train smelled like rotting meat, like something that should have been buried long ago.

The steam still issuing in sudden spurts from the cooling engine smelled bad, too; smelled wrong, unearthly, changed. The few sparks still jumping around the great steel wheels were odd and unnatural colours. The weeds that had choked the railway lines for so long, those that hadn't been chewed up and thrown aside by the train's return, now curled up and withered from contact with the great steel wheels.

JC beckoned urgently to Laurie, and the old man hurried over to join him. He stared at the old steam-engine with fond, almost worshipful eyes.

"She's everything my old grand-dad said she was," said Laurie. "He saw her go into that tunnel, you know, back in the day. He always said she'd find her way home again, eventually."

"Are all the carriages there?" asked JC. "Is anything missing? Is everything there that should be?"

"Oh yes," said Laurie. "But look at the state of the engine! All that . . . stuff, dripping off her! It's a disgrace . . . What have they done to you, girl? You were a classic!"

JC looked at Melody. "Any idea where the Ghost Caller might be?"

"All of my instruments are shot, fried, and dead in the water; but if I had to guess, I'd say probably the baggage-car."

"Look at her," said Laurie, softly and reverently. "Been away so long everything about her has changed. All the metals and alloys are different now . . . the wood of the carriages is rotting, corrupt. And what's inside . . . makes my skin crawl. There's more to this train than there should be. As though the whole thing's alive . . . How can it be alive?"

"How can you tell all this?" said Happy, staring at him. "I'm a telepath, and I'm not getting half of that!"

"I can feel it," said Laurie. "Can't you?"

Happy scowled at the train and said nothing.

"If it is alive, it's not any kind of life we could hope to understand," JC said briskly. "Or would want to, probably. Question is—what forms of life might the train have brought back with it?"

"Really not liking the implications of that," said Happy. He frowned suddenly, his whole face screwing up. "And I'm picking up something really nasty, now. Not a Light or a Voice this time, a feeling . . . like sticking your hand into a mess of corruption. It's the carriages, JC! Look at the carriages . . . Dear God, what's happened to the passengers?"

They all moved slowly down the platform, peering through the distorted glass of the carriage windows they passed. A strange light blazed through the windows, like the blue-green phosphorescence of underwater grottos. People clustered together inside the carriages, staring out at the world they'd come back to; but they didn't act like people any more. Their eyes were empty, faces twisted with wild, inhuman emotions. Driven mad, every one of them, or perhaps beyond madness into something else, through being trapped for so many years in a place never meant for humankind. They beat and pattered against the closed windows with flat hands as though they'd forgotten what windows were, or what hands were for. They were all desperate to get out, crawling and swarming over each other like oversized beetles, staring out at a world they no longer recognised, with blank, insect eyes.

"What happened to them?" said Laurie. "What made these people . . . like this?"

"The Ghost Caller," said JC. His voice was flat and harsh, with rigidly suppressed rage. "It's been active, Calling, all the time it was Away. The passengers in the carriages were all killed, either by the abrupt transition to the Other Place or because they couldn't survive in the alien conditions they found there. But the Ghost Caller wouldn't let their spirits depart. Their souls have been trapped in their dead bodies all this time, driven insane by horrors the human mind was never meant to cope with. These are dead bodies possessed by mad ghosts."

"How can you know all that?" said Laurie.

"I seem to feel it," said JC, a bit dreamily. "Don't you?"

"We can't leave them like this," said Laurie. "It isn't right."

"Of course we won't leave them like this," said JC, immediately all business again. "Helping the restless dead find peace is all part of our job description. But the only way to free these poor souls is to smash or destroy the Ghost Caller. Then they can pass on to their proper places, in the Hereafter."

"Hereafter?" said Laurie. "You mean, Heaven and Hell?"

"Don't look at me," said Happy. "Way above my pay grade. We have enough trouble coping with the Here and Now."

"I'm an agnostic," said Melody. "Mostly in self-defence."

"What matters is sending these lost souls on," JC said firmly. "So they can be made whole and sane again."

"I'm more concerned with what happens if the passengers get out of these carriages," said Happy. "Those windows don't look particularly strong, or secure."

"If they get out?" said JC. "Nothing good, I should imagine. They have enough sense left to know a great wrong has been done them and enough anger to want revenge . . ."

"You know," said Melody, "this would be a really good time for you to produce one of those really powerful and utterly forbidden weapons that you carry about your person, the ones that you're not supposed to have."

"The Boss made me give them all up, after the last case," said JC. "In fact, she was most insistent about it. Had me strip-searched, and everything. And you really don't want to know what the 'and everything' involved."

"She took *all your weapons*?" said Happy. "And you're only telling us now?"

"She's been keeping a very close eye on me," said JC. "I've had to be very careful. I need the Carnacki Institute's resources to help me search for Kim."

"Look, do you have any nasty weapons about you or not?" said Melody.

"Not as such," said JC.

"I want to go home," said Happy loudly.

"Excuse me," Laurie said firmly. "But I have to ask . . . is this a real train or a ghost train? I mean, is it really, physically, here?"

"Good question, Mr. Laurie," said JC. "To which the official answer is, damned if I know. It certainly seems solid enough . . . Best to treat it as though it's real, right up to the point where we decide it's more useful to treat it as though it isn't. We are nothing if not flexible in this business, in the face of utter horror."

"We have to find the machine," Melody said stubbornly. "The Ghost Caller. We have to shut it down."

"Dear Melody, practical as ever!" JC said cheerfully. "I love it when a plan comes together, and all the options narrow to a point where decisions become inevitable. And, given that the light blazing out of the rear carriage is so much stranger and soul-numbingly disturbing than all the others, I think we can safely assume that *that* . . . is the machine, in the baggage-car. Mr. Laurie, please stay right where you are, so we don't have to worry about you. Team Ghost Finders, follow me."

"I'm quite happy to stay with Mr. Laurie," said Happy.

"What?" said JC. "And miss all the fun?"

"Fun is overrated."

"You stand a much better chance of surviving if you stick with me," said JC.

"Right with you, boss," said Happy, miserably.

"Go, team!" said Melody.

            ''''''''''''''''''''''''''

The three of them stuck close together as they moved slowly and cautiously down the platform, maintaining what they hoped was a safe distance from the carriages. Strange phosphorescent lights rose and fell behind the windows as though disturbed by unknown tides. The possessed dead passengers pressed up close against the bulging glass of the windows, crawling over and around each other like so many insane insects. The Ghost Finders did their best not to look at them. Some horrors are harder to bear than others. It wasn't the passengers' fault, what had happened to them, what had been done to them; but that didn't make it any easier to look at. A mad soul is so much harder to consider than a mad mind. Because where sanity runs out, the Outside moves in.

It made sense to have stuck the Ghost Caller in the baggage-car, at the end of the train, as far-away from the passengers as possible; but in the end it hadn't made any difference. JC insisted that they all walk the length of the train at a steady pace because it would have been only too easy to lose control and break into a run; and they couldn't afford to lose control here, in these conditions, not even in the smallest of ways. The light blasting out of the baggage-car's single grilled window was blindingly bright, incandescent almost beyond bearing, so harsh that even JC had to screw up his altered eyes to deal with it. The station gloom seemed to shrink away from the light as though it was afraid or intimidated. JC found the door to the baggage-car and tried it. Locked, of course, with an immense steel padlock. JC tore the heavy door right off its hinges and threw it aside. He pulled himself up into the new opening and entered the rear carriage. Melody and Happy looked at the thrown-aside door, lying on the platform, looked at each other, then followed JC into the baggage car.

The light was easier to bear once they got inside, as their eyes adjusted to the new conditions. It only took them a moment to recognise the Ghost Caller. It wasn't a machine, after all. It was a human corpse, sitting upright in a stiff-backed chair, held firmly in place by a series of heavy leather straps and restraints. Even after so long Away, or perhaps because of it, the body was still perfectly intact. Not a trace of rot or decay, nor any smell of formaldehyde or any other preservative. The three Ghost Finders looked into the set grey face of the dead man and knew him immediately. It was Dr. Emil Todd. The head had been cut open, quite neatly, sawn across above the eyebrows.

JC, Melody, and Happy moved slowly forward, surrounding the corpse. There was nothing else in the carriage worth looking at. They all leaned in, to look inside the dead man's head. There was a brain, but quite clearly it had come from someone else. It slumped to one side, not even close to fitting. A series of brass and copper wires had been threaded through the brain, to hold it in place in the oversized skull. Silver pins protruded from the pink-and-grey matter, set in strange patterns, like a grotesque pincushion. And on top of the truncated head, someone had carefully placed an ornate crown, made of silver, with a dozen human eyeballs set firmly in place at regular intervals, staring unblinkingly out at the world.

"Okay," said Happy, breathlessly, "that is seriously creepy, and I have seen more than my fair share of creep."

"It's also a major disappointment," said Melody. "I was looking forward to examining some glory of steampunk engineering, not this . . . messed-about abomination. What the hell is this?"

"That is my body, given in repentance for all the wrong I did," said a new voice, behind them. They all looked around sharply, and there in the baggage-car with them was the ghost of Dr. Todd. Staring sadly at his own corpse. "This is what I gave up my life for and why I have spent my death here, trying to prevent its return. There were supposed to be protections set in place, to prevent the Ghost Caller from activating. They promised me there would be protections . . . A defensive circle around the chair, binding Wards and Signs carved into the wooden floor . . . But they lied."

"They?" said JC, carefully.

"My partners in crime," said Dr. Todd. His voice was clear, but distant, as though it had to travel some unknowable interval to reach them. "Let their worthless names be forgotten by history. I let them kill me, and make use of my body, to create this wonder . . . and repair my reputation. I never meant to cheat people. When I started out, I wanted to give comfort to the bereaved. But I was tempted—by the money, and the fame, and the women . . . and I fell. This was to be my recompense. A device to summon ghosts, real ghosts . . . To do what I could not.

"I sat down in that chair, and they tightened the straps around me. A terrible experience, to sit down, knowing you will never stand up again. Almost as bad as having the top of my head sawn off. They couldn't give me opiates, you see; it would have interfered with the process. I can't remember if I screamed. I probably did. I passed out long before they cut and levered my brain out of my skull, and I died. Imagine my surprise when I discovered I was still there, as a ghost. I watched as they removed my brain, according to my instructions and specifications, and replaced it with the stolen brain of Oliver Lando, a genuine medium, with quite amazing psychic powers. The man who'd replaced me in the public affection, with his very successful tour of the provinces.

"I could have chosen someone else, some other genuine medium; but he was so very powerful . . . and I regret to say I could be a very petty man, back when I was alive. He was the real thing, you see: no tricks, no showmanship, a genuine Voice for the dead. Everything I'd aspired to be. I like to think he would have approved of what we made from his stolen brain. After I had him murdered."

"What's that thing on his head?" said Melody.

"That, dear lady, is the Crown of Tears," said Dr. Todd. "My associates brought the design to me, the one thing I needed to be sure my Ghost Caller would work. Twelve human eyes, removed from the heads of six genuine psychics. I insisted we take only their eyes, not their lives. I saw no need to be cruel. Twelve psychic eyes, in the proper setting, to amplify the power of Lando's brain, boosted by what was done to my body. Part engineering, part magic, part . . .

"I had help. That's all you need to know."

"Your Ghost Caller is still operating," said Happy. "I can hear its false Voice, see its rotten Light. It's still summoning ghosts, right now. And they will come like moths to a consuming flame. You can't let this go on. Your . . . device must be shut down."

"I don't know how," said Dr. Todd. "I never did. Operation of the marvellous device was to be left to my associates as they toured the country, in all the biggest theatres. Bringing back the dearly departed, to give comfort to those they'd left behind."

"You thought the authorities would allow a corpse to be exhibited, and call up ghosts?" said Melody. "No wonder Julien Advent shut you down."

The ghost smiled thinly. "Is that what it says in the history books? No. My associates heard he was coming and made haste to load the device onto this train. To get away and hide, and make plans for the future. They didn't know I was still there, watching. I'd seen how powerful my device was and how much damage it could, would, cause. So I used the last of my power over the Ghost Caller to send the train Away. And I have stood guard in this place ever since, preventing its return. Until now."

"Maybe we should tear this . . . thing apart," said Happy. "You said there aren't any protections."

"It can't be broken," said Dr. Todd. "I had it made too well. It will . . . defend itself. And I can't help you. I've been dead too long, worn too thin . . . That isn't my body any more. Not a body at all, really. An infernal machine; and no human hand can undo what I have wrought. God damn me."

"Lucky I'm here, then," JC said cheerfully. "Because I'm not merely human and haven't been for some time now."

He reached inside the dead man's head, thrust his fingers deep into the soft grey tissues, and ripped the brain right out of the skull, along with all its brass and copper and silver attachments. He threw the brain on the floor and stamped on it hard. Pink-and-grey matter exploded under his foot. Melody and Happy retreated quickly, mak-

ing loud sounds of distress and disgust at what had splat-
tered over their shoes. The ghost of Dr. Todd looked on
blankly as JC tore the Crown of Tears from the dead
head and broke the silver frame in his strong hands. He
turned it inside out, so that the human eyes were all staring at each other, then carefully replaced the Crown on
the empty head. JC stepped back and smiled about him
easily.

"Time to leave, I think. Our work here is at an end."

ııııııııııııııııııııı

Out on the platform again, the three Ghost Finders
looked hopefully around them. Evening had descended
into night. Moonlight dappled the length of the platform.
Eerie phosphorescent glows still spilled out of the carriage windows, interrupted here and there by the shadows of human shapes moving in inhuman ways.

"Nothing's changed," said Happy, nervously.

"It will," JC said confidently. "Ripping out the stolen
brain and reversing the Crown? Bound to do the job. Sym-
bolic logic, very big in magic circles." He turned to the
ghost of Dr. Todd, trudging silently along beside them.
"The rest is up to you, Doctor. If you really want to put a
stop to all the horrors you're responsible for."

"You know I do," said Dr. Todd. "I gave my life to
creating them, so it is only proper I give my death to ending them. What do you want me to do?"

"I need you to re-enter your old body for a while and
make it yours again," said JC, as kindly as he could. "You
can do that now Lando's brain is gone, and the Crown of
Tears has been turned around. Repossess your old body,

and you'll be able to bring the Ghost Caller, or what's left of it, under your control."

"Yes," said Dr. Todd. "A fitting punishment for a foolish old man. Wait here, please. There are some things . . . that should be done in private."

He disappeared abruptly, and all three Ghost Finders jumped. They'd got too used to the ghost of Dr. Todd still doing things in human ways. And then they all looked back, as the light blasting out of the baggage-car's single grilled window shut off abruptly. There was a pause, then the body of Dr. Todd stepped slowly and stiffly out of the rear carriage and down onto the platform. The body walked slowly along the platform towards them as though every step, every movement, was a conscious effort. Dr. Todd lurched to a halt before the Ghost Finders and worked his dead mouth for a long moment before words finally emerged, dry and dusty and determined.

"Of course," he said. "It's all so clear to me now, what I must do."

"Then maybe you'd explain it to me," said Happy, testily. "Because I haven't got a clue what's going on!"

The dead lips smiled, briefly. "Time . . . to go home. The end of every life, and every death. We all get to go home."

He strode off down the platform, lurching this way and that, and all the passengers' heads in all the windows turned to watch him pass. Cracks had appeared in some of the windows; but the passengers seemed to have lost interest in that. Happy leaned in close beside JC.

"He's doing something. I can feel it. He's not the Ghost Caller any more; but he's still . . . reaching out, to

Something. I think . . . it's another weak spot in reality, another door or potential door, but at the other end of the tracks! Talk to me, JC; tell me what's happening here, or I am leaving!"

"Where's your curiosity?" said JC.

"I had it surgically removed!" said Happy. "It kept getting me into trouble!"

"It's true," Melody said solemnly. "I held his hand while they did it. We keep it in a jar on the mantelpiece now."

"Watch, my children," said JC. "And learn . . ."

The dead body of Dr. Todd climbed into the engine cab and started it up again. Steam blew thickly from the chimney-stack, curled up from the great steel wheels, and howled through the whistle. The passengers in the carriages were all utterly still, waiting for something they couldn't quite bring themselves to believe in. JC stepped forward, took off his sunglasses, and stared down the platform.

"It's not a weak spot," he said, "And it's not a door. It's a tunnel. I can see the tunnel; and it's full of light."

Suddenly, there was a tunnel. An exact duplicate of the old brick-lined tunnel-mouth the train had arrived through, but standing at the opposite end of the railway tracks. Full of a warm and inviting light instead of darkness. The train lurched forward, gathering speed, leaving JC and Melody and Happy behind on the platform. The engine roared into the tunnel, steam-whistle blowing triumphantly, and, one by one, the carriages roared into the light after it. The tunnel entrance disappeared after the train; and all the tension in the night was gone. The air was as clear and calm as a summer night after the storm has passed, and all the shadows were only shadows again.

"Mission accomplished," said JC, replacing his sunglasses with a flourish. "I wish all our cases were this simple."

"You speak for yourself," said Happy. "Hey, where did old man Laurie go?"

They all looked around, and called out after him; but there was no sign of the old man anywhere, and no reply. Melody shrugged.

"Everyone has their limits. Pity he didn't stick around; he could have told the Preservation volunteers it was safe to return. Now, somebody find me a brush and some sacks, so I can clear up what's left of my poor machines and take them home with me."

"Don't pout, sweetie," said Happy. "You know the Institute will give you some new toys once we get back."

"It's not the same," said Melody, pouting.

"The important thing," said JC, "is that my Kim appeared to me, in my hour of need. Which has to mean . . . that she isn't being held against her will, any more."

"We can't know that for sure, JC," Happy said carefully.

"I know," said JC. "But there is hope now."

"We can't be sure it was really her, JC," Melody said carefully.

"Right," said Happy. "I mean, if that was Kim, why did she disappear again? Why didn't she stay?"

"Maybe she couldn't," said Melody.

"It was her," said JC. "I'd know my Kim anywhere. Why didn't she stay? Who knows why the dead do what the dead do?"

"Hey!" said a new voice. "Are you the experts from London?"

They all looked around to see a middle-aged man in workman's overalls and sensible shoes hurrying down the platform towards them. He held an old-fashioned storm lantern out before him and smiled at the Ghost Finders in an agreeable enough way.

"Sorry I'm late; I got held up. Hope you haven't been here on your own too long. It's not a comfortable place here, once it gets dark."

"Who are you?" said JC.

"I'm Howard Laurie, representing the Bradleigh Preservation Trust. Seen any ghosts yet, have you?"

"I think you'll find the station peaceful enough now," said JC. "You're Ronald Laurie's son? He's very kindly looked after us, in your absence."

Howard looked at all three of them in turn. "You've seen my dad?"

"He's been very helpful," said JC.

"Then you've seen one ghost at least. My old dad's been dead these past ten years."

THREE

||||||||||||||||||||||||||||||||||||||||||

HANGING ABOUT IN THE LOBBY, WAITING
FOR THE SHOW TO START

Why do so many theatres have resident ghosts? After all, ghosts are supposed to be the result of bad places, and the theatre is where we go to enjoy ourselves. But what are plays but voices from the past, memories preserved in amber, ghost images of the way we thought we were . . . And even if what we see on the stage isn't real, there are still real triumphs and tragedies, joys and terrors, little deaths and bad-tempered madness going on backstage. All human life is there; and some of it is bound to leave its mark. Players come and go, but some of their lives remain, preserved in the brick and stone, the sawdust and the limelight of old theatres.

Ghosts are still mainly unfinished business; and no-one bears a grudge like an old trouper.

|||||||||||||||||||||||

The three Ghost Finders were heading from Leeds to Leicester by train, from the north of England down to the Midlands; and they were travelling in a first-class compartment. It was all very comfortable. The Carnacki Institute had decided sometime back that its operatives in the field could only claim travel expenses for standard-class rail tickets, in the name of efficiency and belt-tightening, and keeping field operatives from getting above themselves. But Happy had finally figured out how to use his telepathy to make the ticket inspector believe he was looking at three first-class tickets. So he punched the air somewhere near the standard tickets, then wandered off to have a nice little sit-down and nurse the pounding headache he'd only recently acquired. Happy grinned broadly, entirely unmoved, put his feet up on the opposite seat, and made a pig of himself with free food and drink from the complimentary trolley. He took one of everything and two if he liked the look of it, and piled it all up on the table before him so he could gloat over it, like offerings to a somewhat shabby god.

"You couldn't eat and drink all of that if we were travelling all the way to Land's End," Melody said sternly from the seat opposite him, studying him over the top of her new briefing file.

"It's the principle of the thing," said Happy, ripping open a packet of Jaffa Cakes and delicately dipping one into his cup of Pepsi. "I don't know why I didn't think of this before!"

"Because it's illegal and immoral; and messing with people's heads is just wrong?" said Melody.

"No . . ." said Happy. "I'm pretty sure that isn't it . . . Ooh, chocolate HobNobs!"

Melody sighed loudly and went back to her briefing file.

Sitting on his own on the other side of the compartment, staring out the window without seeing anything of the scenery racing by, JC ignored them both. He was still thinking about Kim's unexpected reappearance at Bradleigh Halt. The same questions kept coming back to him, rolling over and over in his head. Why had she chosen to appear to him there, after all this time? Why not before? Because he was in danger . . . No. He'd been in peril of his life on any number of previous occasions; and she hadn't shown up for any of those. Had something changed . . . with her, or with him? Could it be she'd finally broken free from her unknown captors and was waiting for him to come and find her . . . ? So many questions, and not one answer he could trust.

So stick with the cases that came his way, keep himself busy and occupied, and be ready to jump when the opportunity arose.

Happy stuffed his face with junk food, drank fizzy stuff straight from the can, and made a point of looking down his nose at the various smart-suit-and-tie business men sharing the first-class compartment with him. All of them tapping busily away at their laptops and doing their very best not to stare too openly at the strange creature that had invaded their territory. *Work for the Man, monkeyboys!* Happy thought loudly but had enough sense not to say out loud. He sniggered, and turned his attention back to the latest issue of *FHM* magazine.

"The train will be coming into Leicester soon," said Melody, glaring meaningfully at Happy and JC. "And, for once, it would be nice if we could all arrive knowing why we were there."

"She's going into lecture mode," Happy said to JC. "Indulge her. She'll only make a fuss otherwise, and I can feel one of my heads coming on. Try and keep it down to a précis, Melody, there's a dear. Some of us have important eating and drinking to be getting on with. Or important existential brooding, in JC's case."

"Go ahead, Melody," JC said courteously, not looking around. "Distract me. I could use something else to think about."

"We've been called in to investigate a suspected haunting at the old Haybarn Theatre, in the city of Leicester," said Melody.

She looked around to see if any of the business men were paying attention . . . but they all gave every appearance of being absorbed in their work. Possibly in self-defence.

"Ooh, the theatre!" said Happy, unexpectedly. "Does that mean we'll get free tickets for the shows?"

Melody actually lowered her file to get a better look at him. "Since when have you ever been interested in going to the theatre?"

"Take your freebies where you can find them, that's what I say," Happy said complacently.

"Well, unless we can sort this mess out, it doesn't look like there's going to be any more shows at the Haybarn," said Melody, returning to her file. "Says here, the place was shut down twenty years ago. It was about to be restored and reopened . . . But recently there's been a series of unnatural happenings. The workmen have downed tools and scattered, and restoration has ground to a halt."

"This is all starting to sound depressingly familiar," said JC.

"There's no way this case could turn out as complicated as Bradleigh Halt," said Melody.

"God, I hope not," said Happy. "I mean: Ghost Callers, trains full of insane souls, and people wandering around with sawn-off heads . . . Why can't things be simple, now and again?"

"Quiet in the stalls," said Melody. "Keep the noise down and pay attention; or after all this is over, I won't take you back to our hotel room and play medical experiments with you."

"Far too much information," said JC, shuddering genteelly. He turned around to look at Melody, doing his best to appear professional and interested. "What kind of unnatural happenings are we talking about here, Melody? Actual ghosts, with names and histories and legends?"

"No actual visitors from the spirit realms, as far as I can see," said Melody. "Only voices, glimpses, bad feelings . . . all the usual atmospherics. General unease and a certain amount of What Was That?"

Happy frowned. "Why have we been called in for such a minor haunting? I thought we were officially an A team now? Not that I am in any way keen on throwing myself into danger; but I'm damned if I'm giving up on the danger money. It's not the principle of the thing, you understand; it's the money, every time."

"Apparently," said Melody, in that particular tone of

voice that meant she suspected much but could prove little, "a homeless guy found his way into the Haybarn and was discovered there the next day, quite dead. Possibly frightened to death. The workmen and restorers have refused point-blank to go back into the building, until Something Is Done . . ."

Happy sighed heavily. "That still doesn't explain why we . . ."

"The Boss is sending us in as a personal favour for an old friend," said JC.

"Wish she'd do one for us," growled Happy. "Like approving my expense claims without laughing in my face."

"Dear Catherine Latimer, our revered Boss and leader of us all, spoke to me personally about this," said JC, and the other two immediately gave him their full attention. JC smiled faintly. "I was phoning in a preliminary report on what had gone down at Bradleigh Halt, when she broke in. Which is a bit like going to confessional and having God herself butt in. She said some very nice things about how we'd handled the mission, which should have been a warning in itself. The Boss has never been one for honeyed words when a whip and a chair are so much more effective. She said that she wants us on this case precisely because we did such a good job at Bradleigh. Which, of course, suggests to me that there must be a hell of a lot more to this theatre haunting than we are being told."

"No good deed goes unpunished," said Happy. He glowered at the food piled up before him and pushed it away, his appetite gone. For the moment.

"I have to wonder," said JC, "whether Catherine Latimer, her own bad self, is deliberately keeping us busy and occupied with one case after another, so we won't go off on our own to look for Kim."

There was a pause then as JC looked meaningfully at Happy and Melody, and they both looked at each other so they wouldn't have to look at him. None of them had to say anything. They'd already talked themselves hoarse on the subject and knew exactly what the others thought and believed. None of them was ready to give up their various positions.

"The Boss says she's got all her best people investigating the infiltration of the Carnacki Institute," Melody said finally.

"She *says* . . ." Happy said darkly.

"No," JC said immediately. "We have to trust the Boss in that, at least. Or we're completely on our own."

"When you spoke to her," Melody said carefully, "did you happen to mention seeing Kim at Bradleigh Halt?"

"No," said JC.

"So we don't trust her that much . . ." said Happy.

"When we've got anything worth telling her, then I'll tell her," said JC. "One sighting doesn't make a summer."

"Or one swallow make an orgy," said Melody.

"Who knows?" said Happy. "If Kim really is your guardian angel now, guardian ghost, whatever . . . Maybe she'll turn up again, at the theatre."

"Stranger things have happened," said Melody. "Usually to us."

She carried on reading aloud from the briefing file, and

the others pretended to listen to her. Happy leaned back in his seat and closed his eyes, the better to concentrate.

,,,,,,,,,,,,,,,,,,,,,,,,,,

A very modern taxi took the Ghost Finders straight from the railway station to the Haybarn Theatre, situated right in the middle of the city centre. It was a grey, overcast day, with lowering clouds and the threat of thunder. The taxi had Thank You For Not Smoking signs plastered all over the interior, along with half a dozen little pine-tree deodorant things, and the interior still smelled like something large and unpleasant had recently been very ill in it. The driver had a great deal to say about the immigration situation, none of it helpful, and ignored all attempts to shut him up, including *Please shut up or I will have to kill you* from Happy, who then had to be physically restrained by Melody and JC.

When the taxi finally arrived at its destination, Happy volunteered to pay the driver. He fumbled crumpled notes and assorted change from his pockets while Melody hauled her precious scientific equipment out of the taxi's boot, and JC wandered over to stare thoughtfully at the exterior of the Haybarn Theatre. Happy slapped a bunch of well-worn notes into the driver's hand and carefully added the right amount of change. The driver looked at his hand, then glared at Happy.

"What? No tip?"

"Okay," said Happy. "Here's a tip. Wash your mind out with soap, and try to at least slow down for the red lights. Now piss off sharpish, or I'll set my girl-friend on you."

"I heard that!" said Melody, slamming the taxi's boot

shut with unnecessary force. "Don't make me come over there!"

"See what I mean?" said Happy, smiling calmly at the driver.

The taxi departed at speed. Happy wandered over to watch Melody load her assorted high tech on the collapsible trolley.

"Is that it?" he said, after a while.

"The rest of my equipment, all the really important stuff, that I specially ordered in advance, is apparently en route in a separate van," said Melody. "Under armed guard. For insurance reasons."

"I'm sure it'll all turn up," said Happy. "Eventually . . ."

"They're not fooling me!" Melody said loudly. "They're trying to see how little tech I can work with! I cannot be expected to do deep research on dead things with such limited resources! I'd have better luck catching ghosts by running after them with a bloody-big enchanted butterfly-net!"

"I think I saw one of those in the Boss's office, one time," said JC, not looking around. "On the wall, behind her desk, right next to the enchanted grenade-launcher."

"I wish I thought you were joking," said Happy.

He and Melody moved forward to stand on either side of JC, and they all took their time studying the exterior face of the Haybarn Theatre. None of them was particularly impressed. Time and the weather had not been kind to the brick and stone though it was surprisingly free of graffiti. Unlike most of the surrounding office buildings. Apart from the Haybarn's name, still spelled out in cold grey neon tubing, above the closed main doors, there was nothing obvious to mark the old building as a theatre. All the colour and glamour had been stripped away long ago, and now it looked like any other old-fashioned building, silent and unoccupied.

"Has this place really been empty for twenty years?" JC said finally. "I mean, this is prime location, if nothing else. Right in the middle of the business section. The land alone must be worth a fortune . . ."

"Maybe the building has a reputation, as a bad place," said Happy. "Last thing a developer wants is a poltergeist running wild in the lanes of his supermarket. Or restless spirits grinning out of the changing-room mirrors in a women's fashion outlet."

"There's no mention of anything like that in the briefing files," said Melody. "No trouble at all until the renovations started. Are you picking up anything yet, Happy? Any bad vibrations?"

"There's a curry house not far away," said Happy.

"You can't be hungry already, not after everything you stuffed down yourself on the train!"

"Working for the Carnacki Institute is like serving in the Army," Happy said solemnly. "Eat when you can, sleep where you can, because you never know when you might get another chance . . ." He sniffed loudly. "I'm not getting anything from this building, which is a bit odd. I mean, this place has to be at least a century old. I should be getting something . . ."

Melody looked at JC. "Do you have any idea who this important friend of Catherine Latimer's might be, the one we're doing this for?"

"She didn't say anything," said JC. "But then, she never does."

"Are we supposed to go in through the front doors, or should we go round the back and enter through the stage door?" said Happy.

"Hell with that," JC said firmly. "I do not use the back door. Except sometimes as an exit in times of high peril."

Melody moved forward and tried the front doors. They both opened easily before her. "Not even locked," she said. "That can't be right. Not in this day and age."

"Someone is expecting us," said Happy.

"A sign from Above!" JC said merrily. "Inwards and onwards, my children! Danger and excitement await us!"

"If I didn't know better, I'd swear you'd been at my pills," said Happy.

"We are going in!" said JC.

"You first," said Happy.

"Of course!" said JC.

"Hold it," said Melody, and it was a measure of their professionalism that both men stopped immediately and looked at her.

"What?" said Happy. *"What?"*

"We're supposed to wait here," said Melody. "Because we're being joined by the two actor-producers responsible for renovating this place."

"Oh, wonderful," said Happy. "Passengers! Why are we going to put up with these civilians, exactly?"

"Because they know the history of this theatre," Melody said patiently. "And, they know all about the haunting. If it is a haunting and not a bunch of grown men jumping at shadows. I blame those *Most Haunted* shows on television."

Happy looked innocently at JC. "Do we really have to put up with this? You know they're going to get in the way and make the job ten times harder."

"Yes, we do have to put up with them," said JC. "The Boss said so. And you don't say no to the Boss if you like having your organs on the inside. In fact, she was most insistent about making these actors a part of our investigation. Do try and keep them alive."

"You try," Melody said immediately. "I am going to be busy trying to follow electromagnetic fluctuations and orgone spikes with an old barometer and a bent penny."

JC looked at Happy, who shrugged briefly. "She's suffering from equipment withdrawal."

"Ah, to hell with this," said JC. "I am not standing around here waiting for thespians to turn up. The traffic's deafening, the air's so polluted you could shake hands with it, and the rain's coming on. Besides, I don't wait for anyone. It's bad for the reputation. I am going in. Tally ho, Ghost Finders!"

He barged straight through the main doors and disappeared inside. Happy and Melody looked at each other and shrugged pretty much simultaneously. Happy held a door open, and Melody hauled her trolley full of equipment up the raised steps and into the theatre.

∴∴∴∴∴∴∴∴∴∴∴∴∴

JC was already striding round and round the oversized lobby, head held high, looking at everything with keen interest. His ice-cream white suit seemed almost to glow in the gloom. JC lurched abruptly to a halt, hands stuffed deep into his pockets, looking and listening and sniffing the air, getting a feel for the place. The lobby was big enough to be impressive without being imposing, made to hold crowds waiting for the curtain to go up; but it was dim and dusty now, with more than its fair share of shadows. All the windows were boarded up.

Melody hauled her trolley into the exact centre of the lobby, looked briefly around her, sniffed loudly when nothing immediately dangerous presented itself, and began assembling her various bits and pieces. Happy stood alone, some distance away from the others, looking cautiously about him. The lobby floor was bare, and so were the walls. Though there were a few large empty wooden frames, here and there, that had presumably once held bright and gaudy posters, advertising past triumphs and tragedies. The lobby looked . . . depersonalised, anonymous. As though all the glamour and character and history had been deliberately removed, long ago. Several doors led off from the lobby, going who knew where because all the signs and directions were gone. All the doors were very firmly closed.

Everything seemed peaceful enough; but Happy wasn't fooled. There was a definite air of . . . something. An atmosphere of something not easily named.

JC moved quickly from one door to another, opening each one in turn and shouting a cheerful *Hello!* into the gloom beyond. But there was never any response. JC shut each door firmly, in turn, just in case. He finally came back to join Melody and Happy, rubbing his hands briskly together. Happy pointed out the Ticket Office, which had been boarded shut.

"There's something very sad about that," he said. "A real sense that the party is over; everyone get your coats and go home."

"Softy," said Melody, not unkindly, not even looking up from fitting her various bits of tech together and hitting them if they didn't cooperate fast enough for her liking.

"Is that really all you're going to use?" JC said innocently because he liked to live dangerously.

Melody slammed down a sciencey thing and glared at him. "This is deliberate!" she said fiercely. "It's all part of downsizing; if they prove I can do the job with a minimum of equipment, then that's all they'll let me have."

"So what are you going to do?" said Happy. "Deliberately sabotage a mission to prove the accountants wrong?"

"Don't think that hasn't occurred to me," growled Melody.

"I think I'll go and hide somewhere safe until you're in a better mood," said Happy.

"We're not going to be here that long," said Melody.

While the two of them were preoccupied, JC spotted a door on the far wall that he would have sworn hadn't been there a moment earlier. He moved slowly over to stand before it. He looked the door up and down, and it looked like all the other doors. He reached out very carefully, very cautiously, and tried the door handle. It turned easily under his hand, almost invitingly, and he pushed the door open. It swung weightlessly back before him, revealing a deep, dark gloom.

"JC?" The voice came from deep inside the gloom; and he recognised it immediately.

"Yes, Kim," he said. "I'm here."

He stepped forward into the dark, and there was Kim, standing right before him. Glowing so brightly, she threw back the gloom. JC stood very still, careful not to do anything that might frighten her away. His breath caught in his throat, and he could feel his heart hammering painfully fast in his chest.

"Kim?" he said. "Is it really you?"

She smiled at him, her eyes shining. She was hovering a few inches above the floor, rising and falling slowly. She looked like she wanted to say something; but she didn't.

"What are you doing here, Kim?" said JC. "Am I in danger again? Are you? How did you get away . . . ? Or, is someone still holding you?"

She didn't respond to any of his questions, but her gaze never wavered, fixed entirely on him.

"Please . . ." said JC. "Tell me who's got you, where you are, and I will come and get you! I will!"

She smiled sadly at him. JC reached out to her, and she backed away from him, drifting slowly down the endless, dark corridor. JC started forward after her, only to slam face-first into the wall before him. The door was gone, with no trace left behind to show it had ever been there. JC beat at the wall with his fist, once, then tiredly leaned forward to rest his forehead against the cold, implacable surface. He took a deep breath, stood up straight, squared his shoulders, and turned away from the wall to find Melody and Happy both staring at him.

"I saw Kim again," he said.

Happy and Melody looked quickly around the empty lobby, then back at JC, who shrugged briefly.

"I'm not picking up anything," Happy said carefully. "If a ghost had manifested here, even popped in for a moment, I'm sure I would have sensed it."

"Nothing on my instruments, either," said Melody. "Are you sure you saw . . . something?"

"Don't look at me like that," said JC. "It was Kim. I saw her. Spoke to her . . ."

He turned away from what he saw in their faces, his back stiff and straight, hands clenched into fists at his sides. Happy moved over to stand with Melody at her instrument panels. Lights came and went on her monitor screens, signifying nothing.

"She was there, at the railway station," Happy said tentatively.

"Was she?" Melody said quietly. "The image we saw looked like her, but it never said a word; and normally you can't get a word in edge-ways with ghost girl. It'll take more than a brief look-alike image to convince me. So I have to wonder if someone is playing mind-games. With us in general, and JC in particular. Showing him what he wants to see, to distract him from what's really important."

"Oh great," said Happy. "Fantastic. That's all I need, something else to be paranoid about."

"Unfortunately, you're not as paranoid as you used to be, sweetie," said Melody. "There really are dangerous forces in the universe out to get you."

"Life was so much simpler when I was merely mentally ill and chemically deranged," said Happy, glumly. "Now every case we go into feels like a trap."

"That's situation normal where the Ghost Finders are concerned," said Melody.

"I want danger money," said Happy.

"We are getting danger money."

"I want more danger money."

"It's nice to want things," Molly said briskly. "I saw the sweetest French Maid outfit in an Anne Summer's, the other day."

"I told you," said Happy. "I'm not wearing it."

"You can be very unadventurous sometimes," said Melody.

They looked across at JC, on the far side of the lobby. His head was bowed, and he was frowning, lost in thought. He might have been a thousand miles away. Unreachable. Happy shrugged, uneasily.

"Do we know where the homeless guy died?" he said. "Was it here? Because I'm not picking up anything to suggest a recent death, natural or otherwise. In fact, I'm not picking up anything. Just . . . dead air."

"Ho ho ho," said Melody, concentrating on her instrument readouts. "Telepath humour. It's all in the mind."

Happy scowled, moved away, and lowered his mental shields, slowly and methodically opening himself up to his surroundings. Nothing happened until he was completely open and defenceless; and then everything hit him at once. The lobby was suddenly packed full of people, men and women, from all times and fashions, milling back and forth, overlapping and passing through each other. Memories, ghosts, of all the people who'd ever been in the theatre lobby. A hundred thousand audiences, all of them talking at once, a terrible clamour of raised voices from out of the Past, filling Happy's head to bursting. He clapped both hands to his ears, a practiced psychological trick to keep voices outside his head; but it didn't help. There were too many of them, layer upon layer of people pressed upon people . . . Voices determined to be heard.

And slowly, one by one, then in small groups, heads turned to look at him. Faces focused on him, becoming aware of his presence. They could see Happy because they weren't memories, they were dead. Ghosts of people who'd died in the lobby, or the theatre, or returned there because it had special memories for them. They drifted slowly, implacably, towards Happy, passing inexorably through all the other presences in their way. Drawn to him like moths, to the bright light of his living soul. Happy looked about him desperately, but everywhere he looked there were more, coming right at him, their dead faces distorted by an awful, endless hunger.

Happy slammed down all his shields at once, forcing his mental defences back into place, until every last bit of his telepathy was shut down and he was as blind to the world as everyone else. Until he couldn't have seen a ghost even if it walked right up to him and glared into his face. Or, at least, he hoped so. He stood very still, breathing hard. He could feel cold sweat on his face. When he finally lowered his hands, they shook violently. Happy looked quickly around the lobby. JC was still wrapped up in himself, but Melody was looking at him steadily. She came out from behind her instruments, walked over to Happy, and put her arms around him. She held him close, while he hung on to her like a drowning man. She patted his back gently, giving him the warmth of her body to drive out the cold of the dead. Giving him her steady presence to anchor him in the world again.

"Bad one?" she said, her voice carefully calm and neutral.

"Bad enough," he said, when he could find his voice. "My own fault. I should have known better than to lower my guard in a place bound to be soaked in people and memories. Still . . ."

"Yes?" said Melody.

Happy took his arms away from her, and she immediately let go of him and stepped back. Beyond a certain point, Happy didn't like to be fussed over.

"That . . . didn't just happen," said Happy. "That felt much more like an ambush. Which means we're not alone here. Someone, or Something, targeted me."

Melody studied his face carefully. "You need some of your little chemical helpers, don't you?"

"No," said Happy. "I'm stronger than that, now. I don't need them. You showed me that."

"But you still want them," said Melody.

"Oh, God, yes, I want them," said Happy. "Luckily, I want you more."

"That's the nicest thing you've ever said to me," said Melody. "I really wish it was true."

And then they looked round sharply, as the main

doors slammed open and their theatrical guests arrived. A man and a woman, both well into their forties, both clearly fighting for every inch, both of them that little bit too deliberately glamorous. Because they felt it was expected of them. They stopped directly inside the doors, realised they had an audience, and immediately fell into flattering publicity poses without even realising they were doing it. There was a pause, as everyone looked at everyone else, then JC strode briskly forward to stand with Happy and Melody, to present a unified front in the face of civilian outsiders. The two actors looked the Ghost Finders over and gave no impression of being in any way impressed.

"Are you the . . . experts?" said the woman, in a rich clear voice.

JC gave them both his best professional smile. "We are, indeed, the experts. Allow me to introduce your team for tonight. I am JC Chance, ghost finder extraordinaire, exorcist without portfolio, and leader of the pack. Despite everything I can do to get out of it. The short sulky thing on my left is Happy Jack Palmer; team telepath, portable psychic, and general pain in the arse. Feel free to ignore him or throw things. We do. Finally, this sweet and very dangerous young lady is Melody Chambers, geek girl nerd technician and *Take That* fan. Don't get too close, she bites. Do not be fooled by the way we look; we are in fact very experienced and very efficient."

"So . . . ghosts don't scare you?" said the man, in a mellifluous, carrying voice.

JC grinned. "Hell no . . . ghosts are scared of us."

"I'm not sure whether that makes me feel any safer, or not," said the woman.

"Lot of people say that," said Happy.

"Only because they know us," said Melody.

"I'm Benjamin Darke," said the man, a bit grandly. "And this is my wife, Elizabeth de Fries."

They both stood a little taller, clearly expecting to be recognised. When it became clear that wasn't going to happen, Benjamin announced their names again, a little louder and more distinctly, as though that might make a difference.

"Oh come on!" said Elizabeth. "You must have heard of us! We've been jobbing actors for twenty years now! We've been in everything, both stage and screen!"

"Exactly!" said Benjamin. "We've done everything, from soaps to period dramas, police procedurals to sit-coms! I was in a *Doctor Who* and she was in a Sherlock Holmes! Recently!"

"Sorry," said JC. "We're usually out working, of an evening. Our business is with the dead, not the living."

Benjamin and Elizabeth looked at each other. Their shoulders slumped, and they stood more closely together, as though they could only depend on each other.

Benjamin Darke was tall and stocky, with a certain physical presence. He dressed well, if not actually expensively, with a smart sweater and slacks under a navy blue blazer, and a white silk cravat at his throat. He carried himself with a certain youthful vigour, through sheer force of will, and long stage training showed in his every disciplined movement. He was still handsome, in a severe sort of way, though middle age had clearly got a grip on him. His receding hair was suspiciously jet-black. He smiled a lot, a bright, professional smile that probably fooled most people.

Elizabeth de Fries was short and well-made, showing off her perfectly preserved figure in a carefully cut pale blue dress and very high heels. Up close she was clearly into her forties, but with the right makeup and camera lens, she could still knock ten years off that. She had a pleasantly pretty face under a mop of tight blonde curls, and sparkling blue eyes. She still had charm, as opposed to Benjamin's practiced presence.

And then Happy had to go and spoil it all by walking right up to them and prodding them both hard in the chest with his forefinger. Benjamin's eyes widened, and Elizabeth let out a brief squeak of surprise. Happy looked them both over carefully, nodded quickly, and went back to JC and Melody. The two actors looked at each other, then at JC and Melody for an explanation. They didn't get one. JC tried hard to look solemn. Melody didn't even try.

"Just making sure," said Happy. "After what happened with Roland Laurie . . . Still can't believe I didn't spot him . . . Don't get fooled again, that's my motto."

"He prodded me in the bosom!" Elizabeth said loudly. "And . . . he didn't even say please!"

"I did notice, darling," said Benjamin.

"Then don't just stand there, darling, do something!"

"Like what? Go over there and prod him back? I wouldn't lower myself."

"You never did have any spine, darling," said Elizabeth.

And then they all jumped a little and looked around, as the main doors crashed open again as a bright-eyed girl in her late teens came striding in. She stopped, accepted everyone staring at her as her right, and smiled happily about her.

"Hi!" she said cheerfully. "I'm Lissa Parr! It's Melissa, actually, but everyone calls me Lissa. Sorry I'm a bit late."

Lissa was a tall, slender brunette, with flat, shoulder-length hair and a heavy dark fringe falling right down to her penciled-on eyebrows. She wore tight blue jeans, and an even tighter white T-shirt, the better to show off her marvellous figure. Happy took a step forward, then stopped when Melody glared at him.

"Are you sure?" he said. "You might thank me, later."

"You go anywhere near her bosom, and I'll tie your finger in a knot," said Melody.

The three actors took it in turns to kiss the air somewhere near each other's cheeks, then stepped back to look each other over in a professional kind of way. None of them offered to kiss any of the Ghost Finders, which was probably just as well.

Lissa was very pretty, perhaps despite rather than because of all the character in her face. Her lips were very red and very thin, but her constant smile looked real enough. Her eyes were dark and full of humour, with a hell of a lot of blue eye make-up. She still had as if by right what Elizabeth was fighting to hang on to. Which was probably why Elizabeth was the only one not mesmerised by her. The young actress stood happily in her favourite loose-limbed pose, basking in the attention she was still young enough to take for granted. It was clear she'd been taught to stand that way in public if there was even a chance of a photographer . . . drilled into her until it was second nature; but she still managed it unconsciously and unselfconsciously. She threw in the charm at no extra cost, without even realising she was doing it.

"Sorry," said JC, and actually sounded like he meant it, "but who are you, exactly? Are you another name we're supposed to recognise?"

Lissa's smile slipped for a moment. "You really don't know me? Damn. I am clearly not getting my money's worth out of that new publicist. Look, I was in that controversial indie film, *Jesus and Satan Go Jogging in the Desert*. And that big disaster movie, *Werewolf on the Titanic*."

"Oh, I remember that one!" said Happy. "Not even a little bit accurate."

"We weren't expecting you until next week, darling," said Elizabeth, with a hint of chill in her voice. "The theatre isn't nearly ready yet."

"You know her?" said JC.

"Of course we know her; we hired her!" said Benjamin. "She's going to star in our play! As our female lead. But, as Elizabeth was saying . . ."

Lissa shrugged prettily. "Don't blame me, sweeties; I got a phone call from my agent, saying drop everything and get straight round to the Haybarn, they need you. So here I am! You are glad to see me, aren't you?"

"Of course we are, Lissa," said Benjamin, shooting Elizabeth a quick warning glance. "It's simply that the renovators have encountered some . . . unexpected difficulties."

"Oh, I know all about that, sweetie," said Lissa. "My agent couldn't wait to tell me!"

"How very helpful of him," said Elizabeth. "It would seem word has got out . . ."

"Ghosts and ghoulies and things that go Booyah! in the night! How terribly thrilling!" Lissa looked at JC and his team with new interest. "Are you the experts?"

"I do wish people would stop using that word, in that particular tone of voice," said Happy. "Yes, we are quite definitely experts; we are the Ghost Finders! Hauntings a speciality, no spook left unturned. We are very expert! Very!"

"Gosh," said Lissa, completely unmoved by Happy's histrionics. "What larks, eh?" She looked around the lobby, and some of her natural exuberance fell away. "Bit of a dump, isn't it, sweeties?"

"It wasn't always like this," said Elizabeth, frostily. "Back in its heyday, the Haybarn was one of the finest theatres in the Midlands. Very smart, very elegant, very fashionable; the most prestigious vehicle for any up-and-coming young actors looking to make their mark. We had critics from all the broadsheets turning up on opening nights."

"But that was . . . sometime ago," said Benjamin. "The Haybarn has been shut down and abandoned for twenty years. It's going to take a lot of hard work to smarten the old girl up again. And we can't do that until we can persuade the renovators to return."

"Why has it been left empty for so long?" said Lissa. Benjamin and Elizabeth looked at each other, then at the Ghost Finders. "It was to have been our greatest triumph," said Benjamin. "The play that would change all our lives."

"Change everything," said Elizabeth. "But it all went wrong, so horribly quickly . . ."

"We were the established leads, back then," said Benjamin. "Starred in everything the Haybarn put on, took everything in our stride, from classics to modern. The public loved us, the critics thought we could do no wrong. We had the world at our feet, and we thought it would last forever. We wrote a play together, Elizabeth and I: *A Working-class Messiah Is Something to Be*. Something . . . very different, very special. We would direct and cover the two supporting leads, and we had one of the major stars of the day committed to the lead. Frankie Hazzard."

Everyone nodded quickly. They all knew that name.

"Tall, dark, and handsome," said Melody. "Didn't half fancy himself. He played that spy, what's-his-name, in that film; *Index Finger, Left Hand*."

"I saw him on a chat show once," said Happy. "So far up himself he was hanging out his own nostrils."

"Pushing that unfortunate mental image firmly to one side," said JC, "perhaps we could concentrate on the matter at hand. What happened? What went wrong?"

"The play crashed and burned," Elizabeth said flatly. "Didn't even make two weeks before the theatre shut it down. The critics hated it, and nobody came. The theatre's owners had sunk considerable funding into it, and they lost all of it. They had no choice but to close the theatre."

"We were wiped out," said Benjamin. "Lost every-thing we had."

"And, of course, no other theatre would touch us, after that," said Elizabeth. "The stink of failure clings like leprosy in our profession."

"Our play was supposed to make everyone's careers, and make everyone a lot of money," said Benjamin. "But it didn't. Not the play's fault, though . . . We always said that, didn't we, darling? Well, after all these years, we have funding again. A chance to reopen the play, right here. The play as it should have been, before Frankie Hazzard got his grubby hands on it and insisted on all those unnecessary rewrites. Our production will reopen the Haybarn, with the very talented Lissa Parr as our female lead."

"I'm still waiting to hear who's going to be playing opposite me," said Lissa, in a pretty, smiling, and very pointed way.

"We're still in negotiations," Elizabeth said quickly. "We're almost there, only a few last details to hammer out with his agent."

"We can't name him yet, for obvious reasons," said Benjamin. "But he is very enthusiastic. Loves the play . . ."

Happy leaned in close beside Melody. "You think the theatre's owners could be Catherine Latimer's old friends?" he said quietly. "And that's why we're here?"

"Wouldn't surprise me," said Melody.

"So!" Lissa said brightly, turning the full force of her charm on JC. "You're the experts. But what are you, ex-actly? Spookbusters? Exorcists R Us?"

"No-one's reported seeing any actual ghosts," Benjamin said quickly. "Let's not get ahead of ourselves, eh?"

"It could still all turn out to be nothing," said Elizabeth.

"Or nothing important, anyway," said Benjamin.

"What exactly happened?" said JC, and something in his voice stopped Benjamin in mid flow. He looked at his wife.

"The workers we hired to renovate this building, at very expensive rates, were all very vague about what they'd encountered here," Elizabeth said steadily. "In fact, we couldn't get a straight answer out of any of them. But every single one of them was out of here inside of twelve hours; and not one of them would agree to set foot inside the building again, no matter how much was offered them, until we'd agreed to Do Something . . ."

"Oh, that's us!" JC said cheerfully. "We're great ones for Doing Something!"

"Suddenly and violently and all over the place," said Happy.

"But what actually happened here?" Melody insisted. "What did the workers see, or hear . . . ?"

"They'd barely been in here a few hours before the problems started," said Benjamin, reluctantly. "The men saw and heard . . . things, though they wouldn't say what. There was a constant feeling of being watched, apparently, of being observed by unfriendly eyes. Things, tools, would disappear from right under their hands, then reappear somewhere else. Voices, in the dark, saying things . . . bad things. Someone crying who wouldn't stop. Someone they could never find calling for help.

And a constant sense of someone standing right behind you, close enough to reach out and lay a hand on your shoulder . . ."

"And then they found the dead tramp," said Elizabeth. "Right there on the main stage."

"And that was the end of that," said Benjamin. "The final straw. No-one would go back in after that."

"How did he die exactly?" said Melody.

"Heart attack," Benjamin said carefully. "That's what the doctor put on the death certificate."

"It was a reporter from the local paper who claimed that the man died of fright," said Elizabeth. "Apparently he saw a photo of the tramp's face . . . Anyway, that put it on the front page of the local rag. After all, died of fright is a headline. Died of a heart attack is nothing more than filler. Page twelve, if you're lucky."

"Still!" Lissa said brightly. "Paranormal encounters, eh? Isn't it exciting?"

JC, Melody, and Happy all looked at her in a pitying sort of way, which she entirely failed to pick up on.

"We insisted on being here, to oversee your work," Elizabeth said to JC. "To ensure the theatre's interests are represented while you work out what's going on here."

"What's really going on?" Benjamin said heavily. "I'm still not convinced by any of this."

"You sounded pretty convinced a moment ago," said Happy.

"We need to get this all done and sorted!" Benjamin said stubbornly. "Nothing can be allowed to get in the way of our play's revival!"

"Nothing," Elizabeth said flatly. "We've waited too long for this." She looked straight at JC. "You have to get to the bottom of this, Mr. Chance. Before the theatre's owners lose faith and whip the funding out from under us. Again."

Lissa looked sharply at Elizabeth and Benjamin. "Is there a problem with the funding? Is there, in fact, some doubt as to whether this play will actually go on? I turned down a really good part in a good film because my agent said this would be a good career move! I can't afford a mis-step in my career at this point!"

Elizabeth and Benjamin looked fondly at each other. "Doesn't she remind you of us, at that age?" said Elizabeth.

"Answer the question!" said Lissa, actually stamping one small but perfect foot.

"The funding is in place and perfectly secure," Benjamin said soothingly. "The play will go on. As soon as the experts here have put everything to rights. Which shouldn't take too long; right, Mr. Chance?"

"We're not going to have to get a medium in, are we?" said Elizabeth. "They're always so expensive . . ."

"I worked with a medium, once," said Benjamin. "Doing the knockings for him, banging a pair of tap shoes against the underside of the stage. It was all killing effective . . ."

"Was that the one who used to do the cold readings?" said Elizabeth. "And then used what he knew to get the more susceptible ones into bed with him, so he could scam their pin numbers . . . ?"

"Does this theatre have a history of ghosts?" asked JC, cutting in firmly.

"Well, of course; every theatre does," said Benjamin. "But they're just stories. Something to pass the time back-stage, when you're not on for ages, and give the chorus line something to squeal and giggle about. No-one ever takes them seriously."

"What stories do you have here?" said Melody, not very patiently.

"There's the Lady in White," said Elizabeth. "If you see her drifting around the dressing-rooms on opening night, that's supposed to guarantee a good run for your show."

"And then there's the Headless Panto Dame," said Benjamin. "Nasty accident with a trap-door, back in the sixties. Traumatised a whole pack of Cub Scouts in the front row."

"Is she bad luck to see?" said Happy.

"For anyone who sees him, yes," said Elizabeth.

"But," said Benjamin, very firmly, "there have never been any . . . unexplained incidents in the theatre before this. Not one. No nasty business, nothing properly fright-ening, and certainly never anything bad enough to send dozens of hardened workmen running away from very well-paid work."

And then they all looked round sharply again as the main doors slammed shut. And there, standing before them, smiling gently, was an old man with stooped shoul-ders, a long brown overall, and a flat cap perched slightly off skew on his bald head. He looked to be well into his seventies, with a heavily lined face, a weak smile, and a really unfortunate attempt at a moustache. He nodded vaguely to everyone present, regarding them all with pale, watery eyes.

"Sorry about that, ladies and gents; didn't mean to startle anyone. I'm Old Tom; used to be caretaker here, back in the day. Called out of a well-earned retirement to give a hand with the . . . current situation."

Benjamin looked at him suspiciously. "We didn't hire you."

"Bless you, no, sir," said Old Tom, blinking quickly. "The theatre's owners contacted me personally, asked me to come back and help out. I couldn't say no, not after they were so good to me, all those years. Spent the best years of my life here, looking after the old place. No-one knows the old Haybarn better than me. Seen them all come and go, I have. The stories I could tell . . . Anyway. Couldn't leave the old girl in the hands of strangers. No-one knows the ins and outs of the Haybarn better than me, ladies and gents. Shall I show you around?"

"Hold it," said JC. "Who are the theatre's owners?"

"Mr. and Mrs. Lovett, sir," said Old Tom. "The Lovetts have owned the Haybarn for generations."

"Why didn't anyone buy the theatre while it was closed?" said Melody.

"Because it was never put up for sale, miss," said Old Tom. "They'd never sell this old place. Far too much sentimental value. Of course, it helps that the Lovetts aren't short of a bob or two, if you catch my drift." Here, Old Tom did his best to wink roguishly. "No; they've been waiting for exactly the right time to reopen their theatre again."

"And the right play," said Benjamin.

"As you say, sir," said Old Tom.

"Then lead on," said JC. "Show us everything there is to see."

Old Tom gave them all another of his vague smiles and shuffled over to one of the larger doors. It was only then that the others realised that he'd come out still wearing his carpet slippers. They all looked at each other, but no-one felt like saying anything. Old Tom pushed the door open and disappeared through, letting the door slam shut behind him. JC leaned in close to murmur to Happy and Melody.

"No-one said anything to me about a caretaker. Just the actors."

"Want me to prod him?" said Happy.

"Don't you dare!" said Elizabeth, who turned out to be a lot closer than any of them had realised. "The last thing we need is the theatre's owners getting involved, saying we're not respecting their wishes."

JC looked at Elizabeth. "My, what big ears you have."

"All the better for not being left out of things, darling," said Elizabeth. "I don't want Old Tom upset. A good caretaker is worth his weight in gold."

"In oh so many ways," said Benjamin.

"Would he be likely to know the theatre's private and personal history?" said JC. "All the tales told out of school, the secrets and scandals?"

There was a brief pause while Elizabeth and Benjamin

looked at each other, and something went unspoken between them.

"Caretakers were often spies for the owners, back in the day," Elizabeth said carefully. "Reporting back on all the gossip, on every little bust-up and whispered confidence. Never let us get away with anything."

"You think that's why he's here now?" said Happy.

"Why else?" said Benjamin. "We didn't hire him; did we, darling?"

"Never met him before in my life," said Elizabeth.

JC looked at them sharply. "You don't know Old Tom personally?"

"Benjamin and I weren't actually here all that long," said Elizabeth. "A bit over four years, in all. He could have been before our time."

"Or, he might be someone from the local press, passing himself off as a caretaker!" said Benjamin. "Looking to see if their story has legs!"

"He did come across a bit Central Casting," said Elizabeth. "But you know, that might not necessarily be a bad thing, darling. We could use a little useful publicity, to get the theatre's reopening noticed . . . If we play this right . . ."

Old Tom poked his head back through the door. "Is there a problem, ladies and gents?"

"What have you heard about the . . . current conditions?" said JC.

"The dead tramp and the hauntings?" Old Tom tried out his roguish wink again and laid one finger along the side of his nose. "I've worked here man and boy, sir, and never seen a thing. Take more than a few rumours to keep me out. I ain't afraid of no ghost!" He chuckled silently for a moment, enjoying his little joke. "You come along with me, ladies and gents. Old Tom'll see nothing happens to you! There's nothing to be scared of here . . ."

He disappeared back through his door again, and the others hurried after him, JC making a point of leading the way. Melody briefly glanced back at her instruments, then shrugged angrily and went along with the others. The door swung quietly shut behind them. Silence and shadows held sway in the empty lobby. And then the intercom speakers turned themselves on. For a while, there was nothing but the quiet hissing of static; and then, a voice.

"Welcome back, my friends, to the opening night of a brand-new production. Seats available at all prices. The curtain is going up. Prepare yourselves . . . for a show you'll never forget."

FOUR

STAGE BUSINESS

When an audience comes to the theatre, all they usually see is the lobby and the stage. They may notice, in passing, the Ticket Office . . . posters on the walls, maybe some concession stands, but that's it. But what an audience sees is only ever the tip of the iceberg; most of the work and most of the world of the theatre is the nine-tenths of the iceberg that remains hidden from view. For the same reason that most patrons never get to see the kitchens of the restaurants they visit. Because if you could see what went on behind the scenes, what really goes into everything, all the illusion and glamour would be stripped away in a moment. Acting is like athletics—a lot of effort goes into making it all seem effortless.

So getting from the lobby to the stage isn't always a straightforward affair. Old Tom led them all through a warren of narrow backstage corridors, so they could see everything there was to see, cheerfully pointing out all the various points of interest. Everything from dressing-rooms to costumes to props . . . Everyone was very polite, of course, while silently wishing he'd get a move on. JC did his best to keep an eye out for signs and landmarks, so he could be sure of finding his way around on his own if the need arose. But most of the signs had been taken down long ago, and all the doors and all the corridors looked eerily alike. JC quickly lost all track of where he was, or even in which direction the lobby lay. He looked across at Benjamin and immediately realised that the actor looked as lost as he did. JC fell in beside him.

"Something wrong?" he said quietly.

"I'm not sure," said Benjamin, frowning. "It's just . . . I don't remember its taking this long to get to the stage, back in my day. And I'm almost sure the layout was never this complicated. It almost feels like we're going round and round in circles."

Elizabeth nodded vigorously. "I do have to wonder, darling, whether Old Tom is so far gone that he doesn't actually remember where he's going and is too proud to admit it. Or even . . . if he isn't really the caretaker he claims to be and some journalist trying to bluff his way through. Or could he be deliberately trying to disorientate us? I don't know what's going on here, Benjamin, but I don't like it. Something doesn't feel right."

JC left Benjamin and Elizabeth muttering uneasily together and fell back to walk with Happy and Melody. Happy was scowling even more fiercely than usual.

"Something is definitely not kosher with these corridors, JC. The amount of time we've spent walking, we should be through the back of the theatre and half-way down the street. It feels to me . . . as though there's more space here than there should be. As though the local geometry isn't as properly nailed down at the corners as it should be."

"I wouldn't argue with that," murmured JC. "This whole theatre feels wrong to me."

"Maybe we should start leaving a trail of bread-crumbs," suggested Melody.

As she was saying that, Old Tom took a sharp right turn, led them up some steps, and out onto the main stage. All the lights were on, bathing the entire massive stage in a fierce illumination. Everyone stood together, blinking through the harsh glare at the gloom of the massive auditorium, laid out before them. It was like standing on an island of light, peering out at a sea of darkness.

"Who the hell left all these lights on?" said Elizabeth. "The workmen assured me that everything had been turned off when they left! I really don't need the theatre's owners adding their energy bills to our running costs."

"There weren't any lights on in the lobby," observed JC.

"So why are they on here?" said Benjamin.

He strode forward across the stage, Elizabeth sticking close beside him. Lissa wandered after them, smiling happily about her as though she was finally where she belonged. Old Tom stayed by the wings, at the far side of the stage, as though he knew his place and wasn't prepared to venture beyond it. JC moved cautiously forward. To his surprise, he found he didn't like being on stage. It felt too open, too exposed, too vulnerable. He glared out into the shadowy auditorium, and the rows upon rows of empty seats stared silently back at him. JC knew what the workmen meant, now, when they talked of being watched by unseen, unfriendly eyes. He slipped his heavy sunglasses down his nose, so he could peer over the top of them, but even his augmented eyes couldn't make out anything useful. He pushed the glasses back up his nose again. He didn't want his glowing eyes to freak out the civilians; and he was getting really fed up with having to come up with clever answers to distract them.

Happy and Melody stuck close together, braced and ready for an attack that never came.

"Must bring back memories, eh?" Old Tom said cheerfully to Benjamin and Elizabeth. "All the plays you appeared in, all the characters you played; must feel like coming home. I suppose."

Benjamin and Elizabeth walked to the very front of the stage, as though drawn there. They stood arm in arm, looking out into the Past, smiling reflectively.

"This was our kingdom, once upon a time," said Benjamin. "Where we were Kings and Queens, angry young men and femmes fatales . . . We played Shakespeare and Marlowe, Becket and Brecht, Oscar Wilde and George Bernard Shaw, bless his declamatory speeches . . . Hell, we did it all, didn't we girl, one time or another. For everything from standing ovations to sullen silences. Because you can't please all the people all of the time, the ungrateful bastards . . ."

"I sometimes think we had more fun backstage," said Elizabeth. "Applause is what it's all about, of course; but there's more to theatre than the smell of the crowds and

the roar of the grease-paint. For happy times and camaraderie, give me a theatre bar any day. Do you remember
the one time we did the Scottish play."

"Ah, the Caledonian Tragedy," said Benjamin.

"Do you by any chance mean *Macbeth*?" JC said
innocently.

Everyone except the Ghost Finders winced.

"Please," said Benjamin, with all the dignity he could
muster. "Don't do that. It's unlucky."

"And I really don't think we're in any position to push
our luck at the moment," said Elizabeth.

"Anyway," said Benjamin, "you remember young
Dicky Moran, dear; playing Seyton, MacB's second in
command? He was lumbered with one of the most familiar lines from Shakespeare: *The Queen, my lord, is dead.*
Well, what can you do with that that hasn't been done a
hundred times before? Particularly if you're young and
ambitious and keen to be noticed, like Dicky? We got all
the way to the technical rehearsal, before Dicky came up
with his Big Idea and presented it proudly to the director.
He wanted to walk on stage with the Queen lying limp
in his arms, present her to the King, then say the line!
Would have been very effective. You were up for it,
weren't you, darling?"

"It would certainly have made a big impression," said
Elizabeth, which JC couldn't help noticing wasn't exactly
the same as agreeing, "But the director wouldn't wear it.
Complete sense-of-humour failure . . . Which is probably
why Dicky did what he did the next evening, at the dress
rehearsal . . . You remember, darling; it was right at the
end, with half the cast on stage celebrating MacB's death,

and the rest of us watching from the stalls. Hoping it would all end soon, so we could get a drink in. Someone has to bring on a fake severed head and say it's MacB's, then the big names go into soliloquy mode. Well, Dicky noticed that the actor holding the head was surreptitiously turning it back and forth so that it seemed to be looking at whoever was speaking. Well, once Dicky saw that, he couldn't help himself. He started going *Gottle of Gear* from the front row, and other ventriloquist classics, like *Get back in the box! I don't want to get back in the box!* And, of course, the moment he pointed it out, everyone else could see it, too! We rocked with laughter, all of us! We fell about, we leaned on each other, we laughed till we cried. Completely ruined the atmosphere . . ."

"The director blew his top," said Benjamin, nodding happily. "Wanted to fire young Dicky, right there on the spot. But I put my foot down."

"Indeed you did, darling," said Elizabeth, "and quite right, too. Though the first night we had to go on without a severed head because no-one could look at it with a straight face any more. And might I point out, darling, you could be just as bad yourself. I've never been able to forget what happened with *Cider with Rosie* . . ."

"Oh God, yes," said Benjamin, grinning broadly and not looking in any way ashamed of himself. "It was the technical again, when evenings grow long, and nerves grow short. We'd been running the play for hours, and we were all exhausted. We wanted to go home, or to bed, or both. Anyway, we'd finally made it to the last scene, where young Laurie Lee is in the hay-cart with young Rosie, and she's about to give him a glass of cider and show him what life is all about . . . Except, neither of the two youngsters could get their lines right! They kept stopping, or jumping, or getting it wrong, over and over and over . . . The rest of the cast were all out there in the auditorium, watching from the shadows, getting more and more impatient. Until finally a voice was heard, rising out of the dark, saying *For God's sake, Rosie, will you please wank him off, then we can all go home!*"

There was general laughter, while Elizabeth shook her head in mock condemnation. Benjamin smiled innocently.

"Might have been me. Might not. Who can say?"

Lissa wasn't laughing. She had her arms folded tightly across her chest and was trying very hard to look as though such unprofessional behaviour was entirely beneath her. Elizabeth smiled at her frostily.

"You haven't done much stage-work, have you, dear? You mustn't worry—it's the little moments of madness that keep us all sane. And after our play, you'll be able to command every stage you walk onto. You really must try some Shakespeare; nothing like the Bard to stretch the acting muscles."

"I have always fancied putting myself up for Lady MacB," said Lissa. "But if I do, I'll stick to the words. I really don't have any time for sparking up the material with special bits of business, like certain actresses who've played her nude, or peed on stage during the sleep-walking scene."

"Yes," said Benjamin. "I remember that. I do recall being a bit nervous about which way the stage was sloping . . ."

"It's all about the performance," Lissa said firmly. "Shakespeare doesn't need improving."

"It's all about getting noticed," Benjamin said wisely. "But, then, you've probably never had any problems with that, have you?"

They all stopped and looked around sharply. Suddenly, without any warning, there was the sound of loud footsteps approaching from off stage. No build-up, no quiet sounds growing louder; only very heavy footsteps in the far wings, heading towards the stage. Everyone turned to look. The footsteps grew even louder, and heavier, as they drew nearer, slamming down with more-than-human weight and an inhuman sense of purpose. The stage itself seemed to shake and shudder with every step as though in anticipation. As though it was frightened. The footsteps reached the edge of the stage, left the wings, and continued on; but there was no-one there. Nothing to see, nothing at all. Only the sound—one loud crashing step after another, heavy enough to break the world, loud enough to raise the dead, crossing the stage with horrid determination, heading straight for the living.

Benjamin and Elizabeth clung to each other tightly, stupefied by what was happening, unable to move. Lissa fell back to stand behind Old Tom, who didn't seem to know what to do. He stood there, staring blankly at the approaching footsteps. As though it were all happening to someone else. JC moved forward to face the sounds and place himself between the advancing footsteps and the civilians. Melody started after him, realised Happy wasn't moving, grabbed him by the arm, and hauled him along with her. The three of them stood shoulder to shoulder, facing the approaching sounds.

"Talk to me, Happy!" said JC. "What is this?"

"I don't know!" said Happy. "I'm not seeing anything! Anything at all!"

JC whipped off his sunglasses and turned the full force of his glowing eyes on whatever was before him; but the footsteps kept coming, and he couldn't see a damned thing. He held his ground, and the footsteps walked right up to him and stopped. Silence fell across the stage, the quiet broken only by the strained harsh breathing of the living as they waited for something to happen. But no-one appeared, and there weren't any more footsteps. JC carefully extended one arm and waggled his hand back and forth before him; but there was nothing there.

JC put his sunglasses back on and frowned thoughtfully. "Okay," he said finally. "That . . . was a bit odd."

"Really?" said Happy, mopping at his damp face with a grubby handkerchief. "You think?"

"I was expecting whatever was making the footsteps to turn around and walk away," said JC. "But they didn't. The sounds just stopped. As though they'd served their purpose, accomplished everything they were supposed to . . ."

He turned around and looked back at the civilians. Benjamin and Elizabeth had let go of each other and were looking around a bit self-consciously. Old Tom was standing very still at the wings, as though he didn't know where to look or what to do. Lissa emerged from behind him, looking pale and strained and quite decidedly spooked.

"I didn't like that at all!" she said loudly. "I thought ghosts would be . . . thrilling. Exciting! But that was nasty. Horrid."

Elizabeth moved over quickly to put an arm across Lissa's shoulders and comfort her. "It's all right, dear. We understand."

"Do you want us to call you a taxi?" said Benjamin. "You could always go back to your hotel and wait there, till this is all over. We have to be here; but you shouldn't have to put up with this."

Lissa's chin came up. She straightened her back and shrugged off Elizabeth's arm, almost rudely. "No. I'm not going. Nothing's scaring me off."

Benjamin gave her his professional smile. "Brave girl."

Happy moved in close beside JC. "Look at the stage," he said quietly. "There's a layer of dust. See? If you look behind us, you can see all our footsteps, crossing the stage from the wings to here. But there are no footsteps in the dust before us, not a mark anywhere between us and the far wings. Which leads me to believe that there never was anything here. No physical presence, at all. Just the *sound* of footsteps . . ."

"Could be an echo out of Time," said Melody. "Sounds from the Past. Stone tape memory, past events impressed on the surroundings, playing back in the Present."

"Why are we still calling it a stone tape?" Happy said suddenly. "Shouldn't we be calling it a stone CD, these days? Or even a stone download . . ."

"Concentrate, Happy," murmured JC. "That was no echo. Those sounds had a deliberate aim in mind. A purpose . . ."

"How very theatrical," said Melody; and then they all looked at each other for a long moment.

JC looked across the stage at Benjamin and Elizabeth. "Is this the kind of . . . event you were expecting?"

"Well, sort of," said Benjamin. "You have to understand; we never experienced anything first-hand."

"And I have to say," said Elizabeth, slowly, "that the whole thing seemed to me more menacing than scary. Almost . . . a threat. We should never have come back here, Benjamin."

"We had to," said Benjamin. "We owed it to the play."

And then they all froze in place again as they heard something moving about, under the stage. They all looked down, listening hard, concentrating. Some distance underneath the stage, somebody was walking back and forth, loudly whistling a merry tune. JC stamped hard on the stage; but the whistling didn't stop, or even interrupt itself for a moment. JC looked sharply at the actors and Old Tom.

"Is there supposed to be anyone else in the building?"

"No, sir," said Old Tom. "No-one. I'd have been told."

"No-one whistles in the theatre!" Elizabeth said sharply. "It's bad luck!"

"Anyone recognise the tune?" said Happy. There was a general shaking of heads.

JC looked at Old Tom. "What's down there, under this stage? Is there any way to reach it?"

"Of course, sir," said Old Tom. "That's the understage

area, easy to get to. There's a way to everywhere, and I know them all. Follow me, ladies and gents!"

....

The way down turned out to be an old iron stairway that spiralled around as it descended into the gloom of the understage area. The stairway didn't feel properly attached or supported, worn loose through many years of hard use; and it swayed dangerously and made loud, complaining noises as Old Tom led the way down, one careful step at a time. Though whether his pace was due to the infirmities of old age or sensible caution, JC couldn't tell. He stuck right behind Old Tom, peering down into the gloomy depths in search of the phantom whistler. Happy came next though he didn't want to. Melody had to drive him down ahead of her, with fierce encouragement and appalling language that the actors pretended not to hear as they brought up the rear.

The whistled tune cut off abruptly the moment Old Tom and JC emerged from the bottom of the stairway. The understage area was completely empty. Nothing to see, nothing to hear, not even the faintest echo. The light from a single hanging naked light bulb spread a grubby yellow glare across a wide-open space much bigger than the stage above. Everyone relaxed. With no phantom whistler, no footsteps, and nothing in any way unnatural, the open area seemed safe enough. Benjamin made a point of smiling easily around him.

"Well, this place brings back memories! Remember when we were playing the leads in the Restoration comedy, *She Stoops to Conquer*?"

"Oh God, it's another anecdote," muttered Happy. "I think I'd rather have a ghost . . ."

"Of course I remember!" said Elizabeth, seizing the moment to lighten the mood. "We had a real pit band, you see, in the open area before the stage, to play real Georgian music; but at the end of the play, they had to leave the pit and come up onto the stage to accompany the final banquet scene. At the end of which, I would walk forward, the curtains would close behind me, and I would deliver the long closing speech straight to the audience. This was to give the other actors time to race off stage and change into their final costumes for the final walkdown. But it also meant the pit-band had to hurry down here, via that awful old stairway, charge across the understage area, and re-emerge in the pit in time to play music for the walkdown. Well, to begin with, all went well. But by the end of the run, I was belting through the lines so we could all get off stage and get to the bar that much earlier; which meant the poor pit band had to run like fun to get to the pit in time. Many the night I heard muffled curses drifting up from down here, yelling to me to slow down . . ."

Everyone managed some kind of smile if not actually a laugh.

"Scratch an old actor, find an anecdote," said Lissa, and Elizabeth glared at her.

"Did anything ever . . . happen down here?" said JC. "Anything significant?"

Benjamin and Elizabeth looked at each other. "No," said Elizabeth.

"Nothing," said Benjamin.

And then they both looked at JC, as though defying him to contradict them. Which, thought JC, was interesting . . .

A great roar of angry sound blasted through the whole understage area, filling the place from end to end. Huge, deafening, overpowering; a fierce and vicious sound, like the outrage of an angry god. As though something had given rage and fury a voice and let it loose. Everyone put their hands to their ears and squeezed their eyes shut, whether they wanted to or not. It was an instinctive, protective thing; and it didn't help at all. The roar went on and on, beating at them like some living creature but continuing on long past the point where any living thing could have sustained it. The sheer anger and malice in the terrible sound was almost palpable.

Benjamin held Elizabeth tightly in his arms, cradling her head to his chest. "Leave her alone!" he shouted into the face of the roar. "Leave her alone, you bastard!"

JC yelled at everyone, straining to be heard above the appalling sound. "Stick together! Don't let it separate us!"

He forced his eyes open, a bit at a time, but even with his augmented vision he still couldn't see anyone, or anything. There was only the sound and the rage within it.

And then it stopped. No falling away, no quietening down; it simply broke off abruptly, without even leaving an echo behind it. For a long moment, everyone stood where they were, opening their eyes and lowering their hands from their heads, all of them suddenly limp with relief. The end of the sound was like the ending of a physical assault. It had beaten and battered them like some unseen bully; and now it felt good, so good, that it was over. One by one, they all started to relax and look around them. Benjamin and Elizabeth let go of each other and stepped back to look each other over, make sure everything was all right. So did Happy and Melody.

They were all of them shaken, amateur and professional alike, by the sheer fury in the sound. And, it seemed to JC, a very human fury. He strode back and forth across the wide-open area, glaring into shadowy nooks and crannies, finding nothing. He didn't like being caught by surprise. He looked back at the others, and was surprised to see Lissa standing on her own, calm and quiet and apparently entirely unaffected by what she'd been through. She didn't look scared, or shaken; she stared straight ahead of her, her face calm and quiet and completely empty. As though she couldn't be bothered if there wasn't an audience . . . JC stopped and considered her thoughtfully. Shock, perhaps? He started towards her, then Benjamin suddenly spoke up.

"Hold it; where's Old Tom?"

Everyone stopped where they were and looked quickly about them; but there was no trace of the old caretaker anywhere. They all called his name; but there was no response. And even with the single light bulb and the many concealing shadows, there was nowhere in the understage area where he could have hidden himself.

"Where could he have gone?" said Elizabeth. "There's no way he could have gone back up that creaky iron stairway without us noticing."

"Is there any other exit?" said JC.

"Not that I know of," said Benjamin, looking vaguely about him.

"Maybe something . . . reached out, and took him," said Lissa.

Her voice was very small. Almost lost. For a moment everyone stood still, then Benjamin snorted loudly.

"Just because we don't know of any other exit doesn't mean there isn't one! Come on, you all heard the man— *There's a way to everywhere, and I know all of them.* I don't believe he ever was a caretaker; he's a journalist who's done some research. That moustache never did look real to me."

"He could be back up on the stage," said Lissa. "Where it's light . . ."

JC led the way back to the iron stairway.

"""""""""""""""""""""

Back on the open stage again, they all called repeatedly for Old Tom; but there was still no reply. The brightly lit stage was something of a relief, even a comfort, after the claustrophobic gloom of the understage area. It might not actually be any safer on the stage; but at least here they could all see nothing coming towards them.

"He's got to be around here somewhere," said Benjamin, with more hope than certainty. "He can't have come to any harm. We'd have heard."

"It's just struck me!" said Elizabeth. "No-one's been hurt, have they? I mean, yes, of course, it's all been very scary . . . but it's all threats and menaces. Nothing that could actually do us harm."

"Then where's Old Tom?" said Lissa. "What happened to him?"

The stage lights flared up suddenly, blazing into blue-white incandescence, then went out, all at once. Darkness fell across the stage, and everyone huddled together. In-dividual lights blazed up, here and there, sudden flares and flashes . . . and then the bulbs began to explode, one after another. Everyone on stage flinched away from fly-ing slivers of glass, but none of it came close enough to hurt anyone. A heavy, ponderous gloom filled the stage, only held back by brief surges from individual lights. JC grabbed Happy by the shoulder, and he shrieked loudly. JC shook him hard till he stopped.

"What's happening here, Happy? Talk to me! What's behind all this?"

"I don't know!" said Happy. "I'm not picking up anything! And since I sure as hell bloody well should be picking up something, someone or something must be deliberately blocking me. Which isn't easily done . . ." Happy took a deep breath to calm himself, thinking it through. "It's all tricks, JC! Shock and awe, smoke and mirrors, all of it designed to distract us, draw our atten-tion away from what really matters. But don't ask me what this is all about . . . I can't sense a damned thing. It's like being deaf and blind and wrapped in poisoned cotton wool, all at once."

"You are seriously underperforming on this case, Happy," said JC. He looked at Melody, who immediately shook her head.

"No use looking at me. You know I can't tell a damned

thing without my instruments. I should never have left them behind. You're the leader! You do something!"

"There's nothing to do," said JC. "Happy's right, for once. This is all 'sound and fury, signifying nothing.' Carefully orchestrated bits of theatrical business. Someone's putting on a show."

Suddenly, all the house lights came up. Steady, dependable light filled the whole of the vast auditorium and spilled out across the stage, pushing back the darkness. JC looked quickly back and forth across the rows of raked seating, but every seat in the house was empty. The normal, everyday electric light was peaceful and reassuring, and everyone began to relax again. JC looked at Benjamin and Elizabeth.

"Could someone be overseeing all this business with the lights from the lighting control room?"

"I don't see how," said Elizabeth. "It hasn't been wired up properly yet. And even if Old Tom isn't who he claimed to be, and he was only here to mess with us, he couldn't have got all the way to the lighting booth in time."

"Unless he isn't working on his own," said Lissa.

JC turned to Happy. "Are you sure you're not getting anything?"

Happy looked past JC, swallowed hard, and said, "Uh, JC, I am quite definitely seeing something now."

JC turned around quickly, to follow his gaze, and everyone else looked, too. A horribly emaciated figure, dressed only in rags and tatters and dark splashes of dried blood, was lying full length on the stage by the far wings, facedown, pulling itself laboriously forward by digging its broken fingers into the wood of the stage. The figure crawled slowly forward, in sudden, painful lurches, leaving a long, heavy trail of blood behind it. The head came up slowly, to reveal a ravaged face: a mask of blood with one dark, empty eye socket and a single eyeball hanging down onto the cheekbone from the other. The mouth was gone, the lips torn raggedly away, to reveal blood-stained teeth bared in an endless, horrid grin. The figure hauled itself along, every movement a slow, agonised effort, full of desperate determination. The sound of broken fingertips scratching and scraping across the wooden stage filled the horrified hush on the stage.

Benjamin and Elizabeth clung tightly together, all the colour fallen out of their faces. They didn't want to look at the awful figure, but they couldn't bring themselves to look away. JC snapped his fingers at them several times, to get their attention.

"Has either of you ever seen anything like this before?"

"Of course not!" said Benjamin.

"We would have said!" said Elizabeth. *"What is that thing?"*

Happy and Melody stood close together, studying the slowly crawling figure with professional interest. They might not like the look of it, but they'd seen a lot worse, in their time. JC looked across at Lissa. She was standing very still, staring, wide-eyed; but once again, not nearly as scared as JC would have expected. Most civilians, with no experience of ghosts and monsters, would have screamed or run or even fainted dead away. Lissa looked . . . as though she'd been expecting this. Or something like it. But that could wait. First things first. JC turned back to Happy.

"Is it real?" JC said urgently. "Is that thing really there? Physically present?"

"Not physically present, as such," Happy said immediately. "And it's definitely not what's left of Old Tom, if that's what you were about to ask. I'm finally getting something . . . but don't ask me what. There's a strong sense of *presence*, but . . . whether we're looking at a ghost, or a manifestation, or a stone tape memory . . . is beyond me. I can't see! There's so much power here, JC . . . It's swamping the aether and saturating all the psychic channels!"

"You made that bit up!" said Melody.

"There's so much power, I can't tell what's what!" Happy said stubbornly. "It's like staring into the sun, with different radios blasting into each ear . . . This whole building is soaked in some kind of overwhelming presence. A real *genius loci* . . ."

JC glared at Happy for a long moment, then turned away to give the crawling figure his full attention. It had dragged itself half-way across the stage, shaking and shuddering with effort, heading straight for them.

"All right, Happy," said JC. "Go and talk to it."

"*What?* You go and talk to it!" Happy said immediately. "Whatever that is, it doesn't look like it's got anything to say that I would want to hear."

"For once, I am in complete agreement with Happy," said Melody. "I may be a big brave Ghost Finder, but that thing is officially creeping the hell out of me."

"Damn right," said Happy. "You couldn't drive me an inch closer to that thing with a whip and a chair and an electric cattle prod."

"Stay here," said JC.

"You got it, boss," said Melody.

JC slowly walked forward and took up a position right in front of the crawling figure, blocking its way. It stopped, and slowly raised its bloody face to JC. The dangling eyeball rolled slowly back and forth across the crimson cheekbone. JC knelt before the figure, lowering his face so that it was on a level with the thing before him.

"Can I do anything to help?" he said. "Who are you? What do you need? Who did this to you?"

On the last question, the figure raised one hand and pointed a single finger past JC, at Benjamin and Elizabeth. Blood dripped thickly from the pointing, accusing finger. Everyone turned to look at Benjamin and Elizabeth; and when they looked back again, the crawling figure was gone. And so was the long, bloody trail it had left behind it. There wasn't a single trace remaining to show that the awful thing had ever been there. Lissa giggled suddenly, and perhaps a bit hysterically.

"My agent is so going to hear about this . . ."

Elizabeth looked hard at her, and Lissa turned her back on Elizabeth. JC joined Benjamin and Elizabeth.

"Did that figure mean anything to you?" he said.

"No," said Benjamin. "Nothing."

"Then why did it point to you two?" Lissa said loudly, having moved some distance away. "Why did it point only at you? What do you know that you're not telling the rest of us? You're the ones who've got a history with this theatre! What did you do here, twenty years ago?"

"This is nothing to do with us!" Elizabeth said sharply. "Nothing!"

Happy moved in quietly beside JC. "The figure may be gone, but I'm still getting that strong sense of *presence*. Something's still here with us."

JC scowled about him, frustrated. "I hate it when there's nothing solid to get a grip on, literally or metaphorically. But it does seem to me that a lot of what's been happening here doesn't mean anything. As though . . . we're stuck in the middle of someone else's game."

"Unfinished business?" said Melody.

"Almost certainly," said JC.

"Doesn't this all strike you as more . . . dramatic than anything the renovators described?" said Melody.

"As though it was saving the best stuff for us," said Happy.

"Or some of us," said JC. "The question has to be, who is this aimed at, us, or the civilians?"

"I need my instruments," said Melody.

"There must be something, something specific, in this building that's powering this haunting," said JC. "Something must have happened here, and in a sense is still happening, to make this theatre a bad place." He looked steadily at Benjamin and Elizabeth. "Has there ever been a murder in this theatre? Or perhaps some major accident? A fire? Some sort of catastrophe?"

"No," said Elizabeth, immediately.

"Nothing at all," said Benjamin.

"Right!" said JC, clapping his hands together hard, then rubbing them briskly. "I have had enough of this. We need to split up and search this place thoroughly. See if we can find Old Tom, see if he's behind any of this . . . And see if anyone else has got into the building. If not, we need to turn this place upside down and shake it to see what falls out. Search everywhere, people, for something that will make sense of all this. Presumably, we'll know it when we see it. Come along, my children, we need clues, we need evidence. Happy, you go with Benjamin and Elizabeth. Look after them and try very hard to keep them alive."

"Who, me?" said Happy.

"Lissa, you stick with me," said JC. "Melody, I want you back in the lobby. Fire up your equipment and scan this whole building to within an inch of its life."

"You do know," said Lissa, "that in nearly every horror movie, when people split up and go off in different directions, it nearly always turns out to be a really bad idea?"

"Ah," said JC. "But I and my associates are professional supernatural arse-kickers, and very experienced in these matters. We don't take any shit from the Hereafter."

"I want to go home," said Happy.

FIVE

||||||||||||||||||||||||||||

STARDUSTY MEMORIES

Happy stood alone at the edge of the stage, looking out over the vast and empty auditorium. As someone who mostly preferred not to be noticed, even by the people he was working with, the whole concept of standing on a stage and being stared at by an audience made no sense to him at all. He'd never even been to a theatre to watch a play. Or a cinema. Happy didn't like crowds, even when he was part of one. It was hard enough keeping the voices outside his head under normal conditions. Put too many people together in one place, and it was like the whole world wanted to force their way into Happy's thoughts.

On the few occasions when he did let his mental defences down, to look on the hidden world and all it contained, then reality became a very crowded thing indeed. With no room in it at all for a small, unhappy thing like him. It's one thing to know the world is infinite and quite another to be able to see it for yourself. Happy only had an ego as a form of self-defence, so the idea that someone could give a damn about him, like JC . . . or perhaps even love him, like Melody . . . was a whole new concept to him. Happy worried that if people could notice him, then maybe the whole hungry world might, too.

If anyone had ever suggested to Happy that he was a hero, for fighting the good fight as a Ghost Finder, he would have been honestly surprised. Maybe even shocked. He had done some amazing things in his time, it was true, but only because the only other option had been dying horribly.

The pills made things so much easier. His little helpers; his chemical crutch to lean on; something to make him brave when he didn't have it in him. Melody could put his demons to rest, she could hold him in the early hours and make him feel safe in the dark; but she couldn't make him brave. Happy still hadn't got the hang of that. So it bothered him that JC had put the two actors in his care and expected him to keep them safe. That was JC's job, not his. JC knew all there was to know about being brave. And cocky, and arrogant . . . Surely, JC hadn't dumped the actors on him so he could go off with the lovely Lissa and impress her with how brave he was? No; JC wasn't that small. That was Happy. He smiled slightly, looked out over all the empty rows of seats, and wondered what it would feel like to be applauded.

Behind him, Benjamin cleared his throat, politely. He didn't need to. Happy knew where everyone was, all the time. Even with all his mental shields in place, Happy could tell where everyone was, by the way their presence pressed against his shields. The world always wanted in . . . Happy looked back. Benjamin and Elizabeth were standing together, looking at him uncertainly. Happy turned around and gave them both his best professional smile, the one he'd copied from JC.

"Relax," he said because he thought he should. "Everything's going to work out fine. I am a professional Ghost Finder. I do this for a living."

"Where do you think we should start looking, Happy?" said Elizabeth.

"Beats the hell out of me," said Happy with a certain gloomy affability. "It's your theatre. Your past, your history. Whatever's going on does seem to be linked to your time here, twenty years ago. Apart from the stage . . . which part of this theatre would you say was most important to the two of you?"

Elizabeth and Benjamin looked at each other, and something passed between them that they clearly didn't feel like sharing with him. Happy could have reached inside their heads and dug it out, but he didn't. This was partly because the Carnacki Institute had pounded it into him, in a number of very firm ways, that doing so was *wrong*, and that if they caught him at it again, they would lobotomise him with a rusty ice-pick (and Happy didn't think they were in the least bit joking, or even exaggerating), but also . . . Because opening his mind that much, in a place like this, definitely qualified as a Really Bad Idea. The psychic seas of the Haybarn Theatre were choppy and disturbed and full of killer sharks. So Happy waited patiently for Benjamin and Elizabeth to finish not saying the things they didn't want to say out loud, in front of him, and finally Elizabeth nodded, almost imperceptibly, and Benjamin sighed heavily.

"Well, you said it yourself, darling; the best times we ever had were backstage. So I think our best bet would be to go check out the dressing-rooms, those shabby little corners full of dreams and ambition, terror and exhilaration, adrenaline rushes and panic attacks. And home to some of the best after-play parties ever. All human life was there . . ."

"You always were the eloquent one, darling," said Elizabeth.

"Yes . . ." said Happy. "Strong emotions are good— exactly what we need. They always evoke the best memories and the most significant ghosts. Ghosts are memories, and vice versa. Are these dressing-rooms a long way away from the stage?"

"Yes," said Benjamin.

"Oh good," said Happy. "Let us go, right now."

"You're not very brave for a Ghost Buster, are you?" said Elizabeth.

"Brave gets you killed in this business," said Happy, quite seriously. "I prefer to hang around at the back, out of harm's way, shouting helpful advice while the big, brave, alpha types throw themselves forward into an early grave. There's nothing like being able to see ghosts, to make you very determined never to become one. I have been in this business a while now, and I stay alive through a combination of applied caution and a complete willingness to turn and run like fun at a moment's notice, and I suggest you do the same. If you can keep up with me.

Show me these dressing-rooms. Maybe I can pick up some useful mental impressions from them."

"After twenty years?" said Elizabeth.

"Time means nothing to the dead," said Happy. "The Past is always with us, not least because most people never learn to put it down properly."

••••••••••••••••••••••••••

Benjamin and Elizabeth led the way down from the stage, then strode briskly up the long, narrow central aisle of the auditorium. They hurried along, chatting easily to each other, while Happy slouched along behind them, bringing up the rear. He didn't mind that they weren't talking to him; he honestly wouldn't have known what to say if they had. Happy wasn't one for small talk, or most other people skills. And then he stopped, half-way up the aisle, to look back at the stage.

JC hadn't budged an inch. He was still holding his position at centre stage, smiling broadly, and discoursing loudly on something important. Though, to her credit, Lissa didn't seem to be nearly as impressed with JC as JC clearly thought she ought to be.

Melody was already heading off the stage, going in search of her precious scientific equipment back in the lobby. She didn't look back at Happy, even for a moment. Happy was used to that. He knew he was only really real for Melody when he was right in front of her. Or sometimes behind, depending on her mood . . .

Happy stood in the middle of the vast, sprawling auditorium and felt very alone and very vulnerable. He didn't like to work on his own; he preferred being part of a team, if only because it meant there would always be someone there for him to hide behind. But JC had put him in charge of the actors, and Happy had always had a lot of respect for JC. Though, of course, he had never let JC even suspect that because JC would have taken advantage. So Happy quietly decided that he would do his job and do it well. Because he needed someone to be proud of him since he couldn't manage it for himself. He sighed deeply, did his best to square his shoulders in a convincing fashion, and followed Benjamin and Elizabeth up the central aisle to the great swing doors at the top.

The actors swept through the swing doors, still talking, without even glancing back to see if Happy was following. He was used to that, too. He sometimes wondered wistfully if people forgot about him when he wasn't actually making a nuisance of himself. Which might be why he did it so often. He paused again at the swing doors, for one last look out over the auditorium. He didn't dare open his mind for fear of being swamped and overwhelmed by all the prowling memories and emotions of past audiences, like in the lobby . . . but he was quite definitely picking up something. A strong feeling of being watched, observed, by unseen and unfriendly eyes. Happy stared back defiantly, and hurried through the swing doors after Benjamin and Elizabeth.

ıııııııııııııııııııııı

The actors led him down a corridor or two, then took a sharp left turn into actors' backstage territory. One whole corridor had been given over to a long row of dressing-rooms, stretching away into the brightly lit distance.

Happy gave the fierce fluorescent lighting a long, suspicious look; but since Benjamin and Elizabeth didn't say anything, he didn't either. On both sides of the corridor, the doors to all the dressing-rooms stood open, falling back into the rooms, like open invitations to enter. Happy slammed to a halt and looked thoughtfully at the open doors. The two actors realised Happy wasn't with them, stopped, and looked expectantly back at him as he tried to decide whether the doors' standing open was a good sign or not. On the whole, he rather thought not because that was what he thought about most things. But after all, why would all the doors be open . . .

He made Benjamin and Elizabeth stay where they were and stand still, while he slowly and very cautiously peered into the first dressing-room. He eased past the open door without actually touching it (noticing absently that it didn't have a star on it), and looked around the room—brightly lit by a single hanging light bulb. The door was open, the light was on, but nobody was home . . . And then Happy almost jumped out of his skin when Benjamin and Elizabeth got impatient and barged into the dressing-room after him.

"I told you to stay put!" said Happy, doing his best to sound angry, as JC would have.

Elizabeth looked down her nose at him. "I have been shouted at and verbally abused by the greatest directors in the industry, darling, and I didn't take any notice of them, either."

"It's true," Benjamin said solemnly. "She didn't . . ."

Happy decided to let that one go. He wasn't much of a one for taking orders, himself. The three of them stood together, looking around. Though there wasn't much to look at, in the dressing-room. A bare table, pushed up against the left-hand wall, with a mirror fixed to the wall above the table. A few chairs and an empty costume rack. No window, no comforts, only faded linoleum on the uneven floor.

"Is this it?" said Happy. "This is all you get, in a dressing-room? Bit basic, isn't it?"

Benjamin and Elizabeth both smiled the same knowing smile.

"Theatres don't believe in spoiling their actors. Might give them ideas above their station," said Benjamin.

"It's expected that you customise your room, according to your own needs and wishes," said Elizabeth. "Put up your own photos, messages of support, good reviews. Flowers. Whatever you need to feel good."

"And anything lucky," said Benjamin. "Because actors are always great ones for superstitions, on and off stage. Because in this business you need all the good luck you can buy, beg, borrow, and steal."

"Exactly," said Elizabeth. "Given all the things that can and will go wrong, often out of sheer cussedness, on any given night, on even the meanest of productions, it is us against the gods, darling, and don't you ever forget it. In the theatre, lucky charms are ammunition. I've known dressing-rooms where you couldn't move for holy medals, support gonks, and rabbits' feet."

"I never did get that one," said Happy. "What's lucky about a rabbit's foot? I mean, it didn't do the rabbit any good, did it?" He glanced at the door, to make sure it was still open and his escape route was still clear, before turning back to the actors. "Do all the dressing-rooms look the same?"

"Pretty much," said Benjamin. "Stars get one to themselves, of course. Supporting roles double up; and everyone else gets crammed into whatever rooms are left. On some of the bigger Shakespearean productions, I've seen lesser roles and walk-ons filling up the corridor and hanging off the fire-escape. We actors do like to say *We're all in it together*, but some of us are always going to be deeper in it than others. If you think the theatre is a democracy, try asking the leading lady if you can use her mirror to do your make-up. Or sit down even for a moment on the leading man's chair. You'll hear language that would embarrass a sailor on shore leave trying to get his money back from the tattoo parlour."

"We guard our privileges jealously," Elizabeth agreed. "Because we have to work so bloody hard to get them."

"But we're all good companions once the play's under way," said Benjamin. "Because we're all equal when we're standing in the wings, waiting for the curtains to open. When it's only you and your talent and the lines you've beaten into your head versus an audience that will eat you alive if you weaken for one moment. It's not a cast and an audience then; it's Christians and Lions. That's where camaraderie and fellowship come in. Because it's always going to be us versus them."

"And afterwards, in the theatre bar or the nearest pub, or right here in the dressing-rooms if we finish late, it's party time till you drop!" Elizabeth said gleefully. "All

for one and one for all; and do your best to respect everyone else in the morning. If these walls could talk, you'd
have to be over eighteen to get in here."

"Elizabeth!" said Benjamin. "Look!"

Happy's first thought was to check whether the door
was still open and whether anyone was in his way if he
decided to leave in a hurry. The door was still open, so
he looked back at Benjamin. He was staring at the mirror
on the wall and pointing at it with an unsteady hand.
Happy and Elizabeth followed his gaze, to a single photo
wedged into the left-hand frame of the mirror.

"That photo wasn't there a moment ago," Elizabeth
said steadily. "Not when we first came in here . . ."

"Are you sure?" said Happy.

"It's not something you can be wrong about!" said
Benjamin. "You said it yourself: no frills or fancies. If
there had been a photo on that mirror, I would have
noticed it. No-one is supposed to have been back here in
twenty years. The renovators didn't get this far before
they all quit."

They all stood awkwardly before the mirror, maintaining a respectful distance while still leaning in to get
a better look at what was in the photo. Elizabeth finally
reached out a hand to touch the photo, but Happy quickly
stopped her.

"Best not," he said. "Might be real, might not; might
even be booby-trapped."

"What?" Benjamin said sharply. "Why would anyone
do that?"

"Ghosts like to play tricks on people," said Happy.
"You don't get to be a restless spirit by being sane and

well-adjusted. Most ghosts run on bad feelings, or an undying need for revenge on a world that's moved on and left them behind. So, when in doubt, keep your hands to yourself."

They all studied the photo carefully. A standard eight-by-ten, with slightly faded colours, showing a group of actors filling the photo from side to side and from top to bottom. Three rows of five people, cramming themselves in to get everyone in the shot. Smiling and laughing and full of life. A much younger Benjamin and Elizabeth were right down in the front row, grinning broadly, positively glowing with happiness and good cheer. They looked even younger than twenty years allowed, as though life had not yet got its hooks into them. They looked . . . brighter, sharper, less weighed down by the world. All of the actors in the photo were wearing old-fashioned clothes, costumes from the 1920s. And a hell of a lot of stage make-up, which hopefully hadn't looked quite so . . . dramatic, under stage lighting.

"Costumes and make-up would suggest the photo was taken right after we'd come off stage," said Benjamin. "If we'd been about to go back on again, we wouldn't have been so happy and relaxed. No, this looks more like a celebration . . ."

"So many familiar faces," said Elizabeth. "And I can't put a name to half of them . . ."

"This has got to be from when we first started here," said Benjamin. "But what play was it . . . ?"

In the photo, the young Benjamin and Elizabeth were sitting on either side of a handsome, striking young man their own age. They both had their arms across his

shoulders. They gave every appearance of being the clos-
est of friends, like they belonged together, and always
would.

"Who . . . is that?" said Happy, pointing without
touching.

"That . . . is Alistair Gravel," said Elizabeth.

She and Benjamin looked at each other again. There
was a lot going on in that look, a connection Happy
could see but not understand. He did see a new sadness
in their faces, and a heavy tiredness in their bodies. Elizabeth turned away first, to look at the photo again with
an entirely fake bright smile.

"I know this photo," she said. "I've seen it before. But
what play was it?"

"Got it!" said Benjamin. "That's from *Dear Brutus*,
the J. M. Barrie play. Excellent piece: funny, but very
touching, and very thoughtful . . ."

"I don't know it," said Happy.

"You wouldn't," said Elizabeth. "People only remember Barrie for *Peter Pan* these days, but he was a popular
playwright, back in his day. And *Dear Brutus* was a marvellous piece. All about . . . whatever decisions you
make, the real you will always come out."

"Yes . . ." said Benjamin. "I remember."

Happy looked carefully at the young man sitting
between the young Benjamin and the young Elizabeth.
He was definitely their age, mid twenties or so; but he
was more handsome than Benjamin and more glamorous
than Elizabeth; and his natural charisma easily eclipsed
theirs, even in an old photo. His grin was wide and charm-

ing and effortless; the kind most actors have to practice in front of a mirror for hours, before they can risk going on a chat show. But you could tell this look hadn't been practiced; this was the real thing. He looked as though he had the whole world at his feet. Of all the people in that photo, he was the one you'd naturally point to as most likely to succeed.

Not Benjamin or Elizabeth.

"What was his name again?" said Happy.

"Alistair Gravel," said Elizabeth, and the fondness and sadness in her voice were very clear in the small room. "We did a lot of good work together."

"He was the best of us," said Benjamin. "A good friend and a great actor."

Fondness and sadness and . . . regret, in his voice, thought Happy.

"He was the original lead in our play," said Benjamin. "He would have been magnificent . . . Everyone thought so. And then he died—suddenly."

"An accident," said Elizabeth. "A stupid accident. So tragic."

Her voice trailed away. They all looked at the photo, at the bright young things. Full of talent and promise, not knowing what lay ahead of them. And one by one, Benjamin and Elizabeth called back names to fit the faces, helping each other out when necessary, so no-one would be forgotten and left out. So many of them were dead now: illness, drugs, suicide. Actors tended to dramatic deaths as well as dramatic lives, it seemed. And of those who did survive, only a few had gone on to any kind of success.

The theatre is a harsh mistress who doesn't care how many hearts she breaks or how much you love her.

Judy gave up acting to be a singer. Phil gave it all up to work in the family business. Andy had one big hit on television, then didn't work for years because they said he was type-cast. And poor old Rob . . . he got tired of banging his head against a brick wall, trying to get noticed, for one chance to show everyone how talented he was . . . and disappeared back into the everyday world.

"We were all going to see our names in lights, in the West End," said Benjamin. "Not our real names, of course."

Happy looked at them both. "You mean . . . you're not really Benjamin Darke and Elizabeth de Fries?"

"Well, hardly, darling," said Elizabeth. "I was christened Elizabeth Flook, and he was Bennie Darren. You can't put names like that up in lights."

"Though Alistair really was Alistair Gravel," said Benjamin. "The lucky bastard . . ."

As Elizabeth looked from face to face in the photo, she looked older than ever. "We were so close, then, all of us, and such good friends. But . . . you lose touch with people so easily as you move from job to job, and city to city, from theatre to television to film . . . and back again."

"We've always preferred the theatre, though, haven't we, darling?" said Benjamin. "It is good to be back."

It seemed to Happy that Benjamin was trying to convince himself as much as Elizabeth.

"You've got some nerve, coming back here after all

these years," said a new but still-familiar voice. It was Elizabeth's voice; but she hadn't said it. The voice came out of the photo, as the young Elizabeth turned her face to glare out at her older self, her eyes dark and blazing, her red mouth a flat and bitter line. The young Benjamin turned his head to scowl out of the photo at his older self; and he looked grim, even dangerous. The young Alistair Gravel, sitting between them, didn't move at all, and neither did any of the other actors in the photo.

"You ran away and left us," said the young Benjamin. "Abandoned your dreams, blew off all your hope and ambitions, and settled for what you could get."

"We were going to be someone!" said the young Elizabeth. "All the great things we were going to achieve! Set the British theatre on fire!"

"All the things we planned," said the young Benjamin. "And you threw them all away, in pursuit of that stupid play."

"It wasn't like that!" said Elizabeth. She and Benjamin stood close together, frozen in place, their gaze fixed on their younger selves in the photo. But Elizabeth didn't sound scared, or even intimidated, by what was happening. Her voice was harsh, even strident.

"Wasn't it?" said the young Benjamin. "You can't hide from the truth here. Darling. Not here, not in this place. Where it all went so horribly wrong."

"What is this?" said Happy. "What are you talking about?"

They ignored him, the young and the old.

"Did you really think you could come back here and start again?" said the young Elizabeth.

"After what you did here?" said the young Benjamin. "After the awful thing you did, for fame and glory . . ."

"It wasn't like that!" said Elizabeth. Her face was pale and drawn, but her voice was still hard and steady. "You know it wasn't like that!"

"And even after what you did, you didn't get the fame, or the glory," said the young Elizabeth.

"But what you did here, all those years ago, has never been forgotten," said the young Benjamin.

"And you have never been forgiven," said the young Elizabeth. "Time to pay the piper. Darling."

"Tell him," said the young Benjamin. "Tell the poor little Ghost Finder what you did. And how it was all for nothing, in the end."

The two young people lurched forward suddenly, long-clawed hands bursting out of the photo, good-looking faces stretching and distorting, becoming monstrous, devilish. Benjamin and Elizabeth cried out and fell back, Benjamin putting himself between Elizabeth and what was coming for them. Happy looked at them, then looked back at the mirror; and the photo was gone. Nothing to show it had ever been there. Happy took a deep breath, to settle himself, and looked at Benjamin and Elizabeth. They were clinging to each other like small children frightened by a thunderstorm.

"What the hell was that all about?" said Happy.

"Nothing," said Elizabeth. All inflection was gone from her voice, all the colour from her face. Her eyes were wide, and her whole body was stiff with shock; but she still wouldn't give an inch. "Nothing. Nothing at all."

"It's a trick," said Benjamin. His face was empty and

his voice was flat; but he couldn't hide the fact that he'd been hit, and hit hard.

"It's getting too late in the day to cling to that old line," said Happy, as harshly as he could. "JC said all along something bad must have happened here to make this theatre a bad place. Something really bad, something you did. Because all of this only started up again when you came back. Something's been waiting here for you, for twenty years . . . because of what you did. The crawling figure pointed to you, and only you. Your own faces in the photo accused you of some old crime, some old betrayal. So what did you do? I need to know!"

"No you don't," said Elizabeth, flatly.

"None of this has anything to do with us," said Benjamin.

And then the door behind them suddenly swung open, and they all jumped. Elizabeth shrieked and clutched at Benjamin with both hands. He let out a short, choked cry, his back pressed up against the wall. Happy was startled, but also angry at himself for not having noticed that the door had closed. He moved quickly to put himself between his two charges and the new threat because he knew that was what JC would want him to do. Even though it didn't feel in any way natural; and he didn't have a clue what he was going to do.

They all relaxed, and let out their breaths in long, ragged sighs, as they recognised Old Tom, the caretaker. He stood in the open doorway with his vague smile and watery eyes, seeming even more stoop-shouldered than ever in his long brown overall and flat cap. He blinked at them bashfully.

"Only me, lady and gents! Didn't mean to startle anyone . . . Just checking that everything's as it should be . . ."

"Where the hell have you been?" said Happy, glad to have someone he could take out his frustrations on. "We've been looking for you everywhere!"

Old Tom regarded him vaguely. "I thought I heard someone moving about, when we were down in the understage area. And I thought, that's not right, there's not supposed to be anyone else here. So I went out through the rear exit—you know, the one at the back . . . And I had a good look around. But there wasn't anyone there. So I came back. But you'd all gone, and the understage area was empty. So I had a good look around there, too, made sure everything was as it should be, then I came up on stage. Except by the time I got there, you'd all gone again! You really shouldn't all go running off on your own, you know. Not safe, on your own. The old theatre isn't as forgiving as she once was. Anything could happen. I remember when . . ."

Happy gave up on trying to get a word in edge-ways, stepped forward, and prodded Old Tom hard in the chest. His finger rebounded from the grubby overall, and Old Tom actually stopped talking, to stare at Happy reproachfully. Happy didn't even try to explain. Old Tom might actually be there, might be physically present; but he still didn't *feel* right. There was something . . . off about the old caretaker, something all his cheerful nonsense couldn't quite cover up. So Happy braced himself and lowered his mental shields long enough to check out the figure before him. And found, to his shock and surprise, that, as far as his telepathy was concerned . . . there was no-one there.

All the calm good humour dropped out of Old Tom's face, and suddenly he didn't look real any more. Didn't look human, any more. Happy stumbled backwards, shouting to Benjamin and Elizabeth to stay behind him, not looking back because he didn't want to take his eyes off the thing that had pretended to be Old Tom, even for a moment.

"It's not him! That's not Old Tom, or a caretaker, or anything human! I don't think it's even alive!"

Benjamin surprised Happy then by surging forward past Happy to grab the front of Old Tom's uniform with both hands. He thrust his face right into the caretaker's and shook him angrily.

"Who are you? What are you, really? What's going on? *Why are you doing this to us?*"

Old Tom gave him a slow smile, not even raising his hands to defend himself. When he spoke, he didn't sound like Old Tom any more.

"You know why, Benjamin. So does she. You've always known."

"Leave her alone!" said Benjamin. "Don't you dare hurt her!"

"You haven't changed, have you?" said Old Tom.

His hands came up, inhumanly quickly, and grabbed Benjamin's wrists. He tore the actor's hands away from his coat. And then he threw Benjamin back—so hard that the actor slammed up against the far wall of the dressing-room. He hit hard enough to drive all the air from his lungs, and his legs buckled. Elizabeth was quickly there, to hold him and hold him up. Old Tom laughed at them both, an ugly, scary, accusing sound.

Happy stepped forward, again putting himself between the apparition and the actors. He really didn't want to be there, but he couldn't let this go on. If only because it was his job to detect ghosts, and Old Tom had fooled him completely. Happy might not be brave, but he had his pride, and there were limits. Even for him. He scowled, concentrating, and hit Old Tom hard with a telepathic blast of pure disbelief. The old caretaker looked suddenly surprised, and his appearance seemed to ripple, like a slow wave on the surface of a lake, disturbed by a breeze. A great dark pool of shadow formed around the caretaker's feet, then, standing stiffly upright all the while, Old Tom began to sink slowly into the darkness. The feet first, then the ankles, then dropping slowly and steadily up to his knees. The darkness consumed him, swallowing him up, inch by inch, then foot by foot. His back stayed straight, his hands stayed at his sides, and he never stopped smiling at Benjamin and Elizabeth. It was not a good smile. He ignored Happy completely, his harsh and unforgiving gaze fixed on the two actors as they huddled together at the rear of the dressing-room.

"Who are you?" said Benjamin; and his voice was like a frightened child's.

"Poor Tom's a cold," said Old Tom, still smiling, dropping down into the dark pool. Soon he was only a head and shoulders, and then only a head, and then that too was gone, smiling to the last. The dark pool gathered itself in, shrinking to a few inches in diameter, then that, too, was gone, as though it had disappeared down some unknown sink-hole. The linoleum on the floor seemed entirely untouched and unaffected. Happy strode over and stamped on the place, hard; but it was just a floor. He knelt and ran his fingers over the buckled linoleum; but he couldn't feel anything, with his fingertips or his mind. He stayed crouched, staring at the floor, thinking hard.

That took real power. The appearance, and the disappearing trick. Power and strength accumulated over twenty years . . . Had something really been waiting here, all this time, never showing itself, waiting for these two to return? Waiting for its chance to . . . What? Is this about revenge? What did these two do? What did they sacrifice in order for their precious play to be a success? And why didn't it work?

||||||||||||||||||||||||||

Happy rose slowly to his feet. His knees cracked loudly, a sharp sound in the quiet. He looked at Benjamin and Elizabeth. Benjamin was crying quietly, his shoulders jerking as real tears bumped down his face. No presence now, no charisma, no dignity. He was just a man, remembering something unbearable. Elizabeth held him close, cradling his head to her bosom, rocking him like a child. Her face was completely empty, her eyes far-away. After a while, they realised that Happy was watching them. Elizabeth murmured to Benjamin, and he stood up straight and rubbed the tears from his face with the back of his hand. He took a deep breath and stopped himself crying with an almost brutal act of self-control. He looked defiantly at Happy, silently challenging him to say anything, while Elizabeth stood at his side, regarding Happy with cold, wary eyes.

"So," said Benjamin. "He wasn't a caretaker, and he wasn't a journalist. He was a ghost."

"Looks like it," said Happy.

"I never thought he was a caretaker," said Elizabeth. "Far too broad a character."

So, thought Happy. *That's the way we're going to play it, is it? All right. But you're going to have to talk to me eventually.*

"It was an amazingly strong and coherent manifestation," he said. "Solid to the touch. Real enough that none of us suspected his true nature. That's not easy to pull off."

"I was sure he wasn't what he seemed to be," said Benjamin. "But it never even occurred to me that he wasn't *real*. Are ghosts usually like that?"

"Sometimes," said Happy. "I told you, ghosts love to pull tricks on the living. They're people, after all. With problems and pasts that won't let them rest, won't allow them to move on. They can pass as one of us because in many ways they still are." He looked thoughtfully at Benjamin and Elizabeth. "Did Old Tom seem in any way . . . familiar, to you? Was there anything about him that suggested . . . someone you might have known before?"

"The last caretaker I remember from here was Jerry Clarke," said Benjamin. "About our age, and camp as a row of tents in Tent Land. Nothing like Old Tom."

That's not what I asked, thought Happy.

"What does the ghost want with us?" said Elizabeth. "Why won't he leave us alone?"

"You'd know that better than I," said Happy. But they both fixed him with their stubborn gaze, so Happy sighed quietly and moved on. "The Past has a hold on the dead, as well as the living. Particularly when it involves unfinished business. Now, you two can lie to me all you want about what really happened here twenty years ago. I'm easy to lie to. But that won't protect you from what's here in the theatre. Something here has waited twenty years for revenge. Something has not forgotten or forgiven."

Benjamin and Elizabeth looked at each other, excluding Happy completely.

"We could leave," Benjamin said tentatively. "We could walk out of here, and never come back."

"We can't go," said Elizabeth. "We've sunk everything we have into getting our play off the ground again. This is our last chance, to make it the success it should have been. We're not young any more. Not old, not yet. But I can see old from where I am. We're running out of time . . . to be an overnight success."

"We can make more money . . ." said Benjamin.

"This isn't about the money!" said Elizabeth. "This was never about money! I want our play! I won't be stopped, and I won't be beaten. I won't be driven out of here, by the living or the dead or our own damned past!"

Benjamin smiled suddenly. "That's my girl."

And this time, when they looked at each other, Happy could see exactly what they saw in each other.

|||||||||||||||||||||||||

They all looked around sharply again as they heard foot-steps approaching. Outside, in the corridor, slow and heavy footsteps that didn't even try to seem human were heading their way. The sound came clearly through the closed door, as though carried on something more than the air. Each step more than naturally heavy, like something pressing down on the world, imposing its presence through a sheer act of will. The same kind of footsteps they'd heard before, up on the stage.

Elizabeth clutched at Benjamin. "Not again. I can't stand it again. Make it go away."

Benjamin looked at Happy. "If Old Tom was the ghost, what's that?"

"I think . . ." said Happy, "that Old Tom was a mask for the real ghost to hide behind. As though he was put-ting on a performance. Old Tom may be gone now, but the threat is still here."

He moved forward, to face the closed dressing-room door. It worried him that he couldn't remember exactly when it had closed, or who had closed it. Outside, in the corridor, the footsteps were drawing slowly, chillingly, closer.

"Lock the door!" said Elizabeth. "Keep the bastard out!"

"Do you have a key?" said Happy.

"Of course we don't have a key!" said Benjamin. "The renovators had all the keys. When they left, they gave them to the caretaker . . . Oh God."

"Do something!" said Elizabeth shrilly.

"You really think locking a door will keep a ghost out?" said Happy, incredulously. "They're famous for walking through doors! And walls . . ."

"You're the expert!" said Benjamin. "There must be something you can do!"

"There's no other way out of here," said Elizabeth. "We're trapped!"

"Yes, I had noticed that, thank you!" said Happy.

He didn't want to be there. Being in charge, making decisions, doing something, that had always been JC's role. But Happy was the only Ghost Finder in the room, which made him the man on the spot. Part of him wanted to open the door, run blindly, and hope the actors could keep up. Another part wanted to pull open the door, point at the actors, and shout *They're the ones you want! Not me!* But Happy had always been a man of many parts, and he'd spent a long time learning how to decide which of the voices inside his head he was going to listen to. One of the reasons he became a Ghost Finder, though he'd never admit it to JC or Melody, was that he wanted to become a better person. If only because being a coward didn't half take it out of you. JC had put him in charge of the actors and told him not to let them get killed; so it was up to him to do something. And since his usual tactics of screaming and crying and hiding behind other people weren't really options here, that left . . . doing the right thing.

He thought of the pill bottles he still carried secreted about his person. He could knock back a swift cocktail of reds and blues and yellows, and all the problems would go away. Or they'd still be here, but at least he wouldn't care any more. Or care what happened to the actors. Happy smiled sadly. He couldn't do that. Because he sort of liked Benjamin and Elizabeth, for being as larger than life as he'd always thought actors should be; because he didn't like seeing anyone bullied by ghosts; and because he was damned if he'd let JC down. The man who'd believed in him enough to make him part of his team, despite all the warnings. The man who believed that Happy could be a better person.

Happy needed someone to believe that on the days that he didn't.

He walked up to the closed door and scowled at it without touching it. The idea that you could run right at something that scared you, instead of running away, was a new one to Happy. He closed his hands into fists to stop them shaking. The heavy footsteps came right up to the other side of the door and stopped. Everything was still and quiet. The only sound was the heavy breathing of the three people in the dressing-room as they stood very still, listening.

"Has it gone?" said Elizabeth. "It disappeared, the last time it stopped, on the stage."

"That's right," said Benjamin. "The footsteps stopped, and it was over."

Happy didn't know what to say. Reassurance was another of those people skills that he usually left to JC. It didn't feel like it was over . . . but now that the footsteps had stopped, it was hard to remember why they'd scared him so much. Footsteps weren't so bad, after all. Just sounds. The crawling thing on the stage—that had been bad. With all the blood, and the eye hanging out.

But it had been in no condition to hurt anyone. What was so scary about the footsteps . . . was that there was nothing to see. They could have been made by anyone, or anything. The threat and the menace were all in the anticipation . . .

When Happy was still a child, before his powers kicked in, he was afraid of the dark. And what scared him then was that he couldn't see what it was that scared him. There could be anything in the dark, anything at all. Imagination filled in the details, in the worst way possible. Of course, Happy grew up to be a major-league telepath and discovered that he had good reason to be scared of what was hiding in the dark. Another reason he became a Ghost Finder: to find a way to strike back at the things in the dark. So no-one else would have to know, and be scared, like he was.

"I can't hear anything," said Elizabeth. "Is that good? Has he gone?"

Something knocked on the other side of the door, loud and hard—great crashing knocks that made the door jump and tremble in its frame. Something outside wanted them to know it was there. Something that wanted in. It must know the door wasn't locked, so it must want, or need, to be invited in . . . It knocked again and again and again, hammering on the door with vicious force, barely pausing between each knock.

"Don't let him in!" screamed Elizabeth.

"What is that?" Benjamin yelled at Happy. "What's out there? You're supposed to be the mind-reader! What can you see?"

"I can't tell!" said Happy. "I'm trying, but . . . I can't

see anything! Something's hiding it from me. Something big and powerful that's been waiting here for twenty years, growing more and more powerful, determined to have its revenge! What's out there? You tell me! You made it!"

"Please," said Benjamin. "Please help us. Don't let him get to Elizabeth."

Happy scowled at the reverberating door, his heart hammering like the frenzied knocking. It sounded like all the monsters that ever were, determined to get in, and get him.

I can do this, thought Happy, trying hard to make himself believe it. *I ain't afraid of no ghost. I faced down Fenris Tenebrae, and the New People. And I'm damned if I'll chicken out in front of strangers. They're relying on me. Bit of a new feeling, that. Not sure if I like it, but . . .*

He cranked up his nerve to the sticking point, grabbed the shaking door handle, and hauled the door open. He cried out something incoherent, ready to hit whatever was there with the strongest and most concentrated blast of disbelief he had . . . But there was no-one on the other side of the door. Happy stepped quickly out into the corridor and looked up and down; but there was nothing but shadows and silence, and a feeling . . . That there had been something there a moment before. Something bad. The light in the corridor was calm and steady, and so were the shadows, and Happy . . . wondered what the hell was going on. He would have liked to believe he'd driven the thing away, by confronting it; but that . . . didn't feel right.

He stepped back into the dressing-room. Benjamin

and Elizabeth, backed up in the far corner, looked at him pitifully. Elizabeth was trying to be brave; and Benjamin was standing in front of her, shielding her. Happy smiled and nodded quickly to them, and they almost collapsed in relief.

"Whatever that was, it isn't there any more," said Happy. "But it's getting closer. And stronger. If I'm going to protect you, you have to tell me the truth about what really happened here, twenty years ago."

"I'd rather die," said Elizabeth.

Happy nodded thoughtfully. "Yes. It could come to that."

SIX

LOBBY DISPLAY

Back in the lobby, Melody happily bustled around her precious machines, firing up her scientific equipment, checking that everything was as it should be, and having a merry old time. She always enjoyed putting things in order, making sure they were working right, crossing off things on her list and running through her rituals. She liked machines as opposed to people because, with machines, you only had to punch the instructions in once. Melody understood machines. Whereas people, usually men, remained mostly a mystery. Melody had never had any problems having sex with men; it was the talking to them afterwards that gave her problems. One of the reasons she enjoyed Happy so much was that he was delightfully uncomplicated. He divided the entire world into things that he liked and things that scared him; and as long as Melody was careful as to which category she put herself into, she always knew where she was with Happy.

She patched in the short-range sensors, fed extra power to the long-range sensors, and smiled happily as the readouts flickered calmly before her. This was the part of any Ghost Finders mission that she enjoyed the most, being left alone to set up and calibrate her marvellous machines, without the others hanging around making what they presumably thought were helpful comments. She didn't feel alone, or vulnerable, in the lobby because she was never alone when she was with her equipment. Her machines made her feel safe and protected because she knew she could always rely on them. Machines rarely let her down, and on the rare occasions when they did, she either fixed them or hit them until they didn't. People, on the other hand, were always surprising her, and rarely in a good way.

She thought of JC, off on his own somewhere with the lovely Lissa, and smiled briefly. JC might think he was impressing Lissa, but Melody was fairly confident Lissa wasn't the kind who impressed easily. Melody knew a fellow hard-hearted professional when she saw one. In fact, JC would do well to watch out for himself.

Melody's thoughts then turned to Happy, off on his own with the two actors; and she didn't smile at all. She wasn't at all sure why JC had put Happy together with the oh-so-theatrical Benjamin and Elizabeth. Happy did have some good qualities if you were prepared to dig deep enough to find them; but leadership and responsibility definitely weren't on the list. It was always possible JC thought the actors might relax a little around

Happy and unburden their souls to him where they probably wouldn't talk to JC, or to her. People often felt sorry for Happy and told him all manner of things they'd never tell another soul, so he'd stop looking at them with those big, soulful, puppyish eyes. Personally . . . Melody doubted it. Benjamin and Elizabeth had secrets they only shared with each other. Anyone could see that.

She wasn't worried about Happy. Wasn't worried at all. The actors would look after him.

She moved back and forth before her control boards, swaying sensuously, checking sensor displays and energy readouts, fine-tuning things here and there and having a perfectly wonderful time. Everything in the lobby seemed entirely normal, all conditions as expected. Not even a hint of a cold spot, or an energy spike; no electromagnetic fluctuations; and not even a murmur on the EVP dead-radio channels. Melody looked cheerfully round the lobby . . . and then something caught her eye. There were posters on the lobby walls. Large, colourful posters, leftovers from the theatre's past triumphs. There were half a dozen of them, scattered around the lobby, and Melody had to turn around in a complete circle to take them all in, in turn. Melody's good temper was gone in a moment, her smile replaced by a slowly deepening scowl. Because she couldn't for the life of her remember whether the posters had been there before. She hadn't noticed them when she first entered the lobby, or when she was putting her instruments together; but then she often didn't notice unimportant details like that. Unless someone pointed them out to her or she had nothing else to look at.

Melody came out from behind her carefully arranged semi-circle of equipment and walked right up to the poster in front of her to take a closer look. The poster was a good five feet tall and maybe two or three feet wide, a clear, firm image on good-quality paper, with colours so bright and shiny they bordered on gaudy. The image before her was a portrait of a handsome young woman in a full-length wedding gown of a spotless white so dazzling it was almost painful to the eye. The bride had thrown her filmy veil back over her long jet-black hair, to reveal a grinning, sparkling-eyed face. She was hurrying down a long, curving staircase, perhaps half-way down . . . looking out at the viewer. Melody frowned. It was a pleasant enough image; but what was it for? Was it on display to promote a play, or a character, or some forthcoming production? There were no words anywhere on the portrait, not even a title—nothing to indicate its purpose.

Melody moved on to the next poster, on her left. Just as big and as colourful, this second picture showed an old-fashioned, even traditional image, of a clipper sailing-ship, far out at sea, dashing through the waves with sails full of wind and a proud prow raised high into the air. There was no name anywhere on the ship. Uniformed sailors were captured in traditional poses and occupations, all over the ship. Several were set high up in the rigging, pointing out ahead, at something only they could see. Dark blue waves rose out of the ocean, bonneted with foam, and overhead the sky was a clear and empty blue under a perfect summer sun. Again, there was no lettering or information anywhere on the poster. It seemed to Melody that you might expect to see a painting like this on some office wall but not in a lobby. So why was it here? Strange . . .

She moved on, around the exterior of the lobby, vaguely aware she was drifting always to the left, anti-clockwise; widdershins. Anywhen else, anywhere else, that thought might have worried her. But here she only had eyes and thoughts for the fascinating posters.

The next portrait was of a quartet of fine young fellows, dressed in the formal clothing of the early twentieth century. They stood companionably together, filling the whole portrait, toasting the viewers with brimming glasses of red wine. All four young men looked very smart and very handsome, young gentlemen out on the town, perhaps, smiling winningly at the viewer. Melody decided . . . that she didn't care for them. She deliberately turned away from them and moved on.

The fourth portrait showed a pleasant young woman in a fashionable evening gown, complete with long evening gloves, all in the same faintly disturbing shade of buttercup yellow. The young woman stood beside a half-open door, pulling it back to receive someone. She looked very smart, almost aristocratic, and very pretty, with bobbed blonde hair, innocent blue eyes, and a flashing smile. Whoever she was greeting, she was clearly very pleased to see them. So why did Melody think the woman in the portrait looked scared?

The next portrait was a winter-time country scene. A long, narrow lane sweeping between two fields piled high with a fresh covering of snow. There were no other details. No trees, no stone walls to mark the fields' boundaries, no animals or animal tracks to be seen anywhere on the fields. No snow in the narrow lane; only a beaten earthen track. And up above, a grey and lowering sky with a threat of thunder and maybe an approaching storm. Melody leaned in close. She could almost feel the bitter cold of that winter day on her face. And there, off in the distance, right at the far end of the narrow lane, a small, dark figure, trudging down the lane, toward the viewer. So far off he was little more than a dark shape. There was a sense of . . . anticipation about the scene. As though if you watched it long enough, something might happen. Melody slowly turned her head away and moved on.

The sixth and final portrait was a close-up of a stuffed fox's head, mounted on a wall plaque, set high on some anonymous wall. The fox's head was huge, filling the portrait, depicted in amazing detail. Melody could make out every individual strand of hair in the russet grey fur. The eyes weren't the usual glass marbles you'd expect to find in a stuffed animal; instead, they looked dark and alive and full of a terrible fury. The lips were drawn back on the muzzle in an endless snarl, revealing sharp, vicious teeth.

Melody moved away and found herself back where she'd started, facing the first poster. She slowly turned around on the spot, still widdershins, letting the posters fly past her eyes in a circle. She didn't even glance at her precious equipment. She only had time for the posters. What were they? What were they for? Advertisements, perhaps, for long-forgotten products? But if that was the case, why were there no words anywhere, no information, no details on the products the posters were promoting? Could they be . . . perhaps pieces of art, produced by patrons of the theatre, donated to cheer the place up? No. Whatever these images might be, they weren't cheerful. Melody didn't like them. Didn't like any of them.

She was about to return to the safety and security of her instruments when she stopped abruptly and looked again at the first poster. Something was wrong. Something was different about the image before her. She slowly moved forward, drawn almost against her will, staring intently at the poster. The young bride in her wedding gown was now standing at the very bottom of the long, curving stairway. Not in the middle, where she had been. As though she'd walked all the way down while Melody had walked around the lobby, making her circuit of the posters. And the expression on the bride's face had changed. She was still smiling out of the poster at the viewer, but now it was a hard and nasty, openly malicious, grin. Her teeth were broken, all sharp and jagged points. Her eyes were narrowed and fixed on Melody.

Melody made herself move on, drifting almost listlessly left, to the next poster. To see if that had changed, too. And, of course, it had. The clipper ship was sinking. As though it had hit something, unseen and unsuspected in the time it had taken Melody to come around to it again. The sunny skies were gone, replaced by a raging squall. The masts were all broken, the sails split and torn, the rigging in tatters. The ship was already half-under, and uniformed sailors were throwing themselves into the dark and choppy waters.

In the next poster, the four young men toasted Melody with glasses half-full of fresh and foaming blood. There were dark crimson stains on the rims of the glasses and around the mouths of the fine young men. Their skin was the colourless pallor of the grave, and their eyes were dark and knowing. Thin, dead lips had pulled back in a rictus, revealing razor-sharp shark's teeth. Patches of grave mould showed clearly on the formal clothes they'd been buried in. The fingers wrapped around the fine glasses were broken and split, from where they'd had to claw through their coffin lids to get out.

In the fourth portrait, the woman in the butter yellow dress was still standing in her doorway, but now the door had been thrown wide open, and the dress was soaked in blood because the woman didn't have a head any more. Someone had ripped it right off. Blood had coursed down from the ragged stump, down the whole length of her dress, plastering it to her body with ghastly red stains. More blood had splashed across the open door, coating it from top to bottom. The woman stood where she was, in the exact same pose, as though she hadn't yet understood the terrible thing that had happened to her.

The fifth poster was the same wintry scene as before; but now the dark figure was running down the narrow lane towards her. Already it had covered half the distance, and something about it suggested the dark figure was approaching at fantastic speed. Legs pounding, arms flailing wildly, it was running right at Melody; and she knew it meant to do awful things to her when it finally reached her.

By the time she got to the sixth and final portrait, again, all she could feel was shocked and numb. The way everything kept changing had knocked her off-balance. Kicked her feet out from under her. She couldn't seem to find her mental bearings. Every time she thought she knew where she was, it had changed. There was nothing she could count on, nothing she could depend on. The whole world had become fluid, unreliable, untrustworthy. Because if an image could change, so could anything. The floor might become the ceiling, her precious controls might grow teeth and snap at her fingers. Left could become right, and real become unreal. Sanity and madness could flip-flop, and you wouldn't even know which was which. She looked at the image of the stuffed fox head; and it laughed soundlessly at her.

Just like a dream, thought Melody, as she moved slowly to the left, to stand before the first poster again. *Like a nightmare where everything keeps changing, and changing for the worst. Where sane and ordinary everyday things can become horrible and threatening, and there's no safety anywhere.*

Her head was swimming, and it was all she could do to stand upright. It felt like the floor of the lobby was rising and falling, like a clipper ship at sea. She put out her hands for something to lean on, to steady herself; but there was nothing. She felt hot and sweaty, like a fever she'd had as a child, when it felt like the whole world might melt and run away. Melody growled suddenly, a harsh warning sound from deep in her throat. She was under attack.

That realisation was like a splash of cold water in the face. She couldn't trust her eyes any more. The world might not feel real any more, but that didn't mean she was mad. It meant she was under psychic attack. There was danger close at hand; she could feel that very clearly.

She felt that there was something she ought to be doing, but she couldn't seem to clear her mind enough to think what. So she stared at the poster before her, studying the image with all her concentration as though she could make it behave through sheer strength of will.

The young woman in the wedding gown had left the bottom of the long stairway and come forward to press her face up against the other side of the poster as though it were the other side of a mirror. She glared out at Melody, her face twisted with rage and an inhuman malice. Bloody tears ran down her distorted face from her madly staring eyes and dripped steadily off her chin. Her wide-stretched mouth now had lips the colour of dried blood, and it was packed full of needle teeth. She'd raised her hands and slammed them flat against the other side of the poster, the other side of the glass, as though she were banging against it, trying to break through.

Melody wrenched her gaze away and stumbled off, to the left, to stand before the second poster again. The clipper ship was almost gone, only its pointed prow and the tops of the masts still showing above the raging sea. The sky was full of dark clouds and heavy, sleeting rain. The sea was full of sharks, and there were bits of men and long streaks of blood everywhere in the waters. As Melody watched, crimson-tinged waters dribbled down the lobby wall from the bottom of the poster, as though the sea was breaking through. Melody stepped carefully backwards, away from the bloody sea-water pooling on the floor at the foot of the wall.

She found herself standing before the next poster. The

four young dead men had emptied their glasses of blood and crushed the glasses to bloody splinters in their unfeeling hands. One of them had turned and sunk his teeth deep into the neck of the young man beside him, who smiled foolishly out at Melody. The other two had come forward, advancing on the poster, as though they could see Melody watching them. Their split-fingered hands reached out to claw their way through the poster and into her world.

In the fourth poster, the headless young woman had stepped forward, out of her doorway. She was holding up her severed head with one hand, thrusting it out at the poster, at Melody. So the head could look right into Melody's eyes. The severed head was screaming silently, endlessly, eyes wide with an unbearable horror. Blood fell from the severed neck in a dribbling stream.

In the fifth poster, in the wintry country scene, the dark figure was almost at the end of the narrow lane. He was running full tilt as though planning to break through, smash right through the poster, by sheer speed and impact. He was still only a dark figure, roughly human in shape, limbs flailing wildly . . . but the dimensions were all wrong. As though he was a man from some other world, close enough to ours to be disturbing in its differences.

And in the sixth, and final, poster . . . the huge, stuffed fox head shook and twisted on its wall plaque, laughing and howling soundlessly. It was so much closer now, its whiskered snout protruding right out of the poster, as though it had forced itself half-out of its world and half-into Melody's, through sheer force of vicious intent. It snapped its jaws at her. The sharp teeth were red with fresh blood from some recent kill, and the head was so close now that Melody could smell its rank, damp, musky scent.

She looked into the fox's mad, feral eyes and snarled right back at it. The fox hesitated, caught between moments, not expecting that. Melody stamped one foot hard, to force the floor to feel solid under her foot, and clenched her hands into fists until her nails dug painfully into her palms, and both hands ached from the effort. She laughed harshly into the fox's face, then deliberately turned her back on it, and all the posters, and walked stiffly back to her scientific instruments. She set herself behind them, where she belonged, and looked down at what her readouts were telling her. She concentrated on every little bit of information, holding every light and number with her gaze, refusing to let them change in any way. Because if they said something was real, then it was. And if they didn't, then it wasn't. Her mind might betray her, but not her instruments.

"I trust my readings!" she said loudly. *"I trust my machines and what they tell me about the world, and if they say you're not real . . . You're not real!"*

She looked from one monitor screen to the next, from one readout to the next, concentrating. And bit by bit her head cleared, as her machines told her the lobby was perfectly normal. Her head stopped swimming, her legs became firm again, and the fever snapped off as though someone had thrown a switch. Melody wiped clammy sweat from her face with her sleeve and finally lifted her head and looked around the lobby. There were no posters on the walls. Never had been. If there had, of course she would have noticed them, and remembered them. There were a few empty wooden frames, here and there, where old posters might once have been; but that was all. Melody grinned nastily around her and patted the tops of her machines fondly, like they were pets that had remembered their training.

"Good boys. I can always depend on you when some sneaky bastard is playing games with my head."

She leaned forward, braced herself on top of her instruments with both hands, and let her head hang down for a moment, slowly bringing her ragged breathing back under control. Bringing herself back under control through sheer strength of will. She felt like she'd gone ten rounds with Mike Tyson, with an anvil on her back. But after a few moments, she brought her head back up proudly and sneered around the empty lobby, showing her teeth in a nasty grin.

"That the best you can do? It'll take more than that to break me, you bastards!"

One by one, slowly and unhurriedly and without any fuss, the lights in the lobby began to go out. Melody swore briefly and checked her readouts. None of her sensors were indicating anything out of the ordinary, but the lobby lights were quite definitely dimming and going out. Faulty wiring in the lobby? Melody shook her head quickly. That was grabbing at straws, and she knew it. The last few lights went out in a rush, leaving Melody standing alone in the dark, in a small pool of light generated by her monitor screens and work lights. The dark around her was solid and impenetrable, without even an exit light. Melody kicked in the heavy-duty spotlights she'd incorporated into her equipment stand, for just such emergencies as this; but they didn't make much difference. The pool of light surrounding her instruments grew a little brighter, but it didn't expand one inch. The light couldn't seem to push out into the darkness at all.

Melody made herself check her readings methodically, one by one. Everything was functioning as it should, but none of it was telling her anything useful. She glared about her, into the dark. She couldn't see a damned thing. The lobby was . . . gone. She had a sudden horrible feeling that she was alone in the dark, that the rest of the world was gone, and only she and her small pool of light remained. As though the world had been taken away, or she had been taken out of it . . . like the old steam train at Bradleigh Halt. And now she was trapped, floating forever in an endless sea of darkness . . . She shook her head fiercely and took a firm hold on her thoughts. She wasn't afraid of the dark. Darkness was only the absence of light. The world was still there; all her sensors said so. Which meant that this was another form of psychic attack. And like the posters, it might be scary, it might mess with her head, but nothing was happening that could actually hurt her.

She activated the communications system built into her decks and called Happy on his mobile. It rang and rang and rang, but nobody picked up. Which was odd. If Happy had turned his phone off, it would have gone straight to voice mail. So why wasn't he answering? She tried reaching JC, but he didn't answer either. Unless . . .

someone was shutting off the sound, the same way it was shutting off the light . . .

Melody placed her hands flat on top of her instruments, and said to herself, *I'm not afraid. I'm not. I don't believe in any of this bullshit.*

Her head came up sharply, and she glared out into the darkness. Someone was walking around. There were footsteps, in the dark. Not the loud and crashing impacts she'd heard before, up on the stage . . . but quiet, steady, perfectly ordinary footsteps. Melody listened carefully. On the whole she thought they sounded more like a man's than a woman's. And not a particularly big man, at that. Melody smiled. She could handle men. The footsteps walked round and round her pool of light, taking their time. Sometimes coming close but never actually emerging from the dark to enter into the light. Going on, round and round and round . . .

"Who's there?" said Melody, in her most strident and challenging voice. "Identify yourself! Talk to me! Don't make me come out there and get you!"

There was no reply. Only someone walking unseen, round and round her. Melody reached down, into the special cabinet set under the short-range sensors, and pulled out her favourite machine-pistol. She always kept a gun or two handy, for those moments when diplomacy had clearly failed. She aimed the machine-pistol out into the dark, right at the footsteps; and then hesitated. She didn't want to fire blindly out into the darkness. If she randomly shot up the lobby, the theatre's owners would be bound to kick up a fuss. Not that she really gave much of a damn, but she couldn't justify it to herself, opening fire without an actual target. The others would look at the widely sprayed bullet holes, and they'd know. They'd look at her and think she'd become spooked, maybe even panicked. And she couldn't have that.

And then all the lights came back on at once, quite suddenly, as though they'd never been away. Melody jumped, despite herself. She glared fiercely about her, sweeping the machine-pistol back and forth. The lobby looked back innocently, quiet and empty and ordinary. As though nothing at all had happened. A voice spoke behind her, and she spun round, bringing the machine-pistol up to fire; and then she stopped herself at the last moment. It was only Old Tom, the caretaker, standing quietly by the main doors in his long brown overall, regarding her with his usual vague smile and watery eyes. Melody lowered her gun and sighed loudly as the tension ran out of her.

"Where the hell have you been?" she said sharply. "We looked everywhere for you!"

"Oh, around," said Old Tom. "Are you all right, miss? You look pale. You look like you've seen a ghost . . ."

Melody snorted briefly, embarrassed, and quickly put the machine-pistol away, out of sight. "What are you doing here?" she said brusquely.

"Taking a look around, miss, seeing what needs to be done. Before the whole cleaning crew comes in tomorrow. We're going to have our work cut out for us here, miss, and no mistake. Still, it does take me back, being in the old place again. Good to see Benjamin Darke and Elizabeth de Fries again, too. I remember them, and their old friend Alistair Gravel; thick as thieves, the three of them. Always together, always getting into trouble . . ."

"Funny," said Melody. "Benjamin and Elizabeth didn't remember you."

Old Tom shrugged easily. "No reason why they should, miss. They were important people, lead actors, and I . . . was staff. Actors and staff don't mix, miss. Different people, different worlds. But I remember them; oh yes . . . They had this play they'd written, and Mr. Gravel was going to star in it. A play that would make them all rich and famous . . . And then, suddenly, Mr. Gravel was out! And they brought in this big film star to take over the lead. Can't remember his name, on the tip of my tongue; you'd know it if I said it . . ."

"Frankie Hazzard," said Melody.

"That was it!" said Old Tom, beaming at her. "Bless me; fancy you knowing that, miss. Anyway, the play went on, all right, but it wasn't the huge success that everyone expected. Oh no. Died on its arse by all accounts. Very sad. Still, these things happen . . ."

"I heard that Alistair Gravel died," said Melody.

"Bless you, no, miss!" said Old Tom. "He didn't die. He disappeared. Didn't turn up for rehearsal one day. Everyone looked for him, but there wasn't a trace of him to be found anywhere. Didn't leave a note, or anything. Bit of a mystery, really. You want to talk to Benjamin and Elizabeth, miss. If anyone knows what really happened back then, it's those two. Still, can't stand around here chatting with you, when there's work waiting to be done! I'll see you around, miss. You watch out for yourself."

He nodded briskly, shuffled off, and disappeared through the main doors. Melody hardly noticed. She was thinking hard.

When she did finally look up, she noticed immediately that there was a single photo pinned to the Coming Attractions board, right by the main doors. Melody scowled at the board for a long moment. She hadn't noticed any Coming Attractions board before, never mind a photo. Could she have overlooked it, because she was concentrating so hard on the posters? Or was it an illusion as well, put there to mess with her head some more? Could Old Tom have put it there, on his way out, for reasons of his own?

Melody came out from behind her instruments and advanced slowly and cautiously on the Coming Attractions board. A simple wooden easel, supporting a large plain board with a colour ten-by-eight photo attached to it with a single drawing-pin. Couldn't have looked more normal and ordinary if it had tried. Melody gave the easel the Happy test, by giving it a good hard kick, and the board rocked solidly back and forth. She prodded the photo with her fingertip, and it certainly felt real enough. She took a firm hold of the photo and pulled it free.

She shook it back and forth a few times, still half-expecting the thing to disappear, or fall apart into mists, in her grasp. But it gave every indication of being an actual photograph. Melody held it up before her and studied the image carefully. The photo showed three young people standing together, smiling broadly for the camera. From the artificial way they were posed, Melody assumed it was a promotional shot of some kind. The strap-line at the bottom of the photo gave the names of the three young people standing so happily together. Melody had already recognised the much-younger Benjamin Darke and Elizabeth de Fries, but she nodded slowly as she looked at the darkly handsome one in the middle: Alistair Gravel.

"So that's what you look like," she said finally. "What happened to you, Alistair? Why did you disappear? And why are your old friends Benjamin and Elizabeth so sure that you're dead?"

SEVEN

OFFENSIVE CLOTHING

JC stood at the very front of the stage, looking out over the empty auditorium and bouncing lightly on the balls of his feet. He was enjoying this case so far. Lots of clues, lots of entertaining weird shit, and, best of all, he had no idea what the hell was going on. JC always enjoyed a challenge. Something fiendishly complicated, and horribly fiendish, to test his smarts and his courage. JC never felt more alive than when jousting with death. More so these days because he had nothing else. Kim had been his reason for living; and with her gone, he had to find something else to fill his thoughts, to keep him from thinking about her.

He'd seen her here. In the theatre. That had to mean something.

"So," said Lissa, coming forward to stand right beside him, "here we are, alone on the stage together, just the two of us. That has to mean something . . . Why did you choose me as your partner and send everyone else away, I wonder?"

"Almost certainly not for the reason you're thinking," said JC, turning unhurriedly around to smile at her. "Now that Benjamin and Elizabeth are gone, let us take the opportunity to talk about them behind their backs. How well do you know them?"

Lissa shrugged briefly. "They hired me to be in their play, for really good money. What more do I need to know?"

"You must have made some inquiries before you agreed to take on the role," said JC. "You must have heard something . . ."

"Well, one always *hears* things, sweetie. No-one loves a good gossip more than the acting profession. For us, adoration and backbiting are but two sides of the same coin. I did hear that this play was jinxed . . . A lot of people in my business wouldn't touch it with a disinfected barge-pole. And not simply because it died the death in its first and only run. The original male lead in the play, all those years ago, was supposed to be one Alistair Gravel. Except he didn't get to be the lead, did he?"

JC nodded. "I remember Benjamin and Elizabeth saying he died, in an accident."

"Which is very interesting," said Lissa. "Because I was told Alistair Gravel up and disappeared. Vanished, between one rehearsal and the next. And he was never found again, dead or alive. Not one trace of him anywhere, in the last twenty years, which is a bit odd, sweetie, for such an up-and-coming, talented young actor. Wouldn't you say?"

JC considered her thoughtfully. "You didn't take this role because your agent advised you to, did you?"

Lissa laughed softly. "No. I came here because I wanted to find out what really did happen to my uncle Alistair. I grew up listening to stories about his mysterious disappearance, so when my agent got the offer, to be in a play so unlucky they have to attach a rabbit's foot to every script to get people to read it . . . I jumped at the chance. My agent still isn't talking to me. I think dear Benjamin and Elizabeth know a lot more than they're saying. I think they know what happened here, all those years ago. If we can persuade them to talk."

JC raised an eyebrow. "'We,' dear lady?"

"You want to know what's behind the haunting in this theatre," said Lissa, with an artless toss of her head. "And it's my belief that all these spooky manifestations are directly connected to the missing Alistair Gravel."

"Seems likely," said JC, in his best *I'm giving away nothing at this time* voice. "Every haunting, every bad place, has its starting point—its beginning, in some dramatic moment. And its power source. Ghosts . . . are all about unfinished business." He looked steadily at Lissa. "Do you think your missing uncle Alistair is the ghost here? That he's behind everything that's happening?"

"Seems likely," said Lissa. "Robbed of his chance for fame and glory at the very last moment? Struck down on the brink of stardom? Has to be."

"Do you think Benjamin and Elizabeth killed him?" said JC.

"Now why would they do that?" said Lissa. "He was their friend. Their very good friend."

"People have sacrificed good friends before, for success," said JC.

"But there was no success," said Lissa. "The play that was supposed to do so much for everyone, ruined the lives of everyone associated with it. Still, I'll bet you good money that Benjamin and Elizabeth know the truth. Whatever it is."

She turned to JC, stopping before him just that little bit short of uncomfortably close, and smiled dazzlingly.

"Why did you ask me to stay with you, then send all the others away?"

"Because," said JC, staring into her eyes, "I wanted to talk to you, alone. And see how well we're doing . . . Getting right to the heart of the matter, without interruptions. I don't trust Benjamin and Elizabeth any more than you do. It's obvious they're hiding secrets, things they won't talk about except with each other. That's why I sent them off with Happy."

"Because he's a telepath?" murmured Lissa, her face so close to JC's now that he could feel her warm breath on her face. Her perfume, rich and flowery, filled his head.

"If only it were that easy," said JC, steadily. "No, Happy doesn't read the minds of the living if he can help it. He has enough trouble keeping other people's thoughts outside his head so he can hear himself think. No, that's not it. He's . . . surprisingly easy to talk to, and confide in. You'd be surprised how many people will let their guard down and open up when faced with someone clearly so much more battered and broken than they."

"Well then," said Lissa, the brief puffs of air in the two syllables hitting him right in the mouth. "No ulterior motives? No other reason for wanting to be here alone, with me?"

JC took a single step backwards, separating them. "Don't you point those bosoms at me, sweetie. I have a girl-friend."

"I won't tell if you won't."

"She'd know," said JC. "And so would I. It took me a long time to find the love of my life, my Kim; and I won't do anything that might risk losing her again."

"I don't see her around anywhere," said Lissa. "Is she a part of your team? Why isn't she here now?"

"How do you know she isn't?" said JC. "Kim's dead."

Lissa's smile disappeared. "Okay; that's quite spooky."

"Yes," said JC. "It is."

Lissa looked at him steadily. "Why do you always wear sunglasses? It's not a style thing, is it?"

"No," said JC.

"There's something not quite right about your eyes," said Lissa. "I could tell that from the first moment I met you. Take off your shades, JC. Let me look into your eyes."

"Really not a good idea, Lissa . . ."

"Please. I need to see, to be sure . . . Do it for me, JC."

And without quite knowing why, JC reached up and removed his sunglasses. He expected Lissa to cry out and turn away. Everyone else did. His eyes weren't human eyes any more. But Lissa stood there, very still, staring back into his fiercely blazing eyes, apparently unaffected by a Gorgon gaze that had sent other people running for their lives and their sanity.

"Oh, wow . . ." said Lissa, very quietly. "I had no idea . . ."

The golden light from JC's altered eyes bathed her face in sunshine, and she wasn't in the least dazed or distressed. She looked more . . . dazzled. Her face soaked up the light, and she didn't once blink or wince or look aside. She bathed in the golden glow, smiling happily, her eyes full of a simple, unaffected wonder.

"What do you see, Lissa?" said JC.

"It's like looking into Heaven," said Lissa, softly. And then she turned her head away, but not before JC caught a glimpse of a terrible sadness in her eyes. She walked away, her arms tightly crossed, hugging herself, then stopped abruptly and looked out over the auditorium.

"This is why actors love the stage," she said, without looking around. "Because it's always here for us when we need it."

JC put his sunglasses back on. He wasn't sure what had just happened. He could have gone after Lissa, but he didn't. Because you don't have to be a telepath to know when people need their space. Still, there was a lot more to this eager young actress than met the eye.

"There's something different about you, Lissa," he said.

"Got that right," said Lissa, still not looking around. "Really. You have no idea."

"You haven't told me the whole truth about why you're here, have you?"

Lissa laughed, briefly. "A girl has to have some secrets, sweetie."

"What do you think really happened to your uncle Alistair?" JC asked bluntly.

Lissa looked out over the empty rows of seats, and when she finally spoke, her voice was unaccountably weary. "Oh, I'm pretty sure he's dead. Like dear Benjamin and Elizabeth said. And I think they're probably the only ones left now who know the whole story. What really happened. I'm here . . . because I want the truth to come out. All of it."

JC considered the matter for a moment. "Why would Benjamin and Elizabeth tell us Alistair was dead, that he died in a tragic accident all those years ago . . . when they must have known everyone else believes he's missing?"

"Maybe they didn't mean to say it," said Lissa, turning around, at last, to smile at JC. "Maybe there's something about this place that makes people speak the truth. Whether they mean to or not."

"You haven't been scared by anything that's happened here, have you?" said JC. "I saw you, when that dead thing was dragging itself across the stage . . . You didn't blink an eye. It didn't bother you one bit."

Lissa shrugged easily. "Oh, I've always loved ghost-train rides, sweetie. You couldn't keep me off them when I was younger. Takes a lot to spook me . . ."

JC heard a familiar voice say his name. He looked off

stage, and there she was, standing in the wings—Kim. Smiling at him. JC smiled back at her, and a great wave of warmth and relief washed through him. It felt like he'd put down a great weight. And that he hadn't realised how heavy it was until he could put it down at last. She was here again, here with him; and that had to mean something. Lissa looked at JC, looked to where he was looking, then back at him. She frowned, slightly.

"JC, what are you looking at?"

"This is my girl-friend Kim," said JC. "I told you she was keeping an eye on me."

Lissa took a few steps forward, so she could stare right into the wings, then turned back to JC. "I don't see anything . . ."

"Kim is a ghost," JC said calmly. "That's how we met. She's the only real ghost in the Ghost Finders. My teammate, my soul-mate, and my one true love. I thought I'd lost her, but she came back to me. Apparently to be my guardian angel in times of peril."

"JC, really, *I can't see anybody*," said Lissa. "There's no-one there!"

"You have to learn to see with better eyes," said JC. He grinned and tapped his sunglasses significantly with the tip of one finger. "It's a larger world we live in than most people know or would want to know. Packed full, with the living and the dead. Because sometimes even death can't keep some people apart."

"You are seriously freaking me out here, JC," said Lissa.

JC strode across the stage, towards the wings. Kim waited till he'd almost reached her, then she drifted backwards, still smiling, leading him on. JC plunged into the wings after her, and Lissa trotted unhappily along behind him.

"I really don't like where this is going, JC."

....

Kim led JC backstage, then down into the narrow corridors at the rear of the theatre, and into the deeper recesses of the old building. Always staying just ahead of JC, no matter how hard he tried to catch up. Lissa bustled along beside him, determined to keep up, shooting dark glances in all directions and muttering to herself. JC didn't pay much attention to his surroundings, except to note that he didn't think he'd been this way before. He kept trying to talk to Kim: *Are you all right? Are you still being held against your will or have you broken free? Why won't you speak to me?* But Kim never answered him; instead, she smiled back at him. Sometimes encouragingly; sometimes sadly. But never a word. She drifted steadily backwards before him, her feet hovering a few inches above the floor.

"Can I say," said Lissa, a bit brusquely and half out of breath, "that I am getting seriously weirded out by this one-sided conversation? There's no-one there, JC! I can see the whole length of this corridor quite clearly, and we are the only things in it! Trust me on this!"

"Try to keep up, Lissa," said JC, not unkindly. "My Kim may be dead, but she is definitely not departed. She is a ghost, and not everyone can see ghosts."

"I saw that crawling man!"

"Yes," said JC. "So you did. Interesting, that."

Kim finally slowed to a stop before one particular closed door and hovered there. She rose and fell slowly in mid air, her long red hair streaming away to both sides as though she were underwater. She looked entirely solid, but JC knew that if he reached out to her, there wouldn't be anything there. He loved her, but he'd never been able to touch her. Lissa looked from him to the closed door and back again.

"Is she still there? From the soppy look on your face, I'm assuming she still is. What's behind that door? What's she saying?"

"She isn't saying anything," said JC, sharply.

Lissa sniffed loudly. "No name on the door, nothing to indicate what's behind it. Doesn't look any different from all the other doors we passed to get here. Looks like a store-room to me. Do we go in?"

JC looked at Kim. She drifted to one side and gestured at the door; and it swung slowly back to reveal the room beyond.

"Heads up!" said Lissa. "That door opened on its own!"

"That was Kim," said JC. "Come on . . ."

He started towards the open door, then stopped as he realised that Lissa was hanging back.

"You're not really thinking of going in there, are you?" said Lissa. "There could be anything in there. And in this theatre, anything covers a hell of a lot of ground!"

"Kim brought me here," said JC. "She must have her reasons . . ."

But when he looked at Kim to confirm this, she wasn't there. JC flinched as though he'd been hit. A cold hand closed around his heart and squeezed like it would never let go. It was actually harder for him to deal with Kim's absence now that she was coming and going in his life. Lissa followed his gaze.

"Am I to take it, from that wounded, tragic look on your face, that ghost girl isn't with us any more?"

"No," said JC. "She disappeared. She does that."

"So that makes two of us who can't see her," said Lissa.

JC ignored her, thinking hard as he studied the open door. "Why would she bring me here, then vanish? Unless there's something . . . significant in this room. Something I need to see . . . She only appeared before when I was in danger. My guardian-angel ghost. Am I in danger here? Or do I need to see what's in this room to avoid some future danger?"

"He's talking, but he's not talking to me," said Lissa.

JC shot her a sudden grin. "I'm going in. To kick a few things around, start some trouble, see what I can stir up. You can stay out here if you want."

"Sweetie," said Lissa, "I wouldn't miss this for the world."

::::::::::::::::::::::::

They both plunged through the doorway, ready for anything. They found themselves in a fairly large room, packed from wall to wall with row upon row of theatrical costumes, hanging on metal stands. Hundreds of the things, a massive peacock display of styles and colours. There was nothing else in the room, no tables or chairs, not even a mirror on the wall in which to admire one's new costume. Bare, plastered walls, no window, only a single naked light bulb hanging down, filling the room with an unflattering, almost forensic light. JC looked at Lissa.

"Do you have any idea what these costumes are doing here?"

"Nothing to do with me, sweetie," said Lissa. She looked the costumes over and sniffed loudly to show how unimpressed she was. "I have to say, I don't like the look of them. There's something . . . off about those costumes."

"Presumably Benjamin and Elizabeth ordered them, for the play."

"I hardly think so," said Lissa. "Rehearsals aren't due to start until after the renovations are completed. Why hire and ship in expensive costumes before the new paint's even dry? Besides, the play is set very firmly, not to say remorselessly, in the present day. I mean, look at all this! There are enough costumes here for a dozen plays or one light opera revival! Everything from Shakespeare to Restoration comedy, Victorian formal wear to military uniforms. I don't like this, JC. They shouldn't be here . . . And I don't think we should, either."

"Kim brought me here . . ."

"So you keep saying! But I never saw a damned thing! Forget your ghostly girl-friend . . . Trust a ghost hunter to have a dead girl-friend, which now that I think about it, is decidedly icky . . . You'll be telling me you sleep in a coffin next."

"Never on a first date," said JC.

"Oh, I feel so much safer now," said Lissa.

They shared a smile and looked around them. The costumes stared silently back.

"There must be some good reason for us to be here," JC said stubbornly. "And since the only things here are the costumes . . . I suppose we should inspect them. Maybe there'll be a note in a pocket or something . . ."

He stepped up to the first row, and briskly checked out the clothes, one at a time. Lissa moved reluctantly forward while making it very clear she didn't want any part of it. She wouldn't touch anything until she'd watched JC man-handle a whole bunch of them without suffering any ill effects. And then she sighed heavily and pulled out a costume here and there, looking it over carefully and checking the details.

"Good-quality material," she said, finally. "High-end workmanship. But . . ."

"But?" said JC. "But what?" He held a Napoleon uniform up against himself, to see how he'd look in it, then reluctantly put it back again.

"But," Lissa said firmly, "a lot of the details are *wrong*. Mixed periods in the same outfit, wrong kinds of pockets and trimmings, out-of-period materials, important bits and pieces missing . . . No professional costumier would make mistakes like this. This . . . is more like someone faking it. Producing costumes good enough to fool the eye but only from a distance. Amateur night. These clothes look like costumes, JC; but they aren't."

JC looked across at Lissa. She stepped back from the costumes to look them over, hands on hips, glaring ferociously. She looked . . . suspicious, and JC had to wonder why. Nothing else she'd encountered in the theatre had provoked this reaction.

"All these costumes must mean something," he said, standing back with her so he could study the rows of clothes with a sceptical eye. "They must be important. Or why bring us all this way just to see them?"

"We could always play dress-up," said Lissa, but JC could tell that her heart wasn't in it.

"If we assume that Benjamin and Elizabeth didn't arrange for these costumes to be here . . ." he said slowly.

"And I think we can assume that," said Lissa, very firmly.

"Then someone else must have," said JC, talking right over her. "Which in turn implies that we're not the only people interested in this theatre. And this haunting. We're not the only people in this building. Which would explain a lot."

Lissa glared about her, looking seriously unsettled. "There can't be anyone else here. There just can't. I'd know. I'd feel it . . ." She realised JC was considering her silently and scowled back at him. "I'm very sensitive to my surroundings!"

"A lot of people are," JC said soothingly. "Or believe they are. But one of the first things you learn in the Ghost Finding business is that you can't always trust your instincts. Things, and people, aren't necessarily always what they seem, in a haunting situation. The dead play by their own rules."

"But what would the dead want with a whole bunch of not-particularly-accurate costumes?" said Lissa, bluntly.

A slow, heavy rustle passed through the ranks of hanging costumes, like a breeze through forest branches. Hanging clothes twitched and shook, singly and in groups. Sleeves bent and twisted, jackets expanded and relaxed as though someone was breathing in them, and trousers bent at the knee, again and again, as though dreaming of running. Everywhere, costumes were heaving and flexing, as though bothered by unquiet thoughts.

"Back away, Lissa," JC said quietly.

He glanced back and found that Lissa had already backed all the way up to the closed door, unable to tear her gaze away from the slowly moving costumes. There was a new, uneasy feeling in the room, harsh and oppressive: a sharp tension on the air, anticipating bad things to come. JC glared about him. The feeling of being watched was back again, but colder, more intense. As though someone knew something bad was about to happen and meant to enjoy it.

"It's a trap," Lissa said tonelessly. "We've been lured into a trap."

"Don't get twitchy," said JC. "It's all gone weird, agreed, but . . . it's only a bunch of clothes. There's no-one else here but us, living or dead. Look at them; they're . . . bits of cloth on wire hangers!" He looked back at Lissa, to see how she was taking it, and thought she looked more puzzled than scared. "Come on!" he said, encouragingly. "How much of a threat can clothes be?"

As he was saying that, all the costumes shrugged off their hangers and moved away from the cold, metal racks, standing upright on their own. They stood in silent ranks, empty and uninhabited. The clothing rails were forced to the very back of the room, pushed back through the ranks of standing clothes, so an army of empty costumes could confront JC and Lissa with nothing to get in their way. No heads rose from the empty collars, no hands emerged from the empty sleeves, and the slack trousers and leggings hovered a few inches above the floor, with no trace of a foot, or even a shoe. Only costume after costume, standing together in row upon row, turning slowly and silently to orientate themselves on JC, with a horrid sense of purpose.

"You had to ask, didn't you?" said Lissa. "How dangerous can they be? Look at them!"

A subtle frisson of horror ran through JC as he remembered an old childhood terror. Of how discarded clothes can look on a chair at night, or hanging from a door; of how they could seem to come alive . . . or look very much as though they might. In the dark of a child's bedroom. As a young child, JC had wondered whether clothes ever felt angry at being worn and used and moved around under someone else's control. Made to go places and do things and make movements . . . that they wouldn't have chosen to, themselves. On their own. And sometimes he'd wondered whether, when the clothes were finally taken off and laid aside and left to their own devices till morning . . . whether they might not someday rise and take their revenge?

"Lissa," JC said quietly, not taking his eyes off the rows and rows of silently watching clothes stacked before him. "I think this might be a good time to get the hell out of here."

"About time!" said Lissa.

She went over to open the door, then stopped and looked at it.

"Who closed the door, JC? I didn't close the door."

"Don't sweat the small shit, Lissa," said JC. "Let's get out of here."

Lissa reached for the door handle, then stopped again as she realised JC wasn't coming back to join her. "JC, come on! I'm not leaving without you!"

"It's all right," said JC. "I know what to do. I've been trained to deal with shit like this."

"Like *this*?" said Lissa.

"Well, maybe not quite like this," said JC. "I'm thinking this is probably some kind of large-scale poltergeist activity . . . But either way, I can't run off and leave this happening. Someone might get hurt." He squared his shoulders and took a step forward, to confront the standing costumes. "Listen up!" he said loudly. "I am JC Chance, Ghost Finder in good standing. Licenced to kick supernatural arse. What do you want, clothes?"

There was no response. JC wasn't exactly surprised. There wasn't anyone in the clothes to answer. But the more he looked at the various costumes, the spookier they seemed. The lack of heads, of faces, was particularly disturbing. How can you hope to negotiate with, or even threaten, something that has no head to listen with? The more he looked, the more he found to unsettle him. The clothes had no eyes; but they could still see him. Still know exactly where he was. Every single outfit was orientated on him. And none of them had any of the bulges, or fullness, that you'd expect from the bodies that should be inhabiting them. The sleeves were flat, and the legs didn't bend. These weren't clothes worn by invisible men; they were clothes, moving under their own impulses. Animated, not inhabited. He couldn't decide whether that was worse, or not.

He said as much to Lissa, who nodded stiffly. "It's worse. We're definitely not alone in this theatre. Someone else is in here with us, doing this."

She broke off abruptly, as the costumes lurched forward. Row upon row of the things, advancing on JC and Lissa. There was a horrid sense of purpose, of open menace, in their jerky, deliberate movements. Materials rubbed together in a rough susurrus, as though the clothes were whispering to each other. They bustled against each other in their eagerness; but there wasn't the sound of a single footstep.

"Definitely time to get the hell out of Dodge," said JC.

He turned his back on the slowly advancing clothes as an act of defiance and hurried over to join Lissa at the door. She was looking blankly at the moving costumes as though hypnotised, as though she couldn't believe it was happening. JC grabbed the door handle and rattled it hard; but it wouldn't turn. He stepped back and charged forward, putting his shoulder to the door; but while the heavy wood jumped and rattled loudly in its frame, it wouldn't open.

"That isn't going to work!" Lissa said angrily, snapped out of her daze. "The door opened inwards; remember?"

"Now you tell me," muttered JC, rubbing at his bruised shoulder. "Do you see anything in here we can use to break down the door?"

"No. Nothing. You think maybe that's deliberate? Because I sure as hell do. I told you this was a trap!"

"Try not to lose it just yet, Lissa," said JC. "There are still options." He moved to stand between her and the advancing costumes. "You can't let this get to you. A lot's happened since we entered this theatre, but even though some of it was seriously spooky, and even downright disturbing on occasion . . . there was never a time when we were in any real danger. I'm trained to notice things like that. Somebody has been doing their level best to scare us, but not once in any way that put our lives at risk."

"I don't think that's true any more," said Lissa. "Things have changed. This feels different. Dangerous."

"Come on!" said JC. "What can a bunch of old clothes do? Pelt us with mothballs? Beat us to death with their embroidered cuffs?"

He stepped forward again, closing with the clothes, and raised one hand to whip off his sunglasses, to see if he could stop them with the glare from his altered eyes. The costumes rushed forward and threw themselves on JC, ignoring Lissa completely. As though she wasn't important, as though she wasn't even there. The clothes hit JC hard, driving him backwards and wrapping themselves around him in layer upon layer, squeezing tight. JC tried to fight them, but there was nothing there to fight. The clothes simply gave when he tried to hit them and stretched when he tried to rip and tear them. They dropped upon him in wave after wave, closing tighter and tighter around him, pinning his arms to his sides with inhuman strength, like so many constricting snakes.

The clothes whipped JC's feet out from under him, and he fell backwards. He hit the floor hard, driving all the breath from his body. And once he was down, he couldn't get up again. The clothes wrapped him up like a mummy, his legs strapped together, his arms helpless at his sides . . . He fought and struggled, threw all his strength against the enveloping costumes; but they were stronger than he was. Lissa fought desperately to tear the clothes off him, but even though clothing ripped and tore under her hands, she couldn't do enough damage to tear even one piece of clothing away. The costumes ignored her, piling onto JC in layer after layer, burying him underneath them.

He thrashed around on the floor, throwing his weight this way and that, but it was becoming harder and harder to get his breath as the clothes compressed his chest. And then a single silk shirt dropped down across his face, slapping into place, moulding itself tightly across his features, filling his mouth and nostrils so he couldn't get any air at all. One last breath was forced out of him; and he couldn't draw another one in.

....

The door smashed in as Old Tom, the caretaker, came crashing into the room. Lissa yelled for him to help her, and the two of them ripped the silk shirt away from JC's face and tore it into ribbons. JC dragged in a great breath of air, struggling against the clothes again with renewed strength. Lissa and Old Tom attacked the enveloping costumes with their bare hands, ripping and tearing at them; and the clothes collapsed and went limp. Lissa and Old Tom rocked JC back and forth as they pulled the no-longer-resisting costumes away from him, pulling them off him, layer by layer, until JC could finally find the strength and leverage to break free.

He struggled back up onto his feet, tearing at the last few clothes with an almost hysterical strength, desperate to get them off him. When they finally fell away from him and sprawled unmoving on the floor, he kicked at them viciously, breathing hard. And then he was back in control again, himself again, standing still and forcing his breathing back under control. He smiled easily at Lissa and Old Tom as they stood uncertainly before him.

"Well!" JC said brightly. "That was different. Hello again, Old Tom. Where have you been? We couldn't find you anywhere."

"Oh, here and there, sir," said Old Tom, as vaguely diffident as ever. "I was talking to that scientific young lady of yours, in the lobby."

JC waited, until it was clear he wasn't going to get any more, then he looked thoughtfully at the distressed clothes lying on the floor. He prodded a few with the tip of his shoe, to be sure; but there was no response.

"You don't want to go playing with the costumes, sir," said Old Tom, reproachfully. "You'll damage them. Clothes like that are expensive."

"Do you know how they got here?" said JC.

"No, sir," said Old Tom. "I'm the caretaker; I don't do

costumes. That's a whole other department. More than my job's worth to mess with things that are none of my concern."

JC had already stopped listening, half-way through the old caretaker's response. He was thinking. Why would Kim have brought him here, into a trap, to be attacked? This had to be deliberate. Wait until he was separated from Happy and Melody, then bring him to a room with no escape, where his death would be waiting.

"Why would Kim bring me here?" he said, and only realised he'd said it aloud when Lissa snorted loudly.

"What did she say to bring you here?"

"She didn't say anything," said JC.

"Then there's your answer. How do you know it was really your Kim?" said Lissa. "We've all seen all kinds of illusions in the theatre, things and people that weren't what they appeared to be."

"But like you said, this was different," said JC. "This wasn't just scary; someone meant for me to die here."

"Someone else is here in the theatre with us," said Lissa. "Someone who isn't supposed to be here."

JC nodded brusquely to Old Tom. "Thanks for your help. Have you seen anyone else? Anyone who isn't authorised to be here?"

"No, sir."

JC looked at him thoughtfully. "How did you know Lissa and I were in trouble?"

"I didn't, sir," said Old Tom. "I was checking out the corridors, looking for you, to pass on a message. And then I heard you two crashing about in here, where no-one had any business being, and I thought I'd better take a look."

"A message?" said Lissa. "Who from, exactly?"

"From Mr. Happy, Mr. Benjamin, and Miss Elizabeth," said the old caretaker, a bit importantly. "They want you, and Miss Melody, to rejoin them on the old stage, as soon as possible."

"Go back to the main stage?" said JC. "What on earth for?"

Old Tom shrugged. "They didn't say, sir, and it wasn't my business to ask. Will there be anything else, sir? Then I'll be off. Lots of work still to do."

He smiled about him vaguely and went back out into the corridor. Lissa looked at JC, who stayed where he was, frowning hard, thinking.

"Something's not quite right," said JC.

"Oh, I couldn't agree more," said Lissa. "That moustache really doesn't suit him."

"Why didn't Melody ring me if she knew I was needed?" said JC. He took out his phone and checked, but there were no missed calls.

"Why didn't Happy yell at you with his mind?" said Lissa.

"Because I put a lot of time and effort into training him not to do that except for real life-endangering emergencies," said JC. "Still . . ."

"Oh, to hell with it," said Lissa. "Let's go see what they want. I'm sick to death of this room. Never wanted to come in here anyway."

JC nodded slowly and started to follow Lissa out of

the room and into the corridor. At the last moment, he stopped in the doorway as a thought struck him. The costumes only attacked him. Not Lissa. Not even when she was tearing at them, to save him. Odd, that . . .

He looked around the room. There were no clothes, no costumes. Even the clothing racks were gone. He saw only a bare and empty room, full of dust and shadows.

EIGHT

....

IN THE FLESH

Still in the theatre lobby, and getting more than a little tired of it, Melody frowned over her scientific equipment like a mother with a sick child. She moved back and forth, doing her level best to coax and persuade the various instruments into telling her something she actually wanted to know. But, as far as all her screens, sensors, and scientific readings were concerned, everything in the lobby was wonderful. Nothing out of the ordinary was happening, and all was quiet on the supernatural front. Melody stood over her machines, scowling heavily and tugging at her lower lip as she gave the matter some thought and wondered whether she should get out the operating manual or a really big hammer. Because she knew for a fact that something was wrong with the lobby.

And that was when all her readouts started going crazy, right in front of her eyes. The first to go was the

temperature gauge. The display started climbing, and
wouldn't stop. According to the figure before her, the
temperature in the lobby was already at jungle heat and
rising so fast it was heading for the stratosphere. If it really was as hot in the lobby as the gauge was making out,
the machine would be melting, and Melody would be
crisp and aromatic and ready to serve. And then the reading dropped, just as rapidly, and they kept on dropping.
Shooting down past normal levels and into sub-zero tem-
peratures that would seriously upset a polar bear. Melody
felt a sudden nostalgic twinge for the old-style thermom-
eter, with mercury in it, where if you didn't like the reading you were getting, you could tap the thing with a
fingertip until it changed. You didn't have that luxury
with an electronic readout. She was about to try hitting
the thing anyway, on general principles, when the readout rose sharply again, all the way back to normal, and
steadied itself.

While Melody was still trying to get her head around
what had happened, all her warning alarms went off at
once. The sirens were deafeningly loud in the enclosed
space of the lobby, and Melody moved quickly from one
readout to the next, all of which seemed convinced that
she was surrounded and under attack from any number
of heavily armed hostiles. The short-range sensors were
picking up guns, energy weapons, Objects of Power, and
all kinds of dangerous radiations, while the motion
trackers showed dozens of hostile presences, circling
round and round her instrument station. As far as her
defences were concerned, Melody was under attack from

the walking dead, demonic forces, and bloody big aliens in hobnailed boots. The machines were going crazy, warning her about everything under the sun, all of them shouting and screaming for her attention. Melody looked up and glared wildly about her; but the lobby was quite definitely empty and utterly peaceful.

All the alarms shut off at once; and a slow, steady quiet blessedly returned. All the short-range sensor readings were back to normal, indicating everything was as it should be. It was like they'd all suddenly lost their machine minds, for no reason. And then all the long-range sensors kicked in, lights blinking angrily all across the boards. Melody leaned in close to study the readings, and then shook her head numbly. As far as the long-range sensors were concerned, the theatre wasn't there any more. It was gone, and the rest of the world with it. She couldn't find a single sensor reporting anything: no physical readings, no energy sources, nothing at all. As though she and her ranks of machines were floating alone, in empty space. Melody looked steadily about her, but the lobby stubbornly insisted it was still there, surrounding her, and everything was fine. She stamped her foot hard on the floor to make sure.

Bright lights were flashing everywhere now, everything kicking off at once; and one by one, the monitor screens turned themselves on, showing Melody images of things that weren't there. Brief glimpses of other worlds than this. One screen showed the inside of some vast stone temple, from an age before any known history, lit by strange, phosphorescent glows from long creepers of moss, crawling slowly across the floor and walls, and draping themselves around massive stone carvings of long-forgotten gods with horrid insect faces.

The screen next to it showed a dark, drifting, underwater scene, of some sunken city wrapped in seaweed and studded with pulsing mushroom growths. Strange, unpleasant-looking fish darted this way and that, carrying their own eerie light with them, while huge glass submarines glided past, full of hunched humanoid creatures made out of kelp.

Another screen showed the theatre lobby, soaked and splashed with blood and gore. JC and Happy stared out of the screen, standing together, their clothes and flesh ripped and torn. They were both dead, but they shuffled slowly forward on broken feet, staring out of the screen at Melody with dark bloody holes where their eyes had been, their mutilated faces full of a terrible silent accusation.

The monitor screens all shut down at once, showing nothing. Melody was breathing harshly and scowling so fiercely her face hurt. Either something was wrong with her instruments or something was very wrong with the world. And, since a quick glare around showed the lobby was still there, untouched and unchanged, it had to be her machines. She honestly didn't know what to do. If she started running major diagnostics on everything, she'd still be here running them when JC and Happy came back to tell her the case was over. Checking them all for outside influences would take hours. Though that had to be what this was. Something from Outside was messing with her. First those nightmare posters on the walls, and now this. Someone was messing with her head, trying to make her doubt herself, and now they wanted her to doubt her instruments. Melody took a deep breath and shut all her instruments down. Everything. The lights went out, the monitor screens went blank, and every single piece of highly sophisticated technology was suddenly still and silent. Melody hated to do it, but if she couldn't trust what her equipment was telling her, then it was no damned good at all.

It was all very quiet in the lobby now. The lighting was bright and steady, the shadows blessedly unmoving, and the air was dry and still, as though nothing had happened, and this was just another day. Melody snarled silently at that thought, and rubbed at her aching forehead. *Too much thinking is bad for you,* her mother always said. *It'll give you lines.* Though her mother never was much of a one for thinking, anyway, or she'd never have married Melody's father. Bad cess to the man, wherever he might be. Melody made herself concentrate on the matter at hand. Her hands weren't as steady as they should have been, and her back muscles ached unmercifully from the endless tension. The stress was getting to her; and that wasn't like her. She never let the world upset her; she made it a matter of principle to always upset the world.

But now she felt very much on her own, without her instruments to lean on. Alone and vulnerable. Melody sniffed loudly. She knew what to do about that. She crouched and reached into the arms cabinet, feeling for the machine-pistol; but her fingers couldn't find it. She knelt so she could look right into the cabinet, but there was nothing in it. Nothing at all. She stared into the dark space. She couldn't believe it. She swept her hand back and forth inside the cabinet, banging it against the inside walls; but every single one of her weapons was gone. She straightened up and moved quickly up and down her instrument racks, checking all the other, more secret, defensive caches she maintained in her set-up; and they were empty, too. All her weapons were gone, including all the ones nobody else was supposed to know about. Including her team-mates.

She slowly turned around in a complete circle, taking in the empty, innocent-seeming lobby. Her back muscles crawled, in anticipation of the attack she probably wouldn't know anything about until it was too late. Her hands clenched into fists. She could feel cold sweat on her face. And then she caught a glimpse of someone, out of the corner of her eye, watching her. She spun round to look straight at him, but there was no-one there. She caught another glimpse of the watching, smiling stranger, out of the corner of her other eye. She spun around again; and again there was nobody there. She was breathing really hard now, ready to jump on anyone and beat the truth out of them, about what was really going on. She caught another glimpse, and another, from this side and from that, but no matter which way she looked, or how fast she turned, she couldn't catch him. Only the briefest of glimpses; quick impressions of a man watching her, smiling at her, enjoying her agitation. And every time she saw him, he was that little bit closer, closing in on her. She spun round and round, eyes wide open, then stopped herself with an effort. She stood very still, hands clenched painfully tight at her sides, fighting to get her frantic breathing and heart rate back under control. She let her head hang down, squeezed her eyes shut, and refused to open them again.

Come on, girl. You can do better than this. You've been trained to withstand Outside influences. Trained to keep other people from messing with your mind. So focus! You can do this!

Her breathing slowed, and her thoughts settled. Her back muscles unclenched, and so did her fists. Her mind calmed and cleared, as well-rehearsed mental shields slammed down and locked firmly into place. And when she finally lifted her head again, opened her eyes, and looked around her, the lobby was very definitely empty. Melody sniffed loudly and shook herself roughly, like a dog shaking off a bad dream. She took out her mobile phone. She had to reach Happy and JC, let them know what was happening. Let them know there was someone else in the theatre with them. But there was no signal. Even though she was sure there had been, before. She shook the phone hard, and a voice from the phone said her name. *Melody* . . . That and nothing more. She checked the phone again, but there still wasn't any signal. Not a single bar. So where was the voice coming from? The voice from the phone said her name again. A soft, self-satisfied voice, like a purring cat. Like someone used to having the advantage over other people.

"Hello, Melody," said the calm, malicious, masculine voice. "Tell me. After all these years of hunting ghosts, are you finally ready to become one? You won't like being dead, you know. No-one ever does. The truth always comes as such a terrible shock; and then they cry and they cry and they cry . . ."

"Who is this?" Melody said harshly, looking down at the phone in her hand, clutching it so tightly her fingers ached.

"You spent all this time looking for me, and you don't even know my name. How sad is that? Of course, it wouldn't have helped. I have a lovely new name now, to go with my new and very special nature. I'm the one who took your Kim away. Snatched her right out of that dead man's head and dragged her off, kicking and screaming . . ."

"Who are you?" said Melody.

"I serve The Flesh Undying. Ah, you know that name, at least. And I am here for you, little girl. Do you want your precious machines back? What would you give me to have them all working properly again? To be able to depend on what they told you? Hmm?"

"I don't make deals," said Melody.

"Have them back anyway," said the voice. "I want you fully armed. I want this to be something like a fair fight. It's no fun otherwise."

The phone shut itself down. Melody glared at it. "I really must get a *Fuck off and die* app."

And then she jumped slightly, despite herself, as her machines came alive again. All her instruments were back on-line, all her short- and long-range sensors were reporting in, and everything seemed to be working perfectly; sane and calm and reliable again. Melody put her phone away and moved slowly and methodically from one set of readings to the next. Brightly coloured LEDs blinked reassuringly back at her, everywhere she looked. She checked the arms cabinet, and the machine-pistol was back in place, as though it had never been away, along with everything else. She ran one hand caressingly over the gun, but she didn't take it out. She didn't want the owner of the voice thinking she was afraid of him.

Her head came up sharply, as she heard footsteps approaching from outside. Slow, steady, apparently perfectly normal footsteps, barely audible above the muted traffic noise from the street. Heading straight for the main entrance doors.

"Oh come on!" Melody said loudly. "Not that trick again! Getting really tired of that! It didn't work last time, and it won't work now!"

The entrance doors crashed open, and he came in.

|||||||||||||||||||||||||

Something new and terrible had come to the Haybarn Theatre. Something that was not what it appeared to be.

He came swaggering into the lobby, head held high and hands thrust deep into trouser pockets, bringing with him all the arrogant assured cockiness that JC used to have. He wore a very smart and expensive coal grey suit, complete with a waistcoat of many colours. He had slicked-back jet-black hair and dark, unblinking eyes. Eyes as cold and inhuman as a shark's and just as hungry. He had a smile like Satan's, a smile that never stopped. He sauntered around the lobby and then slammed to a halt right in front of Melody, on the other side of her wall of instruments. Everything about him looked perfect. Impossibly, inhumanly perfect. He was heavily built, though muscle and bulk rather than fat. A huge, overpowering, physical presence. The kind that makes you feel it would be dangerous to look away, not because he was a clear and present danger but because he was always going to be the most important thing in the room; and you might miss something important.

His face might have been classically handsome if there'd only been some character in it; but though everything was in the right place, in all the right proportions, it looked more like a mask. With those eyes, and that smile. Melody made a point of sneering at him, on general principles, to let him know she didn't impress that easily.

"Hello, Melody," he said, and it was the soft purring voice she'd heard coming out of her phone. The voice of a man who'd never lost a fight and wasn't about to start now. "I am the Faust. Horror without end, amen. I made a deal with The Flesh Undying. Didn't sell my soul, in return for the pleasures of the flesh. Rather, I sold my flesh in return for a better soul. Have you any idea what it is you and your fellow Ghost Finders are up against? I gave up ownership of my flesh, to The Flesh Undying, to be its presence in the world; and in return, it promised me I'd never have to die. How cool is that? And now, I am so much more than I used to be. And so much more powerful, of course. Ah, the things I can do . . ."

"Like to make speeches, don't you?" said Melody.

The Faust shrugged easily. "Comes with the job. And the territory."

He turned his back on her and strode off to saunter around the lobby again, taking it all in and looking it all over as though he were planning on buying it, then destroying it, then pissing on the ruins because he could. He ended up back before Melody and sneered equably at her ranks of scientific equipment.

"There is something to be said for improvisation in the face of jeopardy, I suppose. Look at it . . . Something old, something borrowed, something cobbled together at the last minute. None of it of any real use against something like me." He cocked his great head on one side and considered her happily. "Did you enjoy my posters? My little mental movies? Nothing like a good video nasty, I always say."

"You put that shit in my head?" said Melody.

"No," said the Faust. "Everything you saw came from inside your head. All the things you're afraid of, little girl."

"If you were as powerful as you claim, you'd have killed me by now," said Melody.

The Faust smiled and waggled one finger at her, roguishly. "Now where's the fun in that?"

"Are you responsible for the haunting here?" said Melody. "All the weird shit we've been seeing?"

"I just got here," said the Faust. "I don't know what's going on in this dreary little playhouse; and I don't care. I didn't come here for the ghosts; I'm here for the Ghost Finders. Not because you present any real danger to The Flesh Undying, you understand, because you don't. But there is the smallest possibility that you might become a nuisance. Eventually . . . So I'm going to destroy you now. Leave three new ghosts to moan and wander in this dusty old theatre. If it wasn't haunted before, it will be."

"Getting really tired of hearing you talk," said Melody. "In fact, hold that pose. I've got a bloody big gun here, somewhere."

"What shall I start with?" said the Faust. "Something suitably theatrical, I think. What's the point of murder without a little style? Let us call up the dust of ages and set it to work."

He gestured languidly with one meaty hand, and all the dust in the lobby, left untroubled and untouched for twenty years and more, rose everywhere. It sprang up from the floor and jumped off the walls and ceiling to dance madly on the lobby air, forming and re-forming into stretching shapes that bordered on meaning, before abruptly condensing into two dark grey, vaguely human figures. Soft but substantial living shadows . . . and where their faces should have been, the old traditional masks of Comedy and Tragedy. Endlessly laughing, endlessly crying. The ancient symbols of Drama, topping tall and spindly bodies, stretched and stylised, almost art deco. They danced and capered around the Faust, fawning and bobbing their heads, cringing under his shark's gaze and devil smile.

"Here is Drama, come to do my will," said the Faust. "Two small and pitiful things, but mine own. Because I don't see why I should get my hands dirty, dealing with something as small and insignificant as you, little girl. So . . . Go and get her, you nasty little things. Make a mess."

The two grey figures tore themselves away from ador-
ing the Faust and danced towards Melody, throwing
wild, extravagant shapes as they pirouetted in rapid circles around her and her equipment. Dark liquid monsters
of inhuman suppleness and horrible malice, soaked in
menace and vicious intent. Melody sneered right back at
them, holding her ground, refusing to be impressed or
intimidated.

"Get the hell away from my machines!" she said
coldly.

"Dust is the mortal enemy of computers, is it not?"
said the Faust. "Ah, what it is, to put the iron in irony!"

The dark grey figures froze in place while he spoke.
He waved them on with a languid hand, and they surged
forward. Melody grabbed the machine-pistol from out
of its resting place and opened fire. She raked the gun
steadily back and forth, blowing great holes through the
leaping, darting figures; but it didn't harm them, and it
didn't stop them. They were, after all, only dust. The bullets tore right through to chew up the wall behind them.
Plaster cracked and wood chips blew. *To hell with the
theatre owners,* thought Melody, and kept firing. *They
can bill me . . .* The dusty grey figures didn't even slow
or hesitate as they pressed forward; and then suddenly
Melody stopped firing and lowered her gun. The dusty
figures stopped where they were, regarded her suspiciously, and looked back at the Faust. He found the energy to raise one inquiring eyebrow in Melody's direction,
and she smiled nastily back.

"It occurs to me," she said, "that I am wasting perfectly good ammunition that I might have a better use for

later. Let the dust come. My machines are top-of-the-line, and can look after themselves. And the dust can't hurt me. Since those things are really nothing more than the left-overs from an old vacuum cleaner."

"Ah," said the Faust happily. "But I have made them so much more. You can drown in dust, if there's enough of it. And they . . . are all the dust there is. They will fill you up from the inside out, little girl; and I shall stand right here and watch while they do it and laugh and laugh."

"Yeah?" said Melody. "Watch this."

She leaned forward and hit one big red button, and the two grey figures were gone in a moment, blasted apart by an unseen force. Nothing more than millions of dust motes, scattered across the lobby. They hung on the air in a thin, dusty mist, slowly settling, falling back to the floor. No trace remained of the smiling, scowling faces. Melody smiled brightly at the Faust.

"Localised electromagnetic pulse," she said smugly. "Blasting out from my carefully isolated machines so as not to disturb them, and so limited in scope it didn't even affect the lobby's electric lighting. But more than enough to see off your dusty attack dogs."

The Faust sighed loudly. "I tried to do it quickly and cleanly, I tried to deal with you in a civilised manner, but no . . . you had to be difficult. It seems I have no choice but to go all Old School on you, little girl."

"Stop calling me that!" said Melody.

"Why?" said the Faust. "It's all you are, really. Whereas I am The Flesh Undying, incarnate. I have been given power over flesh, all flesh . . . Even yours. Want to come out and play, little girl?"

He took one measured step closer and extended one oversized hand. Melody raised her machine-pistol threateningly, but the Faust ignored her. He gestured imperiously, a harsh, beckoning movement, and Melody lurched on her feet as she felt him draw something out of her. She tried to say something and couldn't, held in place where she was. The machine-pistol dropped from her unfeeling fingers, and her hands rose on the air before her, pulled forward by an unseen force. Long, thin tendrils of some white, spongy substance extended slowly from her fingertips, stretching away from her, hanging unsupported on the air like long white chalk-marks. She shook her hands, trying to break off whatever it was, but the white streaks clung to her, growing longer and thicker. They inched away from her fingertips, across the empty air, growing longer and thicker . . . Melody's hands tingled heavily with pins and needles, but more like the loss of vital warmth than the return of circulation. She opened her mouth to yell or scream or curse, and more of the white stuff erupted out of her mouth, stretching her jaws wide with its presence. Still more jumped out of her eyes and nostrils, to shoot out across the air.

Melody was losing something; or rather, something was being taken from her. She could feel it. The long, chalky, white tendrils were slowly coming together on the air before her, forming one huge pallid mass.

All these years I've been a Ghost Finder, Melody thought dazedly, *and the first time I get to see some ectoplasm, it's mine.*

The white shape was almost human now. Standing upright, with arms and legs and a rough head bulging up from its shoulders. It slowly straightened up, on the other side of the wall of machines, and snapped into focus. Entirely human in shape and form, an exact duplicate of Melody, down to the smallest detail. Including her clothes. The dupe shook her head slowly, then glared at Melody.

"What the hell are you doing, behind my equipment? Get out of there!"

Melody's first reaction was, *My voice doesn't sound like that.* Followed by, *Why did I ever think those glasses suited me?*

"These are my machines," she said coldly. "Because I am the real deal, and you are not. As far as I can tell, you're made out of snot and mucus, and I'm not letting you get your nasty ectoplasm all over my nice clean instruments."

"Girls, girls," muttered the Faust. "Don't argue. Or, on second thought, do. Argue! Dispute! Kill the unworthy duplicate who wants to take your place in the world. I'll hold your coats if you like."

"Shut up!" said Melody.

"Stay out of this!" said the dupe.

Neither of them spared a glance for the Faust; they were glaring at each other, eyes locked. The dupe snarled at Melody.

"I'm the real thing. I don't know what you are."

"You're an ectoplasmic dupe," said Melody. "Which is why I'm standing on the right side of the instruments."

That threw the dupe for a moment, but she quickly shook it off. "That is a mistake, easily rectified."

Melody sank down and shot up again with her machine-pistol in her hand, pointed right into the dupe's face. "Yeah right. Let's see you try, ecto-bitch."

But the dupe had already brought up her hand, also holding a machine-pistol. She pointed it at Melody's head. "Who are you calling a bitch, bitch?"

"Fight, fight, fight!" said the Faust, happily.

"Shut up!" said both Melodys, in perfect unison. And then they both stopped, looking at each other in a new way.

"He's behind all this," said the dupe. "He's the enemy."

"He wants me to shoot myself," said Melody. "Because for all his fine words and grand claims . . . I don't think he's up to the task."

"I don't think we should solve this with guns," said the dupe. "I don't think we should give him that satisfaction."

"Damn right," said Melody. And she lowered her gun.

The dupe hesitated for a second, then lowered her gun, too. "Typical man, getting a woman to tear herself apart. But we've got to sort this out somehow. What do you suggest?"

"Put it to the machines," said Melody. "They can scan us, right down to our DNA, and decide who's who and what's what."

"Sounds good to me," said the dupe. "If we can't trust our instruments, what can we trust?"

She came behind the wall of equipment to stand beside Melody, who was already firing up the short-range scanners and putting them to work. It only took the machines a moment to study both women, inside and out, and come up with a definitive answer. That the dupe was the real Melody Chambers.

The dupe let out a long, slow sigh of relief, before turning triumphantly to face Melody. "See? When in doubt, put your faith in the machines."

"Except when you know someone's been messing with them," said Melody. "Remember before the Faust made his big entrance?"

"No," said the dupe. "No . . ."

Melody brought up her machine-pistol and put a single bullet through her duplicate's forehead. The impact snapped the dupe's head backwards and sent her somersaulting back over the wall of instruments to crash onto the floor beyond. Melody turned to the Faust.

"You bastard. Making me shoot myself. I couldn't let her live; I could never trust her because she was your creation. Not really real . . . But damn you anyway for making me do it."

And then she broke off as she heard low moans and scrabbling noises from the other side of the machines. Melody hurried out, to find her dupe lying sprawled on the floor, leaking a chilly white fluid from the small hole in her forehead and the larger hole in the back of her head. More ectoplasm was leaking from the dupe's fingertips. Drifting on the air, slowly dispersing.

"You didn't really think it was going to be that easy to kill yourself?" said the Faust. "You can't kill ectoplasm by shooting it in the head. All you did was break the surface tension. Oh yes, you've destroyed your duplicate, all right . . . Now all you have to do is watch yourself die slowly. That's me, you see, always two moves ahead."

Melody ignored him, crouching at her duplicate's side. The dupe looked up at her sadly.

"I'm sorry. He made me too well. I really thought I was me. I mean, you . . . And now I'm dying. I'm scared, Melody."

"Don't be," said Melody. "I'm here with you." She glared across at the Faust. "You worthless piece of shit. Don't let her suffer like this. Do something!"

"I am!" said the Faust. "I'm enjoying it! More than one way to skin a cat, or break a spirit."

Melody sat down on the floor beside the dying dupe and took her in her arms. She held her tightly, while the dupe shook and shuddered, slowly breaking up, losing basic coherence as ectoplasm leaked from everywhere at once. Melody didn't know what to do. She'd never felt so helpless. But when the machines can't help you, all that's left is to be human. And care.

"I'm so cold . . ." said the dupe. Her eyes weren't tracking any more.

"Hush," said Melody. "Hush. It's all right. I'm here."

Ectoplasm boiled off the dupe's body, rising like a thin white mist, dispersing quickly on the still lobby air. Melody could feel the dupe's form growing soft and vague in her arms. The dupe grabbed at Melody's hand with her own. Melody took hold of it firmly, and it fell apart in her fingers. The dupe's face fell in, collapsing. The eyes and the mouth were the last to go. The dupe's lips moved.

"Melody. Make him pay."

And then she burst. Great splashes of ectoplasm soaked Melody from top to toe. Her arms were full of a chalky, white, liquid mass, quickly falling apart into mists, which dispersed in the air and were gone. Melody was left sitting on the floor with empty arms. Her clothes were dry, all traces of ectoplasm gone. She got up, clambering awkwardly to her feet, and looked at the Faust with cold, cold eyes. He smiled easily back at her.

"So," he said. "Are we having fun yet?"

"What are you?" she said. "Isn't there anything human left inside you?"

"Why should I settle for anything so small, so limited? I am the Faust. I'm everything that ever scared you, little girl, in one easy, soul-destroying package! Can I get a halleluiah?"

Melody brought up her machine-pistol, and opened fire. The Faust stood sportingly still before her, soaking up every bullet that hit him. He didn't so much as flinch while the bullets hit him, over and over again. The bullets punched into him, but he took no damage, and he didn't bleed. Even the holes in the front of his nice suit healed themselves instantly. When Melody finally gave up, stopped shooting, and lowered her gun, the Faust coughed obligingly and spat the bullets out onto the palm of his hand. He let them drop, to jump and rattle loudly on the lobby floor.

"I'm not soft, everyday flesh like you, little girl. Not any more. I am the new flesh, the better flesh, The Flesh Undying in the world of mortal men. The clue is in the name, really . . ."

"I'll kill you," said Melody. "I will find a way to kill you."

The Faust ignored her, his perfect brow creased with a hint of concentration. "Door!" he said, finally.

And a Door appeared in the lobby, appearing suddenly and silently out of nowhere. It looked like an ordinary everyday door except that it was hanging high up on the air, below the lobby ceiling. Entirely horizontal, facedown.

"I think something terribly theatrical is needed here," said the Faust. "I think this calls for . . . the Phantom of the Haybarn!"

The Door dropped open, hanging down, and something dropped out of it like a bag of garbage. A dark shape that hit the floor of the lobby hard. But it didn't break, and it didn't cry out. Melody quickly covered it with her machine-pistol; and the Faust chuckled. At first, Melody couldn't make out what it was—a hunched figure, crouching on the floor, hidden under a heavy black cape. It rocked back and forth, swaying this way and that; and then it rose suddenly upright and spun around to glare at Melody.

A tall, stoop-shouldered creature, dressed in all the finery of the late nineteenth century, wrapped in a night-black opera cloak. Half his face was hidden behind a grubby, blood-stained mask. The features that could be seen were a sickly yellow colour, as though disfigured by a skin disease. And the eyes . . . were exactly like the Faust's. Dark eyes, shark eyes. The creature's filthy gloved hands dripped fresh blood, which smoked and stained the lobby floor. The Phantom of the Haybarn—a corrupted dream, a living nightmare. He stank of filth and blood and rotting meat.

"What a pretty thing you are," said the Faust. "My very own Phantom, for this tawdry little theatre. Go forth, my child, my own. Be bad. Be scary. Tear this place apart and everyone in it."

The Phantom lurched forward, heading for Melody. He looked human enough, but he didn't move like a man. He swayed and lurched, as though something inside him was broken. He laughed breathlessly, and as he reached out to Melody, she could see that splintered claws had burst through the end of his gloves. He wanted to do things to her. Horrible things. And Melody knew he would take a long time with her before he finally let her die. She was also pretty sure the machine-pistol wouldn't stop him.

So she did the sensible thing. She strode right up to the Phantom, kicked him so hard in the balls she lifted him right off the ground, ran past him, and fled through the swing doors, into the warren of theatre corridors beyond. She smiled as she heard choked, agonised sounds behind her; the Phantom, trying to force air back into his lungs.

She was already deep into the maze of corridors when she heard him coming after her.

The Faust nodded once and turned away, quietly satisfied at having ticked one small thing off his list. He looked up at the Door, still hanging open, hovering below the ceiling. He waved it away with a brief dismissive gesture, and the Door disappeared. The Faust looked quickly around the empty lobby, then he disappeared, too.

\|\|\|\|\|\|\|\|\|\|\|\|\|\|\|\|\|\|\|\|\|\|\|\|

For a moment there was peace and quiet in the theatre lobby, then a figure stirred in the shadows. From where he had been watching all this time, unsuspected and unobserved, Old Tom, the caretaker, emerged into the light, shuffling out across the lobby floor. He stopped and looked at the doors where Melody and the Phantom had made their exit; and then he looked thoughtfully at the spot where the Faust had disappeared.

"You're not one of mine," Old Tom said finally. "So whose little ghost are you, I wonder? It doesn't matter. You won't get to spoil anything; I'll see to that. I've still got a show to put on."

And then he disappeared. And the lobby was finally empty and quiet.

NINE

OLD TRUTHS, COME HOME TO ROOST

Melody ran headlong through the narrow theatre corridors, not once looking back. She didn't need to look back to know that the Faust's Phantom was still hot on her trail. She could feel his presence behind her, feel his hot gaze on her back, feel his rotten breath on her neck . . . She pounded down the dimly lit corridors, arms pumping at her sides, not even trying to pace herself. She had to get to the others, had to tell them about the Faust . . . because they only thought they were dealing with a haunting. They didn't know there was a monster in the house. In the end, she had to look back over her shoulder, because she couldn't stand the tension any more; and, of course, he wasn't there. Never had been. She made herself run a little faster anyway. She hoped she was going in the right direction. All the corridors looked the same to her. She felt like a mouse running a maze, with a cat at every exit. She took a sharp left turn without slowing and pounded down another long corridor that looked like all the others.

The Phantom burst out of a side passage and slammed right into her, lifting her off her feet as though she weighed nothing and throwing her hard against the far wall. She cried out miserably at the impact and tried to struggle; but he held her easily with one hand at her throat, her feet kicking helplessly several inches above the floor. She made herself fight him, flailing wildly; but her human strength was nothing compared to the Phantom's. He pushed his masked face right into hers, smiling nastily with the revealed half of his face. Up close, the grubby mask smelled of rotting leather, while his half-face smelled of rotting flesh.

"You can't outrun me, my sweet," he said, and his voice was a low, hissing thing, full of venom. "I'll always be able to run faster than you because I'm a made thing, not bound by human limitations. I was made to run down my prey, then do awful and unforgivable things to it. I was made to make you suffer, and to enjoy it. And I will! It's good to have a purpose in life."

Melody brought up her machine-pistol, stuck the barrel right under his jaw, and pulled the trigger. The sound of the gun was shockingly loud, and Melody cried out despite herself at the terrible sound and the blinding glare. The sheer velocity of the bullets slammed the Phantom's head back. The repeated impacts broke his hold on Melody and drove him backwards. Melody half collapsed into a crouch before she got her strength and balance back, but she kept firing. The Phantom lurched and swayed this way and that, but she moved the gun with him. The bullets punched right through his formal clothes and cape, but he didn't cry out, and he didn't bleed. Melody quickly realised that the Phantom could heal as easily as the Faust who made him.

A sudden silence fell across the corridor as Melody ran out of bullets. The Phantom smiled at her. She looked blankly at the gun in her hand, as though it had betrayed her, and she shook the pistol for a moment, as though that would do anything. She had more clips for the gun, but they were all back in the lobby, in the arms cabinet. She looked at the Phantom, smiling at her like a shark that's scented blood in the water; and she smiled back at him. He didn't like that. He started towards her, and she went for him, throwing the empty gun into his face. He snatched the machine-pistol out of mid air and crumpled the metal in his inhuman grasp. And while he was preoccupied doing that, Melody punted him good and hard between the legs. The Phantom dropped to his knees, mouth stretched wide as he tried to force a scream through his constricted throat. Melody punched him once, in the side of the head, just to be sure, then ran on.

The Faust really shouldn't have made you in his own image, she thought, as she ran. *Given you two hostages to fortune . . . And you really should have been expecting that. Not terribly bright, this Phantom of the Haybarn.*

‌‌‌‌‌‌‌‌‌‌‌‌‌‌‌‌‌‌‌‌‌‌‌‌‌‌

She rounded the next corner at speed, and there, waiting for her was Old Tom, the caretaker. She stumbled to a halt, and he smiled benignly at her. He didn't seem in the least surprised to see her. She struggled to get her harsh breathing back under control, so she could warn him about the Phantom; but he was already talking.

"You don't want to go this way, miss. You want to go down there, round that corner, then it's second on the right. Take you straight to the main stage area, that will. You can't miss it."

"Get out of here!" Melody said finally.

"What?"

"Get out of here! Get out of the theatre! There's bad people here. Dangerous people."

Old Tom smiled and shook his head. "Bless you, miss, I'm not in any danger. No-one's going to hurt Old Tom. You follow the directions I gave you, and you'll be fine."

He pointed out the direction to her. Melody looked, and when she looked back, he was gone. Not a trace of him anywhere. Melody scowled briefly, gathered up her strength, and ran down the corridor.

''''''''''''''''''''''''''''

She finally saw a familiar set of swing doors up ahead of her, burst through them without slowing, and found herself back in the main auditorium. She stumbled down the central aisle, leaning on end chairs as she went, for support. Up on the stage, JC and Happy, Benjamin and Elizabeth and Lissa, were all standing together and arguing loudly. They broke off to look out at her, caught off guard by her sudden entrance. She stopped, and slumped down onto a padded chair for a moment, to get her breath back. She always felt a little safer when JC and Happy were around, though, of course, she'd never tell them that. It took encountering something like Faust and his Phantom to get her to admit it to herself. She glanced quickly behind her; but there wasn't the slightest sound or sight of the Phantom. Yet. She forced herself up out of her chair and glared indiscriminately at everyone on the stage.

"You stay right where you are! I'm coming up! And I don't care what you're arguing about; I've had a far worse time than you have, so my problems are bound to be much worse than yours, so I am entitled to be in a very bad mood!"

"Never knew you when you weren't!" murmured JC.

"I heard that!"

"You were meant to."

Melody strode down the main aisle, round the side, and up onto the stage, while everyone else stood exactly where they were and looked at her. Melody had that effect on people, sometimes. If only because they knew silent, fuming rage when they saw it. She finally stomped across the stage to confront Happy, who gave her his best *What have I done now?* look.

"Why don't you answer your phone?" snarled Melody.

Happy blinked at her a few times. "It hasn't rung. Did you try and call me? You never call me when we're out in the field. You said constant communication was a sign of weakness."

Melody growled deep in her throat and shook her head in frustration. Happy considered her for a moment and took a tentative step forward.

"Something's happened," he said. "Something bad. I don't have to look inside your head to know that. What was it? What could possibly spook you this much? Are you all right, Melody?"

"No," she said. And then she managed a small smile. "But I do feel a lot better for being here, with you."

"Yelling at me is very therapeutic," said Happy, solemnly. "A lot of people have told me that. After they calmed down."

Melody looked around her. "What's everybody doing back here?"

"That is what we were . . . discussing, when you made your dramatic entrance," said JC. "Old Tom brought Lissa and me a message. Ostensibly from Happy, saying we all needed to meet back here. Urgently. Only when Lissa and I arrived, it was to find Happy and his two actors waiting here for us, demanding to know why I'd called them back."

"Old Tom is a ghost," said Happy. "Or more properly, a ghost in disguise. I saw him disappear into a pool of darkness."

"I said he was too broad a character to be true," said Benjamin. "A performance of a caretaker; not the real thing."

"We were always very suspicious of him," said Elizabeth. "But only because we thought he was a journalist in disguise."

"Never even occurred to us that he might be the ghost

haunting this theatre, said Benjamin. "I mean, walking around with us, pretending to be real, like us . . . That is so creepy, the hairs on the back of my neck are tying themselves in knots."

"Sly," said Elizabeth. "Underhanded. I mean, you don't expect spirits to sneak around and take advantage of you."

"He told Lissa and me that Happy wanted us here, urgently," said JC.

Happy shook his head quickly. "Not me, boss. Nothing to do with me."

"I had gathered that," said JC.

"We're here because we found a note pinned to the wall," said Happy. "Apparently from you, telling me to get the actors back here sharpish."

"And you didn't think to phone me first, to check?" said JC.

"No signal," said Happy. "And no, I didn't try to reach out to you with my mind. After watching Old Tom melt away to nothing, I didn't trust the atmosphere in this place; and I certainly wasn't going to drop any of my mental shields. It's not safe here, JC. For Old Tom to pass as human like that, up close and personal, with none of us suspecting a thing . . . that's almost unheard of. Maintaining something like that takes a hell of a lot of power."

"Have you still got the note?" said JC.

"Sure," said Happy.

But when he rummaged in his pocket, it wasn't there. Happy smiled weakly at JC and tried all his other pockets, sometimes more than once; but the note was gone.

"Someone wanted us all here," said JC. "Old Tom . . . or whatever that really is, hiding behind the appearance of Old Tom."

"A kindly old duffer who no-one would look at twice," said Happy. "So clearly harmless, no-one ever suspected a thing. Good disguise."

"Excuse me!" Melody said loudly. "But I do have something very urgent and extremely dangerous to discuss!"

JC smiled at her easily. "Of course you do. Very well, Melody; what brings you back here? In such an excited and sweaty state?"

"Something is chasing me," Melody said bluntly. "Trying to kill me; and then all of you."

"How very stupid of it," murmured JC. "Where . . ."

Melody gestured back at the swing doors, at the rear of the auditorium; and everybody looked. The doors didn't move. It was all very still and very quiet. Everyone looked at Melody again.

"Who is it?" said JC. "Who's after you?"

"The Phantom of the Haybarn," said Melody.

"You have got to be fucking kidding," said Happy.

He sniggered, until Melody shut him up with a cold glare. She filled them all in on her encounter with the Faust, and his creation, the Phantom. She made it as clear as she could for the actors, while still being careful to refer only obliquely to The Flesh Undying. Some things civilians were better off not knowing. JC and Happy got what she was talking about immediately and shared several thoughtful and meaningful looks. Benjamin and Elizabeth, and Lissa, mostly looked confused. Melody finally ran down, and they all looked at the swing doors again.

"We are in deep shit, people," said Happy. "This isn't just a haunting any more. I say we get the hell out of here, napalm the theatre, then salt the ashes afterwards. It's the only way to be sure."

And then he broke off abruptly. All of them turned around as the sound of quiet, mocking laughter drifted across the stage from the far wings. And there, standing half in the shadows and half in the light, smiling easily, was Old Tom, the caretaker. Except he was standing taller and straighter now . . . and he didn't look like someone who'd take orders from other people. He looked like the man in charge. Benjamin and Elizabeth stared at him, then moved to stand close together. Happy started forward, to put himself between the two actors and danger . . . and then he remembered that JC was here, so he didn't have to be the hero any longer. That was JC's job. With a certain amount of relief, Happy fell back and hid behind Benjamin and Elizabeth, out of harm's way. Melody moved over to join him. JC took a moment to notice that Lissa was giving Old Tom her full attention although she didn't seem nearly as affected as everyone else. JC filed that thought away for future reference and stepped forward to face Old Tom.

"Who are you?" said JC.

"What are you?" said Happy, from a distance.

Old Tom stepped out onto the stage, into the bright light. The flesh of his face had sunk in deeply, right back to the bone, becoming desiccated, mummified. The face of some long-forgotten corpse, brought to light at last.

Dark lips had drawn back from yellow teeth in a never-ending smile. The only life left in him burned in his eyes, shining brightly from his dead face.

"I am the unquiet dead," he said grandly. "The unquiet past, determined to be heard at last."

"Damn," said Benjamin. "He's one of us! He's an actor! We're the only ones who talk like that."

"Ah," said Old Tom. "But not just any actor."

"You've put on a pretty good show, so far," said JC. "All the thrills and chills of a ghost train; but no-one was ever in any danger of getting hurt. So what's really going on here? What's this all about?"

"Why don't the dead lie still in this empty palace of broken dreams?" said Old Tom. He pointed a single skeletal finger at Benjamin and Elizabeth, still huddled together. "Ask them. They know."

And then he faded away, melting into thin mists that blew away and were gone. Even though there wasn't a breath of a breeze, anywhere on the stage. JC, then Happy and Melody, and finally Lissa, turned to look at Benjamin and Elizabeth.

"It's time to tell the truth," said JC, not unkindly.

"Past time, I'd say," said Lissa.

Benjamin and Elizabeth consulted each other silently, with one of their long looks that meant so much, but only to each other. And only then did they both nod briefly, in agreement. They held on to each other's hands, like lost children comforting each other in a dark forest, and turned to face the Ghost Finders, and Lissa.

"It's all my fault," said Benjamin. "Alistair Gravel didn't disappear. He didn't go away. I killed him."

"It was an accident!" Elizabeth said immediately. "We were arguing, at the top of the stairs. Raised voices, shouting into each other's faces, lots of arm-waving. Benjamin shoved Alistair in the chest. And he fell, backwards."

"I'd forgotten where we were," said Benjamin. "And I never meant to shove him that hard. By the time we got to the foot of the stairs, he was dead."

"What were you arguing about?" said JC.

"The play, of course," said Elizabeth. "The bloody play."

"Twenty years ago, we wrote the play for Alistair to star in," said Benjamin. "It was a good play. I mean, really good. Everybody said so. We all knew it was our best chance for fame and glory, to break out of this very small pond and make real names for ourselves. But, we were having trouble raising funding. Until Frankie Hazzard came forward. Mister big-name movie star. He wanted a starring role in the theatre, to give himself some credibility. Someone sent him a copy of our play, and he wanted in. Wanted to star in it. And with his name attached, suddenly there was no problem getting all the money we needed, and then some."

"But Alistair would have none of it," said Elizabeth. "He refused to be pushed aside and replaced. This was his big chance, too, and he knew it. He said . . . he'd contributed so much to the play already, in rehearsal, that he'd sue us if we tried to go ahead without him. We did offer to pay him off, but he wasn't interested. He insisted on his right to play the lead."

"We argued," said Benjamin. "I pushed him, and he fell. And he died."

He couldn't speak for a moment, holding back tears.

"We hid the body," Elizabeth said finally. "Rather than have a scandal that would interfere with the play's production. And success. We did it all for success."

"It was my idea, not Elizabeth's!" said Benjamin. "I couldn't let her stand trial, and go to jail, just for being there. For something that was all my fault."

"It wasn't your fault!" said Elizabeth. "It was an accident! A stupid accident. He fell."

"We buried him beneath the understage area," said Benjamin. "He's still there. No-one ever found him or found out what we'd done. To our oldest friend."

"Our dearest friend," said Elizabeth.

"We kept the secret, all these years."

"Of what we did, for success."

"Except, there wasn't any," said Benjamin. "Frankie Hazzard insisted on major changes in the play. Rewrite after rewrite, that messed up everything. He changed everything that mattered, took all the best lines, and gave them to himself . . ."

"And every time we objected, he threatened to walk," said Elizabeth. "And take the play's funding with him. We had no doubt he'd do it if he couldn't have his own way. And we were all in too deep, by then."

"We were desperate to get the play on," said Benjamin. "After everything we'd done, everything we'd lost . . . if there was no play, then it had all been for nothing."

"And in the end, it was," said Elizabeth. "The changes ruined our play. When we did finally get it on, it died in under two weeks."

"Frankie Hazzard didn't give a damn," said Benjamin. "He walked away. On to his next big movie project."

"We got the blame," said Elizabeth. "Frankie Hazzard was a star. Everybody loved him. So how could it be his fault? No, said the critics, and the commentators, it had to be our play, our lousy words, that buried the production."

"We killed our oldest and dearest friend and covered it up, for fame and glory," said Benjamin. "And we didn't get the fame, and we didn't get the glory. It was all for nothing. And nothing was ever the same after that."

"We left the Haybarn," said Elizabeth. "We didn't have to. The owners still believed in us, we'd made them a lot of money. Far as they were concerned, we were still a good draw. Locally. But we couldn't stay. Not after what we'd done. Not knowing that Alistair was buried here."

"And anyway," said Benjamin, "it was no fun any more, without him. We left. Our careers . . . never really happened. We kept busy, but . . . the spark was gone."

"I sometimes wonder," said Elizabeth, "whether deep down, we felt we didn't deserve to succeed."

"This is all very touching, I'm sure," said Melody, loud enough to make everyone jump. "But why are we all standing around chatting, when I already told you the Phantom is on his way here to kill us all!"

"Because he isn't here yet," said JC. "And this . . . is the job. The mission. We came to the Haybarn Theatre to discover the reason behind the haunting, so we could . . . resolve matters. Now we know, perhaps we can make peace between the various parties."

"Now we know what's been powering all these visions and manifestations," said Happy. "Twenty years of unfinished business. Lying there in his grave, dreaming and plotting, gathering his strength . . . Is there anything stronger than thwarted dreams and ambitions? The loss of the life Alistair Gravel should have had?"

JC stepped forward, to face Elizabeth and Benjamin. She looked tired, beaten down. He looked even worse. But he still had enough left in him to hold Elizabeth protectively as he stared at JC.

"What now?" he said.

"Why did you decide to come back here, after all these years?" said JC. "To revive a play that had only ever brought you pain?"

Benjamin and Elizabeth looked at each other.

"I don't know," said Benjamin, frowning. "The idea . . . came to me, one night."

"Yes," said Elizabeth. "The twentieth anniversary was coming up, and even though Benjamin and I never discussed it, we both knew it was much on our minds."

"And when we did finally discuss it, we couldn't get the idea out of our heads," said Benjamin. "I contacted the theatre's owners, and they said . . . they'd been waiting to hear from us."

"It never occurred to me to question any of this before," said Elizabeth. "But now I come to think about it . . ."

"You were called back here," said JC. "Summoned, by a spirit of great power. But why? To tell you both that you had never been forgiven? To punish you?"

"No," said Melody, caught up in the discussion despite herself. "That's not it. The ghost put on a really scary show, but it's clear no-one was ever supposed to get hurt . . ."

"Old Tom was a mask," said Happy. "A disguise, for Alistair Gravel. A dead actor, playing a part."

"I always said that caretaker was too broad a character," said Elizabeth.

"The moustache didn't help," said Benjamin. "Alistair always was too fond of the make-up box."

"So this has all been about Alistair Gravel," said JC. "Watching us, as Old Tom. I understand everything, now."

"Well, not everything," said Lissa.

They all turned to look at her, and she smiled at them dazzlingly.

"Nothing in this theatre is necessarily what it seems," she said sweetly. "And not everyone is who they appear to be."

And she slowly and silently faded away.

TEN

....

YOU'VE GOT TO GET INTO
THE SPIRIT OF THINGS

The living men and women stood close together on the Haybarn Theatre stage, staring wide-eyed and open-mouthed at the spot where Lissa had been standing. Or, at least, at where the thing they thought had been Lissa had been standing. They moved instinctively closer to each other, feeling the need for mutual support. Real people doing real human things, in the face of something long dead and only pretending to be human. A basic need for human warmth and human presence, to counter the cold of the grave and a close encounter with mortality. They needed to look into each other's eyes and see someone they knew looking back. Actors might be used to dealing with people who aren't who they appear to be, and Ghost Finders might be used to dealing with things that aren't what they seem to be; but that only makes it that much harder to handle, knowing how completely you've been fooled.

Not all that surprisingly, JC was the first to get his mental feet back under him.

"Happy!" he said sharply, and the telepath jumped and gave JC his full attention.

"Yes, boss?"

"Is everyone else here real? Really real?"

"Way ahead of you," said Happy. "I scanned everyone still on this stage the moment after Lissa did her disappearing act. Everyone left is who they appear to be. As far as I can tell. Something in this theatre has been messing with my head, and my abilities, ever since I got here."

"How can we be sure about you?" Elizabeth said bluntly.

"Oh, trust me," said JC. "No-one else could be that annoying."

"You want me to prod you with a finger?" said Happy.

"Later, dear," said Melody.

JC looked steadily at Benjamin and Elizabeth. "You knew Lissa. And you never suspected anything?"

"We never met her before!" said Elizabeth, immediately. "Not in the flesh . . ."

"I talked to her on the telephone a few times," said Benjamin. "We knew her work, obviously, that's why we hired her. But most of our contacts went through her agent. So when she turned up here, early, but looking exactly the way we expected her to, well . . . We never thought! Why would we?"

"So that was never the real Lissa," said Happy. "All this time we've had two ghosts walking around with us, pretending to be people . . . And I never suspected anything!"

"My machines didn't detect anything, either," said Melody. "But then, I never knew the right questions to ask them. If it walks like a person and talks like a person . . ."

"We should have been on our guard," said Happy. "Especially after what happened at the railway station . . ."

"Don't be too hard on yourselves," said JC, cutting in quickly before Benjamin and Elizabeth could start asking awkward questions about the railway station and really confuse the issue. "I'm the one with the special all-seeing eyes, and I didn't see a damned thing I wasn't supposed to . . . But to be able to manifest that strongly, to walk around like one of us, or rather two of us, Lissa and Old Tom . . . there must be something in this theatre, some unusual source of power, to make these ghosts so much stronger than they had any right to be."

The lights dimmed suddenly all across the stage. Dark shadows gathered. And then a single spotlight stabbed down from above, marking out one small part of the stage in a circle of shimmering light. And from out of the darkness and into the spotlight walked the ghost girl, Kim. She took up her position in the pool of brilliant light, standing tall and proud and serene, and smiled dazzlingly at everyone. She looked exactly the same as she had before, dressed in exactly the same way as when she'd been murdered, down in Oxford Circus Tube Station . . . when JC first met her. He started toward her, then made himself stop. He looked fiercely at the others.

"You can all see her this time?"

"Certainly looks like her," said Happy. "But . . . I'm

not getting anything from her, JC. I can't even sense her presence, never mind her personality. And normally, she blazes in my mind like a balefire at midnight. Are you sure this isn't another illusion?"

"You haven't been picking up much of anything recently, Happy," said JC, not unkindly.

"Don't think I hadn't noticed," growled Happy. "Something, or more probably Someone, has been deliberately blocking me. And so thoroughly, and so subtly, I didn't even notice. Until now. After what happened here, I thought it was Alistair Gravel who'd been misdirecting me with his scary visions, so I wouldn't see through the Old Tom disguise he was wearing . . . but now I'm not so sure. This Faust you met, Melody; how long has he been here? How much of what we've seen and experienced could be down to him? And if he can make things, physical things like the Phantom, then maybe . . ."

"That looks like our Kim," said Melody. "But why isn't she saying anything? Normally, you can't shut her up."

"Could Alistair Gravel be behind her?" said Happy.

"How would he know about her?" said Melody.

"He's dead!" said Happy. "The dead know all kinds of things they're not supposed to!"

"Or maybe, just maybe, she really is my guardian-angel ghost," said JC. "Come to save us all in our hour of need."

He moved slowly forward, his footsteps loud and clear and echoing on the open stage. Kim smiled happily at him but made no move to leave the spotlight and come to him. JC stopped, carefully, right at the edge of the shimmering light. It was her face, every detail exactly right. He should know. He'd spent enough time staring at it. He spoke softly to Kim, doing his best to be persuasive without pressuring her.

"Why are you here, Kim? Can you tell me? Can you tell me anything? Something, anything, so I can be sure this is you."

But she looked at him, smiling sadly, her eyes fixed on his, saying nothing. JC reached out a hand to her, and Kim immediately fell back a step. Her smile disappeared, and she looked at him warningly, admonishingly. JC stayed where he was. He wanted it to be her. Needed it to be her. But he didn't trust anything in the Haybarn Theatre any more. Not even himself. He raised a hand to his sunglasses, to take them off and look at her directly with his altered eyes, then he stopped and spun round as the swing doors at the back of the auditorium smashed open, and the Phantom of the Haybarn came crashing through them.

iiiiiiiiiiiiiiiiiiiiii

Everyone turned to look. Both swing doors were blasted right off their hinges, thrown away to either side, by the sheer force of the Phantom's arrival. He struck a pose in front of the great dark gap he'd made, letting everyone on the stage get a good look at him. Stooped, half-crouching like an animal, resplendent in Victorian finery and a night-dark opera cape with blood-red lining. He should have looked like a gentleman, like a civilised man from a civilised time; instead he looked more like some creature from the wild places, a beast that had been raised up to walk like a man but left none of its savagery behind. Murder was in his every move, death in his smile, horror in his rotting half-face and grubby half-mask. He laughed silently at them all, like some terrible predator from the jungle night.

"Told you," said Melody. "The Phantom of the Hay-barn."

"Okay," said Happy. "That is seriously ugly, with a really big side order of disgusting and distressing. But I have to say, although I'm quite definitely sensing its presence, I'm not picking up any thoughts from it. As such. That's not a person. More like a projection from some other mind, further away."

Melody said, "It's a creation of the Faust. He made it. Right there in front of me. It's bits of flesh, shaped by his will and intent."

"Flesh?" said Happy. "Oh ick."

"Not an actual creation, then," said JC. "Not a living thing. Good to know this Faust has his limits."

"It's still butt ugly," sniffed Happy.

"Go on," said Melody. "I'm pretty sure it can hear you. Go ahead and annoy the insanely powerful murderous creature, why don't you?"

"Shutting up now," said Happy. "And hiding behind you until further notice."

"I don't think that . . . thing, that Phantom, is anything to do with the games Alistair has been playing," said Benjamin.

"Of course not," said Elizabeth. "Alistair had more style. Not to mention taste. His imagination was never that . . . grubby."

"You never put on a production of *The Phantom of the Opera*?" said JC. "Nothing this creature could have been derived from?"

"Oh please," said Elizabeth, crushingly. "We were theatre people, not music-hall."

"Snob," said Benjamin fondly.

"So this is nothing to do with our dead actor and his twenty-year-old grudge," said JC. "This isn't about you; this is about us. An old enemy of ours has followed us here." He smiled slowly, and it was not a good smile. "The Faust is really nothing more than a party crasher; and it's up to us to give him the boot. I say first we take down this second-rate Phantom, then we go find the Faust and kick his nasty arse until he agrees to tell us things we need to know."

"Sounds good to me, boss," said Happy, from behind Melody. "You go right ahead and get all violent on the dangerous psychopath in the cape. I'll watch your back. From a distance."

"We have to make the Faust talk," said JC with a cold and deliberate patience. "He knows the truth about Kim. Where she's been, what's happened to her. You think it's a coincidence she showed up here the same time as him?"

They all looked at Kim, standing still and silent in her spotlight. Like a ghost impaled on a shimmering pin. She looked only at JC, with calm, steady eyes. As though she was waiting for something.

"Is there anything you can do to help us, Kim?" said JC. "No. Then you stay here while I go have words with the Phantom."

"Some guardian-angel ghost," muttered Happy.

"I heard that!" said JC.

The Phantom came tearing through the auditorium towards the stage. He didn't bother with the open aisle down the middle; instead, he tore a path right through the ranked rows of seats, in a casual, brutal display of strength. Insanely powerful, he smashed through the bolted-down seats as though they were made of paper, throwing broken pieces aside. The impacts didn't slow him, and he took no obvious pain or damage. He hit the chairs like a runner breasting an endless series of tapes, his arms flailing wildly. The savage sounds of destruction echoed through the vast auditorium, bouncing back from the walls, the sounds of something destroying everything in its path because it couldn't be bothered to go around.

"Show-off!" JC said loudly, to make it clear that he wasn't in any way impressed. He looked down his nose at the rapidly approaching creature and suddenly smiled. "Everyone knows how to stop the Phantom of the Opera . . ."

He strode right up to the edge of the stage and stepped off without slowing. He landed easily then stood there and waited for the Phantom to come to him. He even smiled and nodded and made encouraging gestures to the creature to hurry it up. The Phantom snarled at him, his eyes glowing yellow as urine in the gloom of the auditorium. He finally smashed through the last row of seats, and slammed to a halt right in front of JC. Stooped by a curved back, half-crouched like an animal ready to spring but not even breathing hard, for all his exertions. He smiled a horrid smile, with no humour in it, no human emotion at all, and held up his gloved hands, so JC could see the splintered claws that had thrust through the ends of the fingertips. JC sniffed loudly.

"Am I supposed to be impressed? I've crapped scarier-looking objects than you."

The Phantom lunged forward, clawed hands raised. JC stepped forward at the very last moment and tore off the Phantom's mask. It clung stickily for a moment, then ripped away in his hand. The Phantom stopped dead. But instead of revealing the expected disfigured face, which the Phantom of the Opera would have immediately stopped to hide . . . there was nothing there. Nothing at all behind the grubby half-mask. The left side of the Phantom's head was . . . missing. The right half of the face and head ended abruptly in a twisted mess of gnarled and fused tissues. One glowing yellow eye, a nose bi-sected right down the middle, and half a mouth, still smil-ing its nasty smile. Up close, the half-face smelled of rotting meat.

JC felt something move in his hand. He looked down. The half-mask still had a yellow eye in it, looking up at him through its hole, glaring madly. The mask itself felt like skin, like flesh, in his hand, living materials moulded into shape by the Faust's will. It pulsed in his grasp. JC wanted to grimace with disgust, but he couldn't allow himself to show weakness. He crushed the mask in his grasp, then whipped off his sunglasses with his other hand, to give the Phantom the full benefit of his unearthly glare. The Phantom flinched and turned his half-face away from the golden glow, but he didn't fall back by so much as a step. Instead, he slowly turned his half-

face back, to match the glowing glare with his own inhuman gaze. And then he took one slow deliberate step
towards JC.

"Happy!" JC said loudly. "Really could use a little
assistance down here!"

Happy came forward to the edge of the stage, looked
down at the drop, and the Phantom, and hesitated. Melody came up behind him and pushed him off. Happy let
out a loud cry and landed in a heap beside JC. He quickly
scrambled back onto his feet, checked quickly to make
sure everything was undamaged, then moved reluctantly
forward to stand beside JC. Because once you'd been
thrown in the deep end, you might as well go kick the
snot out of the sharks. Happy was always quite prepared
to be brave—once it was clear there was no other alter-
native. He hit the Phantom with his hardest, strongest
blast of telepathic disbelief. The Phantom slammed to a
halt as though he'd hit a brick wall. JC glared his golden
glare. Happy concentrated on his disbelief till he felt that
his head would burst open. The Phantom opened his
mouth to say something, then fell apart. Unable to hold
himself together in the face of such focused opposition.

The night-black cape dropped off his shoulders, running away like some thick, inky liquid. The legs collapsed, and the arms fell off. The squirming trunk hit the
floor hard and fell in upon itself, melting down and running away in thick rivulets. The clothes dissolved along
with the body, as though they were all part of the same
thing. It slumped down like a melting candle, then dis-
sipated into thick white mists that quickly disappeared
on the still air. The half-face was the last to go, lying in

a white pool on the floor, still glaring silently and malevolently up at JC and Happy, the mouth still working right till the very end, when it disappeared suddenly, like a bad dream.

JC felt something squirm in his hand. He looked down to find that the mask had become a thick sticky liquid, dripping through his closed fingers. He opened his hand and shook the stuff away. JC pulled a face and rubbed his hand clean on the back of Happy's jacket. Happy knew better than to say anything. They both studied the floor carefully, but there wasn't even a stain left to mark the Phantom's passing.

"What *was* that?" said Happy.

"Get back up here!" Melody said sharply, from the stage.

JC and Happy turned and raced around to the steps that led back up to the stage. JC got there first, by a short head, then the two of them ran out onto the stage and looked to where everyone else was looking. Another Door had appeared, at the far side of the stage; a trap-Door, full of darkness. JC looked quickly at Benjamin and Elizabeth, but they were already shaking their heads.

"Hasn't been a trap-door in this stage for decades," said Benjamin.

"Not since that nasty business with the Panto Dame," said Elizabeth.

And then they all cried out and turned their heads away for a moment as a blindingly bright light blazed up out of the trap-Door, like a spotlight in reverse. There was nothing shimmering about this one; it was a stark and brutal light, harsh and unforgiving, casting deep dark

shadows all around it. And then the Faust rose majesti-
cally through the opening, accompanied by the singing
of a heavenly choir and the sound of massed bugles. The
Faust rose smoothly, as though riding an elevator, standing tall and proud and erect, until he was a good foot or
more above the open trap-Door. And it became clear that
he was standing on nothing. He smiled happily about
him, like some visiting dignitary bestowing his grace on
the unworthy, and stepped lightly down onto the stage.
The brilliant light snapped off, leaving everyone else
blinking for a moment. The heavenly choir and the
massed bugles shut down in mid phrase. The Faust
beamed about him.

"If you're going to make an entrance, make an entrance! That's what I always say. I am the Faust, and I'll
be your murderer tonight. I do hope nobody's going to
be bothersome . . . That small thing you destroyed was
only flesh, after all. Nothing more. And I've been given
dominion over all such things by my lord and master,
The Flesh Undying. Ah me; I do so love to see the look
on people's faces when they hear his glorious name. And
know that all hope is gone, the game is over, and the
sentence is death. Because that is, after all, the only fitting fate for his enemies."

"You were right," JC said to Melody. "He does like to
talk, doesn't he?"

Benjamin and Elizabeth looked at the Faust. Anywhen else, they'd probably have been impressed. But
after everything they'd been through and experienced so
far, he was merely another unpleasant visitation. They

looked to the Ghost Finders for some sort of explanation, in a not-terribly-hopeful way.

"Long story," Melody said briskly. "And you really wouldn't want to know, anyway. Settle for knowing that this completely up-himself personage is the only really dangerous thing in this theatre."

"How very harsh," murmured the Faust. "Frankly, I'd expected a better class of dialogue, in the theatre."

JC, Happy, and Melody stepped forward to confront the Faust. Benjamin and Elizabeth backed off a little and let them do it. They knew when they were way out of their depth. JC took another step forward, and the Faust came forward to meet him. They circled each other, like two tigers meeting in a clearing. Two powerful, arrogant beings who had more in common than either of them would ever have admitted.

"What are you?" said JC.

"I am what I've made of myself," said the Faust. "Can you say the same? I doubt it. What are you, Mr. Chance, except another overworked and underpaid civil servant, working for a government department . . . never knowing what's really going on behind the scenes."

JC smiled. "You really don't know me, do you?"

"I chose my master!" said the Faust. "I gave myself to The Flesh Undying. Like the man said, we all have to serve someone. Whom do you serve, really? A Boss? A cause? Or are you only another pitiful little functionary, doing a job to fill in all those long, dreary hours till you die? I have given my life to something greater."

"You gave it to a monster," said JC. "Something that

only came here because it was kicked out of its own dimension. It fell through a hole in the sky like a lump of shit because its own kind couldn't stand to have it around any longer. It doesn't care about you. It doesn't care about anything. It'll tear this whole world apart to get home again."

"What do I care?" said the Faust. "As long as he takes me with him. I never cared much for this world, anyway. Certainly it never cared much for me. And there you have it, ladies and gentlemen, the secret origin of the Faust! Death and damnation to all the world, and everyone in it, because they didn't love me the way they should have! That'll show them. I have been given command over flesh. The new flesh, the bad flesh—I can summon anything through my Door and mould it to my will and need. Call up any shape and form and throw it at my master's enemies."

"You may have the flesh," said JC, stopping his circling abruptly, so the Faust had to stop, too. JC gave him his best confident grin. "Hell with the flesh; I have the spirit at my command. Meet my secret weapon." He stepped back and gestured at Kim, still watching from her spotlight. "Meet my very own guardian-angel ghost! Get him, Kim!"

"Sorry," said the Faust. "But that's not her."

He snapped his fingers, and the shimmering spotlight blinked out. Kim smiled and shrugged briefly at JC, then slumped forward into a melting mass, like a candle in an oven. She collapsed into a pool of sticky white flesh that drained away through the cracks in the stage floor-boards; then she was gone.

JC swayed sickly on his feet, as though he'd been hit. His heart lurched in his chest, and he had to fight to get his breath. He tried to say something and couldn't. He'd been so sure it was her, come back to him at last, to save him as he'd saved her, down in the Underground. He'd believed in her because he needed it to be her. But it wasn't her, never had been her, not his Kim. He stared at the place where she'd been, then slowly turned his head to look at the Faust. And a wiser man would have been very careful about what he said next.

"Another of my little tricks," the Faust said easily. "I sent her to you, to keep an eye on you. To take you where I wanted you to go, to lead you around by the nose and mess with your head, for the fun of it. Some say the greatest trick God ever pulled was to make us believe love is real. It does make people like you so much easier to manipulate."

"You bastard," said JC. "You bastard."

Melody looked uneasily at JC, then raised her voice to attract the Faust's attention. "So that was you at the railway station as well?"

The Faust looked at her. "What? What railway station? Can we stick to the point, please?"

"You see?" Melody said to JC. "He doesn't know anything about a railway station. So what we saw there . . ."

"Yes," said JC, straightening up and squaring his shoulders again. "I see." He looked steadily at the Faust. "I saw Kim at that railway station. So she . . . was nothing to do with you. Which means, if nothing else, that you're not nearly as knowledgeable as you claim to be."

The Faust shrugged briskly. "It doesn't make any

difference. You are alone and powerless before me. Exactly the way I like it."

"Actually, no," said JC. "I have more than enough spirit to throw at you." He turned his back on the Faust and beamed at the others. "Getting to the heart of this haunting has been like peeling an onion. Every time you peel off a layer, you find there's another underneath. Nearly everything we've seen and encountered here has been part of one big extravagant show. But the time for distractions is over. Unless you want to see your beloved theatre destroyed . . . Step forward and take a bow, Alistair Gravel!"

There was a pause, then the sound of loud, heavy footsteps emerged from the wings and advanced a short distance across the stage, with no-one making them. They were followed by a crawling dead man, bloody and ruined, dragging himself across the stage by his broken fingers. A young Benjamin and a young Elizabeth emerged from the wings after him, strolling happily forward, arm in arm. Followed by a smiling Lissa and a quietly grinning Old Tom, the caretaker. They all stood together in a group, ignoring the dumbfounded Faust and nodding easily to Benjamin and Elizabeth and the Ghost Finders. The crawling dead man rose abruptly to his feet, popped his dangling eye back into his socket, and stood calmly with the others. And then they all stepped forward as one and took a deep bow. The performance was at an end. They straightened up, grinned briefly, and disappeared, all of them at once, like blown-out candles. And from out of the wings strode one young man in his twenties, with a very familiar face. He grinned easily about him and took a quick bow of his own.

Alistair Gravel.

"It was *him*, all along?" said Happy. "He was . . . all of them?"

"It was him," said JC. "It was always him."

"Even Lissa?" said Melody.

"Yes," said JC. "I have something to discuss with Alistair Gravel, about that."

"Why?" Happy said immediately. "What happened?"

"Nothing happened," said JC, firmly.

Benjamin and Elizabeth stared at Alistair. They didn't seem scared, or even upset. Slowly, they smiled and relaxed, pleased to see an old friend again, after too long apart. Elizabeth sniffed back tears and wrung her hands together, while Benjamin put a supporting arm across her shoulders. He looked . . . as though a great weight had finally been lifted off him.

"Oh please," said Elizabeth. "Please let it be him. Let it really be him."

"It is," said Benjamin. "I can tell. Can't you tell?"

"Yes," said Elizabeth. "Oh yes . . ."

"It's me," said Alistair Gravel. "And I am so very happy to see you both again, Benjamin and Elizabeth."

The two actors hurried toward him, and Alistair strode forward to meet them. They came together in the middle of the stage and threw their arms around each other and hugged each other tightly. Three old friends who hadn't seen each other in twenty years, separated by far more than years and time. There were a few tears, and some laughter, then they all stood back and looked at each other as though they could never get enough.

"You look the same, Alistair," said Elizabeth. "You haven't changed at all! Oh, don't look at me, Alistair. I've changed so much."

"Not in any way that matters," said Alistair. "Nothing else matters except that we're together again."

"I've missed you so much," said Benjamin. "We both have . . ."

"And I've missed you," said the ghost. "That's why I brought you back here. For one last performance." He looked across at the fascinated Ghost Finders and grinned broadly. " 'All the world's a stage . . . and one man in his time plays many parts . . .' Why should death be any different?"

"So everyone we met here was you?" said Elizabeth.

"All of me," said Alistair. "Everyone you've seen, and everything you've been through, has been down to me. In one guise or another. Until Little Miss Faust here turned up and started interfering." He stuck his tongue out at the Faust, then turned to smile winningly at JC. "The whole costumes thing was down to him. Including the appearance of your ghost girl. Which is why I couldn't see her; he was working directly on your mind. I did rescue you, as Lissa and Old Tom."

"Yes," said JC. "You came on to me as Lissa!"

"I knew it!" said Happy.

"Shut up, Happy," said JC. "Nothing happened."

"Alistair always was very . . . promiscuous," said Elizabeth, and Benjamin nodded solemnly. Alistair beamed on both of them.

"This whole show was for your benefit, my dears. I wanted to prove to you . . . what a great actor I was. Far more talented than that conceited movie star, bad cess to his name. He ruined your play. I hope you told everybody about his toupee . . . Good. I brought you back here so I could have a little fun with you, and to say goodbye, properly. Because we never got the chance. But the performance is over now. Ring down the curtains and get on with your lives. Go ahead with your play. All is forgiven. I always said . . . it was a bloody good play."

"So there was never any real threat here?" said JC. "Never any real danger, to anyone?"

"Of course not," said Alistair. "It was all me, putting on a show. Oh, it's been so much fun, my dears, to have an audience again!"

"But why go to such lengths, to create things to scare the crap out of us?" said Benjamin.

"Because I owed you both a good scare, like the one you gave me," said Alistair. "And, perhaps, a little punishment. But it was all perfectly harmless scars. Think of it as a good old-fashioned ghost-train ride. I always loved those . . ."

"Oh bloody hell, not another one," muttered Happy.

"Hold everything," said Melody. "What about the dead homeless guy?"

"What about him?" said Alistair. "He broke in one evening and died of a heart attack in his sleep. Nothing to do with me."

"Excuse me!" said the Faust, very loudly. "Will you all please shut the hell up and pay attention to me!" He glared around at them all until he was sure he'd got everyone's attention again. "Do you really think I give a damn about some twenty-year-old sob story and some half-arsed ghost who can't take a hint and piss off to the afterworlds where he belongs? Life is for the living, and the flesh is all that matters."

Happy smirked at Melody. "He's talking to you."

"What? Him? That scrawny piece of shit in the off-the-peg suit?" said Melody. "Look at the state of him—no two pounds of the man hanging straight. I'd rather sleep with the dummy the suit came from. He couldn't keep up with me, anyway . . ."

"Not many can," said Happy.

"This is true," said Melody. "Now stop fishing for compliments."

"You'll have to excuse them," JC said to the increasingly frustrated Faust. "They're just being themselves. But they do have a point. For all your fine words, what can you hope to do against trained operatives like us? We only had to give your Phantom thing a hard look, and it fell apart on us."

"The Phantom of the Haybarn was only a bit of fun," said the Faust. "Now it's time to get serious. The best way to overcome an enemy is to make them a part of you. Even if you're clearly not worthy . . . So, I'm going to eat you all up with spoons."

He gestured languidly at the trap-Door, lying forgotten on the other side of the stage, and a great fountain of corpse white flesh erupted up out of the dark opening. It reached almost to the high ceiling—a tower of pulsing, expanding and contracting flesh . . . before finally falling back again to slap onto the stage and spread out in a great pulsating pool. It moved slowly but inexorably across the stage towards the actors and the Ghost Finders, in sudden spurts and rushes. More and more of the stuff burst up out of the trap-Door, spilling out in all directions, forming a thick carpet of flesh on the stage. It rose and pressed forward like a slow-motion wave, throwing out sudden extremities, straining hungrily out for prey. Flesh, without form or limit, called up by the Faust and driven on by his will: an endless supply of living tissue, come to eat up everything set before it and make them a part of it.

JC had frozen in place like all the others, but he broke the spell first and gestured quickly for everyone else to back away from the advancing, hungry tide. But they'd barely started moving before more of the shapeless mass burst out of the other wings, spilling across the stage towards them. More welled out from behind the drawn curtains at the back of the stage, and a sudden white wave leapt up over the front of the stage. The actors and Ghost Finders pressed close together, surrounded on all sides by a slow-moving sea of hungry flesh. It boiled and seethed, rising and falling in sudden surges; and as it drew nearer, JC could see narrow traceries of blue veins in the white material. It was alive in its own way. JC didn't need to ask the Faust what this stuff would do when it finally reached its prey. He could feel its hunger pulsing on the air. It was here to swallow them all up, render them down, and absorb every last bit of them into itself.

Flesh at its most basic, all appetite and menace, here to serve The Flesh Undying.

Alistair Gravel lifted his ghostly feet and sat cross-legged in mid air, perfectly poised, looking down at the flesh moving jerkily below him with a curled lip of cold distaste. The flesh ignored him. Perhaps because it could tell he wasn't real, that he had no physical presence to absorb.

Happy glared about him, scowling at the gleaming, pulsing mass. "Okay. This is the most disgusting thing I've ever seen. And I've been around."

"Are you picking up anything, from this . . . stuff?" said JC, looking quickly about him for anything that might serve as an exit and not finding one.

"Yes," said Happy. "It's not an illusion. Unfortunately. It's really physically here even though I do wish ever so much that it wasn't. It's alive, and it's hungry. Don't let even the smallest part of it touch you."

"Way ahead of you there," said Melody.

"It's like that movie, with Steve McQueen," said Elizabeth, clinging tightly to Benjamin while trying hard to sound brave.

"Hush, dear," said Benjamin. "You're showing your age."

"Oh come on, darling. Who remembers anything about that awful remake? Benjamin, it really is getting awfully close . . ."

"Stay close to me, love. Stick close to me."

By now, they'd all been herded together in the middle of the stage while the flesh urged slowly forward on all sides at once. It was almost half a foot deep, and growing taller and thicker all the time, as more and more of the sickening stuff burst up out of the trap-Door. It advanced in sudden leaps and spurts, throwing up into the air sticky projections, projections that fell back to be absorbed and vanish into the main mass. The flesh oozed straight past the Faust without touching or bothering him, and he smiled happily at his victims, huddled together before him.

Benjamin looked urgently at JC over Elizabeth's shoulder as she hid her face against his chest. "You and Happy destroyed the Phantom! You're the professionals here! Can't you do anything?"

"I am," said JC. "I'm thinking."

"What?" said Benjamin. "You're *thinking*?"

"Yes," said JC. "The Phantom was flesh but a small thing. There doesn't seem to be any end to this . . ."

"Where's it all coming from?" said Happy.

"From The Flesh Undying, I assume," said JC. "Directly or indirectly. It would appear the name is more literally descriptive than we realised. I'd been hoping it was a metaphor . . . Still, spirit trumps flesh every time. Because flesh begins and ends in life, while spirit transcends life . . . So, to counter this much flesh, we need more spirits. Logic. Alistair Gravel! Come on down! This is your theatre, your place of power. We need a helping hand here, and you need to put a stop to this unwelcome intrusion. If you really have forgiven your friends, and don't want them to die . . ."

"Of course I don't!" said Alistair. "But what can I do?"

"We need spirits, darling!" Elizabeth said, turning

away from Benjamin without leaving his arms to stare desperately at Alistair. "Spirits like you, to throw against this awful Faust person. Can you oblige?"

"Glad to," said Alistair. "Sorry if I'm a bit slow, my dears, but this is all new to me. And rather more than one poor ghost can handle. Fortunately, I'm not alone here." He lowered his legs to stand on the stage, right in the middle of the fleshy sea. The pulsing white mass cringed back from him, repulsed by his very nature. Alistair sneered at the Faust. "How do you think I achieved all my many illusions, and manifestations? My power comes from the theatre: a place of dreams and dramas, created by the living to be timeless. So that the Past and the Present and the Future could always be with us. Visions and fantasies become eternal truths, on this stage. History becomes legend; ordinary men and women become immortal. The Haybarn is full of the spirits of performances long past and audiences long gone. They're all still here, in spirit, because they loved this place too much to ever leave it completely.

"So rise up, dear friends! Let us fill the stalls with our English dead, and drive out this soulless, heartless wretch and the mess he's made of our glorious stage! Rise up, you players all! 'The play's the thing!'"

Suddenly, the whole stage was full of costumed men and women. Packed from front to back and wing to wing. With lords and ladies, character roles and spear-carriers, and every actor who ever created magic for an audience . . . with words and gestures and perhaps a knowing look. Whole armies from Shakespeare, crowds of comic actors and proud tragedians, uncounted heroes and villains, and any number of attendant lords proud to swell a scene. Drawn back to the stage, by the pride and glory of their ancient profession, to set their great hearts and hard-learned lessons against the simple, spiteful malice of the Faust.

Great in spirit, no matter how small they may have been in life, because deep down every one of them knew that everything they did on the stage was not for them but for their audiences.

And there they were, too, all the audiences that ever were, countless bodies filling the ranked rows of seats in the vast auditorium. A sea of faces, come in celebration of the magic they saw made before them every night, of the lifting of the spirit and the awakening of the heart, that the actors made possible. Come to stand against the empty heart of the Faust.

Actors stood together on the stage, row upon row and rank upon rank, packed so tightly they overlapped each other. And together, they advanced upon the Faust. The audience stood up, as one, and charged the stage, rushing forward in a great tide. The dead actors and the dead audiences fell upon the Faust, and all his vicious flesh was no match for their spirits.

The glistening sea of flesh withered at their touch, unable to cope with so much spirit in one place. It fell back from them, dissipating and disappearing, surging back to the trap-Door. In moments, it was all gone. The ghosts swarmed past Benjamin and Elizabeth and the Ghost Finders, not even seeing them, all their attention focused on the Faust. Benjamin and Elizabeth looked on, wide-eyed and wondering, recognising a face here and there. Even though the ghosts didn't see them. They were not here for the living. The ghostly actors and audiences surrounded the Faust, circling him, round and round and round; while he turned his face away, this way and that, crying out . . . faced with something beyond his powers and his experience. All he knew was the selfishness of flesh. All the arrogance and confidence had been beaten out of him, and he had nothing to replace them with.

Alistair Gravel came forward, and an aisle opened up before him so that he could walk unhurriedly through the army of ghosts he'd called up, to confront the Faust. Alistair came forward, and the Faust spun around to face him, confused and half-mad. The two men stared at each other—the dead man not yet departed and the living man who'd only thought himself so much more.

"There's more to life than flesh," Alistair said finally. "Here, in this theatre, generations of actors and audiences have celebrated all the glories of the human heart and soul. Monday to Friday, twice on Saturdays. The theatre celebrates all the things . . . that life is for. The things more important than life, that make being human worthwhile. The great Dream of Humanity. What is flesh in the face of that?"

"Don't get cocky, little ghost," said the Faust, breathless with shock, glaring desperately about him. "There's more to power than sheer strength of numbers. All of you together are no match for me! I'm the Faust! I'm not just flesh; I am the force that gives flesh form and meaning and appetite. I'm alive; and you're dead!"

"And that . . . is why it will take both body and spirit,

the living and the dead working together, to stop you," said Kim Sterling, the ghost girl.

They all looked round at the unexpected voice, and another aisle opened up among the massed spirits on the stage so that Kim could walk through them, to stand before JC. She smiled at him, and, after a moment, JC smiled back at her.

"You always did know how to make an entrance, Kim."

"Hello, love," said Kim. "Miss me?"

"You know I did," said JC. "I almost died without you. Where have you been, all this time? That was you, at the railway station, wasn't it?"

"Of course," said Kim. "You didn't think I'd leave, walk off and abandon you, did you? But answers will have to wait. There is business to be done here. The Faust must be dealt with. Nasty little thing that he is. We have to do this together, JC. Your flesh and my spirit against the simple brutal thing that is the Faust. Are you ready, my love?"

"Always," said JC.

"Brace yourself," said Kim.

She walked forward, into JC's body, until she overlapped him completely, combining her ghostly self with his physical form. Joining the two of them together, into a whole far more than the sum of its parts. JC cried out, in shock and pain and awe, as his whole body glowed with the same golden glare as his eyes. And both the living and the dead had to turn their faces aside, away from that blinding, brilliant, otherworldly light.

JC and Kim advanced on the Faust, and the ghosts fell

back as something moved through them, shining like a star fallen to the earth. The Faust cried out. He couldn't look away, couldn't back away, held where he was by the power in that light. JC and Kim stopped, right before the Faust, and dropped one heavy hand onto his shoulder. And the Faust cried out again, in agony and horror, as his whole body shook and shattered under that unbearable touch.

He crumbled and fell apart, collapsing in upon himself like the artificial construct he was, like a statue struck by a hundred hammers. He fell into pieces, which melted and ran away, dissipating into streaky mists that hung heavily on the still air, before reluctantly disappearing. His face hung on stubbornly, hanging together on the top of the pile till the very last, through some awful act of will, his glaring eyes fixed on JC and Kim. When he spoke, at the last, his voice seemed to come from far and far-away.

"I won't go," he said. "I can't go, not yet. Not till I've had my say. One last chance to strike at you, JC, and hurt you. I have enough strength left for that."

"Stamp on him, JC," said Happy. "Shut the bastard up. He doesn't have anything to say that you need to hear."

"No," said JC and Kim, with both their voices. "He knows things."

"I didn't sell my soul for power," said the Faust's face, already drifting away at the edges. "I sold my body to be free from the limitations of the flesh, and of the spirit. For a better soul, not trapped within the body. Already my master is calling me away, to a place where you can't reach me. Where he will set me up again, as something new and even more powerful. The new flesh, the bad flesh. You'll see! Oh, don't look so disappointed, JC. We'll meet again. After all, we have so much in common. Because you're no more real than I am!"

"What are you talking about?" said JC.

"You haven't been real since the Outside reached down and touched you in the Underground! Don't you get it, JC? You died down there, on that demon train; and the Outside brought you back!"

"Why?" said JC and Kim. "Why would it do that?"

"For its own purposes, of course. That's why you can love a ghost girl when most living men can't stand to be around them. That's why you can hold her within you now, and use her power, to do this to me! That's why you were drawn together . . . That's why . . ."

His voice trailed away, his gaze fixed on something only he could see. And a look of utter horror passed over his crumbling face. When he spoke again his voice was full of shock and panic, and a terrible, agonised betrayal.

"No! No, Master! You promised me! You promised me . . ."

His voice broke into a heart-rending scream of loss and deception; and then his face collapsed into undifferentiated flesh, melting and running away into the open trap-Door, which swallowed him up, slammed shut after him, and disappeared. Kim stepped forward, out of JC, and for a long moment they both looked at where the trap-Door had been before they turned to look at each other.

"Do you believe him?" said Kim.

"I don't know," said JC. "I don't know what to believe. Does it matter?"

"We found each other," said Kim. "Living or dead, nothing else will ever matter as much."

"Hello," said Happy. "Where's everybody gone?"

Everyone looked around them. The ghosts were gone, all the actors and their audiences, returned to their rest. The stage was empty, the auditorium full of broken chairs again. Happy and Melody stood together, and Benjamin and Elizabeth stood very close together. Alistair Gravel stood to one side, studying JC and Kim thoughtfully.

"I declare this case officially closed," said JC. "The Haunting of the Haybarn Theatre is over. If that's all right with you, Alistair?"

"Oh yes. Certainly!" said Alistair. "Job done as far as I'm concerned."

JC smiled fondly at Kim. "My guardian-angel ghost. Always arriving just in the nick of time."

"I can't stay, JC," said Kim.

"What? Why not?" said JC. "You have to! Or do they . . . Does someone still have a hold over you?"

"No," said Kim. "They never did. They never had me, JC. I had to disappear, but I can't tell you why. Not yet. I saw something, then, and . . . Come after me, JC. Come and find me. And when you do, all will become clear. The real job, the real mission, isn't over yet. Come find me, JC. I'll be waiting for you."

She placed one ghostly hand against his cheek; and he could almost feel it, like a cool breeze passing by. But by the time he'd raised a hand to place over hers, she was already gone. Disappeared in a moment, as though she had never been there. JC nodded slowly, at some hidden thought, or decision, then he turned away and walked back across the stage, to join the others.

"You can't believe anything the Faust said," said Happy. "The Devil always lies."

"Except when a truth can hurt you more," said Melody.

"Really not helping here," murmured Happy.

"I'm not dead," said JC. "I'm not. I'd know."

"There's all kinds of tests I could run," offered Melody.

"I don't think so," said JC. "I think . . . we're in unknown territory, here." He started to raise one hand to his sunglasses, then stopped himself. He smiled, briefly. "I breathe, I have a pulse, I'm solid; I still get up in the middle of the night to take a pee . . . That's real enough for me."

"The Faust didn't actually say you were dead," Happy said carefully. "He said . . . you might have been, but the Outside brought you back. To life. Think of it as a Really Near Death Experience."

"Brought back, to serve its purposes," said JC. "Nothing at all to worry about there."

"Maybe it knew about The Flesh Undying," said Melody. "Maybe it needed some powerful agent of its own, in this world, to fight it."

"And it chose you!" said Happy. "Could have been worse. Could have been me."

"Kim has all the answers," JC said firmly. "We have to find her."

"Of course we will," said Melody. "We're the Ghost Finders."

"Tally-ho," said Happy.

"Excuse me," said Benjamin. "But are we supposed to understand any of that?"

"No," said JC. "Don't worry about any of it. If you like sleeping at nights."

"I thought not," said Elizabeth.

The two actors moved away from the Ghost Finders, to talk with Alistair Gravel. They hugged each other again—not like old friends meeting, more like saying good-bye.

"It's been so good, to see you again," said Elizabeth.

"You know I never meant to hurt you, Alistair," said Benjamin.

"Of course I know," said Alistair. "I've always known."

"Then why did you wait so long, to call us back?" said Elizabeth.

"It's not easy, being a ghost," said Alistair. "It took me years to raise the power to do the job properly. My return had to be . . . dramatic. As was my death."

"You always were an old ham," said Benjamin.

"What do you mean—old?" said Alistair.

They laughed lightly together. Three friends again.

"Go on with your show," said Alistair. "And I'll go on . . . to the bigger show that's waiting."

Elizabeth looked at him searchingly. "You can see it?"

"I seem . . . to sense it," said Alistair. "Okay, that's it. No more hanging around. I'm off. Break a leg, my dears."

"Do you want your body buried properly?" said Benjamin.

"No," said Alistair. "Leave me where I am. Where I've always felt I belonged."

He turned away and disappeared, like a turned-off

light. Gone, finally. They could all feel the difference in the atmosphere: like an actor who's finished his last scene and walked off stage.

||||||||||||||||||||||||

They walked back through the auditorium. Up the central aisle, surrounded by broken chairs and shattered rows, courtesy of the Phantom of the Haybarn. Benjamin and Elizabeth were already quietly discussing how the hell they were going to sell this to the insurance people. The whole place seemed quiet, calm, at peace with itself.

When they arrived at the great gap where the swing doors had been, JC hung back, to let the others go through ahead of him. He stopped, to look back at the stage. And there, in a single spotlight from nowhere at all, the Lady in White and the Headless Panto Dame were waltzing silently together.

Because the show, the great Dream of Humanity, must always go on.

From *New York Times* Bestselling Author

SIMON R. GREEN

THE BRIDE
WORE BLACK LEATHER

A Novel of the Nightside

Meet John Taylor: Nightside resident, Walker—the new representative of the Authorities—and soon-to-be husband of one of the Nightside's most feared bounty hunters. But before he can say, "I do," he has one more case to solve as a private eye . . . which would be a lot easier to accomplish if he weren't on the run, from friends and enemies alike.

And if his bride-to-be weren't out to collect the bounty on his head . . .

M933T0811